Runners and Riders

D1482742

Runners and Riders

GEORGINA BROWN

Black Lace novels are sexual fantasies.
In real life, make sure you practise safe sex.

First published in 1996 by
Black Lace
332 Ladbroke Grove
London W10 5AH

Typeset by CentraCet Limited, Cambridge
Printed and bound by Mackays of Chatham PLC

ISBN 0 352 33117 8

Chapter One

*A*s her horse cantered, Penny's breasts bounced unrestrained beneath her shirt. Touched by the stiffness of the crisp, white cotton, her nipples became hard like small acorns.

Alistair, the man who had been her sponsor within the world of showjumping, rode with her. Was it a mere eighteen months ago that she had first been interviewed by him? Time had flown. She had gained his sponsorship in response to a challenge from her friend Ariadne who had told her she would never be able to seduce him. Ariadne had insisted he was a man who only watched people having sex. That in itself had been enough to fire her imagination.

She had risen to her friend's challenge, had gained Alistair's sponsorship, and had also found out how his sex drive was kept in a state of ferment. After experiencing various sexual scenarios, she had found out about the rubber pants he wore and the power his sister had over him. It was his sister, Nadine, who kept the key to his pants dangling behind her ear. Now it dangled on a chain between Penny's breasts.

Remembering everything that had happened made her smile. Alistair saw her smile and returned it, though weakly. It was as if something were worrying him.

1

You're just imagining things, Penny told herself. All the same, she resolved to ask him what was wrong.

They eventually came to a halt in the shade of an ancient oak. That was where they dismounted.

'This tree must have been young in the days of Queen Anne.' Penny adopted a cheerful voice and tapped the twisted trunk.

Alistair Beaumont smiled, but did not answer. Silently, he tethered the horses, then gently took her by the hand and led her to where lunch was already set out for them.

Penny eyed him quizzically before sitting down. She was loath to let go of his hand. But he took it from her anyway, then pulled a chair away from the table.

Penny took a deep breath and willed herself to be patient. She eyed the rolling landscape as if it were the most important thing in the world. A field of young, green corn curved down to a small wood, pastures, and the river beyond. White-washed cottages and warm brick farmhouses dotted the landscape. In the distance, framing the scene to perfection, the distant mauve hills separated the earth from the sky.

The spot had been pre-arranged and prepared in advance by Alistair Beaumont's chauffeur. White linen topped a fold-up table, and the meal, though light, was presented on white china with a gold trim. The wine was pale and served in goblets of Waterford crystal.

She willed herself to be bright and breezy and to pretend not to have noticed his mood. Her patience eventually paid off. He took her hand, squeezed it and gazed into her eyes.

'You know you're the most sexually exciting woman I have ever come across, don't you Penny?'

'That's a wonderful comment, Alistair. I much appreciate it. But why say this now?'

Alistair sighed as his fingers interlaced with hers. 'I want to ask you something. I have a problem and I think you have the skills I need to resolve that problem.'

Penny frowned thoughtfully. 'If my sexual skills can

help you, then I will do what I can. What sort of problem are you talking about?'

'Superstar, my champion thoroughbred, has been stolen. I need someone to help me get him back.'

'But how can I help?' Penny asked him.

'I believe he's been taken by a very powerful syndicate. The syndicate itself takes a lively interest in sex as well as racing. I need someone of like mind to infiltrate it.' His gaze was steadfast. 'You are the only person I know whose knowledge of horseflesh is matched by a phenomenal sex drive.'

Penny took a deep breath and set her glass on the table with exceptional care. This needed careful consideration.

A sip of wine helped moisten the dryness of her lips as she eyed the handsome face before her. 'You're asking a lot of me. You know that don't you?' she said slowly.

He hung his head. Then, he shook it despairingly. 'I've given it a lot of thought, Penny darling. That horse means a lot to me. He's taken most of the classics this season, and he's a dead cert for those he hasn't raced in yet. Besides that, his stud potential is enormous.'

'So is yours,' she said with a smile, in an effort to lighten the occasion.

A faint smile came to his face too, then melted away. He looked at her. His expression was the same as it always was, and yet today there was a desperate look in his eyes.

He went on to tell her how Superstar had been stolen from the trainer's stable which was in Southern Ireland.

Penny was intrigued by his talk of the syndicate, but not entirely unafraid. She checked her natural thirst for adventure and asked the obvious question. 'What about the police? Shouldn't you have told them of your suspicions?'

He shook his head vigorously. 'I wouldn't dare. If the syndicate think I'm on to them, they might panic and kill my horse. You remember what they said happened to Shergar?'

Penny bit her lip and nodded. What good was a dead racehorse? She ran her finger around her wine glass as she gave his request some thought. How could she not help this man? Just the sound of his voice, his look of casual elegance and the thought of his body against hers determined her reaction. She took a deep breath before she spoke. 'Are you sure all the syndicate members are as interested in sexual adventures as they are in horse racing?'

He looked at her and smiled. She felt she was melting. 'I'm very sure,' he said softly. 'It's a very select syndicate. I should know. At one time, I was one of their number.'

Penny studied her wine glass. She had seen Alistair look vulnerable before, but never like this. She raised her eyes and studied the strong face. Alistair had a sensuous mouth and engaging eyes. His dark hair was attractively threaded with silver and expensively styled. It made her ache just to look at him.

Penny made her decision. 'I'll do it.' She said it quickly.

The tension seemed to slide out of Alistair's body. He sighed and sank back in his chair. 'I'm relieved. It means you travelling all over the place, of course; all over the world in fact. I must warn you that the syndicate members are very demanding people. They are also very rich. All I ask, is that you do not tell anyone about my suspicions or your assignment.'

Penny raised her eyebrows at the same time as raising her glass. 'Not even your sister, Nadine?'

Alistair's eyes left her face and surveyed the meadows that lay between them and the river. 'No one. Not even Nadine.'

Suddenly, what he had asked her to do seemed much more daunting than before. He didn't want his own sister to know. Strange, Penny thought, considering they had always been so close in other things. She took a quick gulp of wine.

'So, when do I get to meet these people?' Casually, she played with a strand of long, dark hair and watched him closely as she awaited his reply. His fingers were tight around his wine glass.

'Ascot. I'll introduce you to the first one at the June meeting.'

'My word! I'll have to get a hat!' She laughed. Alistair managed to laugh too, but it sounded slightly hollow.

'You'll have an invitation to their private box in no time,' he stated.

'Their private box is fine, and I admire your confidence, but what makes you think I'll get a more personal invitation?' Penny asked.

Now his smile seemed more sincere. His eyes twinkled. 'Oh, don't worry about that. I'll make sure they know you're available. I'll also make sure they know what you're capable of.' His hand covered and squeezed hers. He leant further across the table.

Penny smiled bravely. 'You think of everything, Alistair Beaumont.' His lips were warm and soft on hers. Desire swept up from her loins and gathered in her nipples. She shivered with pleasure.

'You're arousing me,' she said in a low, husky whisper.

'Then I'd better do something about it. Let's go.'

As they re-mounted their horses, Alistair's chauffeur seemed to appear from out of nowhere. After nodding politely to both of them, he began to gather up the wine, the food, and the folding table.

'I want you,' Penny mouthed softly to Alistair, as she urged her horse into a canter.

'You can have me,' Alistair called once they were out of the earshot of his chauffeur. He dug his heels into his own mount and cantered beside her. 'Now would be a good time. Don't you think so?'

'The best of times!' she shouted as she galloped past him.

High on an escarpment, they found a pleasant spot among a clutch of silver birch. It was a cool place, secret and shady, where crowds of bluebells nodded among dark, shiny leaves. Overhead, the bright green foliage of late May danced against the blue of the sky.

'You'll need your key,' said Alistair as he pulled off his brown leather riding boots and tight breeches. Next to his skin he wore the usual latex rubber pants that were fastened with a metal clasp at the side. A small padlock hung from it. This was Alistair's secret; a secret Penny shared with him and his sister, Nadine.

Alistair Beaumont was a powerful man whose companies stretched from New York to Sydney. However, his dominance was confined to his business life. By means of rubber pants, Alistair's sex drive was controlled by others. Both Nadine and Penny allowed him to watch others indulging in sexual games. In that way his libido was allowed to build up to explosion point. His rubber pants were accessed by a key of which there were only two copies: one hung on a chain around Penny's neck, the other swung behind an earring worn by his cigar-smoking sister, Nadine.

Penny took the key from her neck and unlocked the padlock and the clasp that held the rubber pants to his body. His penis leapt free. It was already hard and pulsating. Need had been intensified by restraint.

Penny slid out of her cool cotton blouse and delighted in the breeze which now caressed her breasts. She pulled off her brown leather boots, undid the matching leather belt, and pulled off her white jodhpurs and cotton knickers.

Moaning pleasurably, she ran her hands down over her belly as she watched Alistair remove his shirt before his hands dropped to his waist.

'You look good,' she said softly as she eyed his well-muscled chest and the line of hair that dived down to his navel and beneath his waistband.

'Thank you,' he said with a nod. He stood smiling speculatively for a moment as Penny's eyes swept over him. He still wore his black breeches and leather boots.

Eventually his clothes joined hers. He reached for her and she went to him. Slowly, they lay down in the cool carpet of budding bluebells. Above them, the first swallows soared and dived between the escarpment and the river. The smell and sound of summer was in the air.

Aching for each other, they fell together. Bluebells, crushed by the weight of their bodies, released a perfume which spread damply across their backs.

Their lips met and their breathing became as one. As desire became more urgent, arms embraced and legs entwined in a desperate need to fasten their bodies together.

Penny moaned as her desire mounted. Alistair's member was hard and hot as it prodded at her belly.

He muttered beautiful words that she hoped were true. 'You're everything I have ever wanted, Penny. Everything I have ever dreamt of.'

'Keep saying these things. Oh, keep saying them!' Her words were lost on her breath as she writhed beneath his touch. She ran her hands over the firmness of his shoulders, the hardness of his chest. Her fingers luxuriated in the crisp feel of his pubic hair.

Her heart was pounding, her blood racing. She stretched her back muscles and tightened those of her stomach.

Shivers of pleasure ran over her body. With eyes closed, she ran her hands over his flesh and felt the hardness of his buttocks which clenched together beneath her digging fingers.

Hot and moist, the head of his penis nudged between her pubic lips. She raised her hips and entwined her legs with his as he entered her.

They moved in unison, pelvis thrusting against pelvis, belly nudging on belly. They caressed each other, their breath mingling before each hot kiss.

With the sort of dexterity only gained from experience, Penny remained impaled on his phallus as he turned on to his back. He was her mount. She was his rider.

She groaned as his fingers dug into the plump cheeks of her behind. She cried out as he dug more fiercely into her. Spurred to greater effort, she bounced up and down

7

on him. Her breasts jiggled and slapped against her ribcage like they did when she was riding a horse.

Alistair gasped with delight as he watched Penny take one breast in each hand. She held them as high as possible, then bent her head, opened her mouth, and licked each one.

Once her tongue had pleasured each breast, she released them. With her eyes firmly fixed on Alistair's excited expression, she reached behind her and touched the velvet softness of his scrotum.

Alistair groaned, jerked his hips, then reached above his head and broke off a thin branch from a hawthorn.

'What are . . .?' Penny did not finish her sentence. She cried out as the thin stick, bright green leaves, and newly formed thorns, scratched at her breasts. But she did not wince. Neither did she bring her hands around to protect her tender flesh. As before, her breasts pouted firmly forwards, her nipples redder, but hard and erect.

Alistair ignored her cries of protest. His face became red as he watched her body contort and her eyes close as if she were trying to block out what was happening to her.

He could not be entirely sure that she was only feigning pain; pretending that his exertions were truly hurting her. Although Penny's eyes appeared to be closed, she saw enough in Alistair's expression to know he was thinking of something more than the sex they were having. She resolved to do something about it.

As she descended on the downward stroke, she snatched the piece of hawthorn from his hand.

He cried out. She saw surprise in his eyes. There was also a mute request to do exactly what she had in mind to do.

'Get going, my sturdy steed, my beautiful stallion,' she cried, her voice laced with desire and demand. 'Move your hips in time with my whip. Move them to suit me.'

She stretched her arm out behind her.

Alistair yelled out as the switch of hawthorn landed on his sensitive scrotum and the curving cheeks beyond.

Penny was pleased with his response.

Alistair's penis thrust angrily up inside her as his hips rose and fell in perfect time with the stinging hawthorn.

The smell of his masculinity drifted up to her. She inhaled the scent and mewed with pleasure. Then she closed her eyes, threw back her head and lost herself in the thrill of the ride.

Her riding became more vigorous and caused her juices to run down his stem and soak his pubic hair. Faster and faster she bounced on him. Faster and faster fell the prickly hawthorn.

His back arched up from the blue and green of the flowers he lay on. His thrusts intensified. His groans changed to staccato grunts.

Penny's muscles absorbed his thrusts; smoothed them, sucked them in. Her thighs tensed as he thrust one last, almighty time and cried his orgasm to the nodding trees above.

As her own climax exploded, Penny threw back her head, pressed the hawthorn tightly against his groin, and moaned in time with the sensations that washed over her.

They lay together for a while afterwards. The warm breeze cooled their glistening flesh, and the scents and sounds lulled them into mutual peace. His fingers caressed her face and she could feel the warmth of his breath upon her hair.

Soon, thought Penny, opening her eyes and staring at his chest, I will be away from him. I shall miss him and yet I cannot refuse to do what he has asked me to. Was there no other way out?

'Tell me,' she said softly as her fingertips made patterns in his chest hair. 'What makes you so sure it's this syndicate that's taken your horse?'

He stopped caressing her hair. Penny sensed a return of his earlier tension. Instinctively she knew there was something he was not telling her.

Alistair was a while in answering.

'Don't ask me about it now, Penny. If you confirm that I am correct in my suspicions, then I will tell you how I know.' He paused again. 'Will you still do it for me? Will you still infiltrate the syndicate and find out for sure?'

Despite her misgivings and her earlier despair at having to leave his side, Penny did not hesitate. She kissed his chest, then his lips. His mouth tasted like wine.

'Yes,' she said softly. 'I will do it. Not just for you, but for myself.'

Chapter Two

*S*he chose a soft grey outfit for Ascot. Nothing outrageous or vulgar, something stylish yet, at the same
time, erotic.

The skirt was long and resembled a riding habit. It
was made from one piece of material that wrapped
around her, and fastened at the waist. A white jabot
poured delicately from the front of her jacket which
followed the line of her ribs and nipped in neatly at
her waist. White chiffon formed a band around her
grey silk topper. The ends of the chiffon trailed out
behind her like a soft white cloud. Grey, suede boots,
complete with silver spurs, were laced to her knees and
had high thick heels. A matching purse hung from a
thin silver chain around her waist. To finish off the outfit
and maintain the pretence that she truly wore it for
riding, she carried an antique whip that tapered from a
thick silver handle and looped back up to almost
nothing.

'You look absolutely ravishing,' Alistair told her as
she slid into the car seat beside him.

His hand rested on her thigh as he kissed her. She
knew he would have liked things to go further. He took
his hand from her and clenched his fingers. She knew
he was making a supreme effort to hold himself aloof

11

from her charms. She could also tell he wanted to say something important.

He cleared his throat before speaking.

'Look, Penny. If you have second thoughts, please tell me. I know I'm asking a lot of you, but I don't want you to feel pressurised into doing this. You have to want to indulge in some sexual adventure as well as assisting me.' He turned and looked intently at her. His features seemed set in concrete. 'I will miss you, Penny. I can't stress it more forcefully. But I do need to know whether the syndicate really do have Superstar.' He sighed. 'But if you want to back out, I will understand.'

Penny shook her head and covered his hand with hers. Her voice was low and gentle. 'Do you think I can't see the pain you're suffering. I know you practically brought that colt up yourself. I can well imagine how you are feeling.'

He stared at the hand that covered his. He covered it with his free one. 'I'd like to take you here and now, Penny. I know you're not wearing any underwear and how easy it would be. I'd love to roll up your skirt and feel the silkiness of your pubic hair and the satin softness of your thighs. I'd like to kiss your lips as I do this and breathe in the enticing freshness of your hair. I would dearly like to make love to you here and now on the back seat of my car. But I can't. I have to leave you unruffled, hot for someone else to enjoy.' He sighed as despairingly as he had done before. His eyes met hers. 'I'm feeling incredibly jealous. I think I'm beginning to have second thoughts. I even think I should never have asked you in the first place. Are you sure you know what to do? Are you sure you are willing to do this?'

His pain was tangible. She forced herself to smile.

'I know exactly what to do and I am completely willing to help you. Leave it to me.'

'And remember,' he added suddenly. 'If you have to phone Beaumont Place, make sure you speak to me and me alone. No one else. Not even my sister, Nadine.' His expression was deadly serious.

'I won't. I promise.'

She kissed his cheek. It felt cold. Their eyes met. They both knew that Alistair's sister, Nadine, had already been asking questions. Knowing that she would be curious about Penny going away for a while they had agreed a plan beforehand. It was just as well they had.

Nadine was over six feet tall, with sharp features and a lean, angular figure. Her hair was white and cropped close to her skull. Her eyes had a striking metallic look about them. Her skin was pale and made paler by the black clothes she wore which were in her preferred materials of leather, latex or suede.

Usually, a black cigar or Turkish cigarette stuck defiantly from one corner of her mouth. Her white teeth clenched it in a vice-like grip.

Everything about Nadine had a tightness, a no-nonsense straightness about it, though her voice could sound as warm as cognac when she wanted it to.

The other thing about Nadine was that she always liked to be in control. Both Penny and Alistair knew that Nadine liked to be kept informed. Alistair was adamant that she would not be informed of Penny's mission. But Nadine had got a sniff of their plans.

On the previous day at Beaumont Place, she had cornered Penny just as she was unhooking a bale of hay from the pulley-hook that brought it down from the hay loft to the stable. At the crucial moment when she was about to unhitch the bale from the hook, the hook had hitched under the strap of her watch.

'Damn!' Penny had shouted. On hearing the rustling of straw and the clinking of chain, she had tried to look over her shoulder. Suddenly, she heard a motor start. The bale of straw fell to the ground, but the hook – still caught in her watch strap – went up and she went with it. She cried out, but was left dangling, her toes barely reaching the ground.

As the watch strap cut into her wrist, she held on to the hook with her other hand. Although clinging tightly to the hook and the chain above it, she managed to look over her shoulder.

Nadine was leaning against the winch motor. One finger was hanging over the red button that had started the motor. She was grinning broadly.

'You look like an angel in flight, Penny darling.' Nadine's wide mouth displayed strong white teeth as she laughed.

'Nadine! Let me down!'

Alistair's sister patted the chain pulley-blocks with one hand. In the other, she held a half-smoked cigar. She was smiling that wide-mouthed smile of hers. As usual, she was dressed from head to toe in black. The fabric was very shiny and clung tightly to her long, lean form. She wore leather boots that covered her knees and ended halfway up her thighs. The outfit sported a lone metal star above each breast and one above her crotch. Penny knew they were studs that could be undone at a minute's notice.

'I'm not letting you down until you've answered some questions,' Nadine proclaimed.

'Nadine. Please let me down. My watch strap is caught.'

She saw Nadine smile as she clicked the pulley-blocks into a stop position.

Like a predatory cat, Nadine came to her side. Her latex catsuit gleamed as if it were wet. It clung tightly to her small breasts, her narrow ribs and long legs. It clothed her yet moved with her as though it were a second skin.

'Then hold on to the hook with your other hand, my dear, sweet Penny.' As she spoke, Nadine ran her black-painted fingernails down over Penny's shirt. She did not scratch, but only applied enough pressure to scintillate rather than tickle.

Unable to help herself, Penny whimpered. Her cries intensified as her nipples pushed out to meet the selfish fingers. Knowing she could not escape until Nadine was finished with her, Penny held on to the hook.

'I've never had you like this,' purred Nadine as she unbuttoned Penny's blouse. 'I think it will be quite an experience, don't you?' The grey eyes glazed over with excitement. The white teeth flashed, and chewed at the half-smoked cigar. The black earrings – things of jet and dull grey metal – jingled menacingly.

'Perhaps.' Penny's voice trembled. It was all she had time to say. Nadine, who was taller than she was, bent her shorn head and covered Penny's mouth with her own. Penny's lips opened. Nadine's tongue pushed into her mouth. Its tip almost reached the back of her throat.

Long, cool fingers opened the front of her blouse. Soft, icy palms bunched her breasts tightly together. Penny cried into Nadine's mouth as two long-nailed thumbs flicked tantalisingly at her nipples.

Nadine's mouth left hers. She smiled that hungry smile of hers. Penny felt like a sparrow at the mercy of a marauding cat. She gasped for breath. Nadine looked determined to do whatever she wanted to do. Penny was equally determined that nothing of Alistair's plan would leave her lips.

'I'm going to enjoy you,' said Nadine in a low growling voice. 'Whether you like it or not, I'm going to enjoy you. And then, you're going to tell me all the fine detail of why you are leaving here. I know you are leaving, but I want to know more than that. Alistair says it's between you and him, but I want you to tell me the nitty-gritty details, my pretty pussy. You will tell me won't you?'

In order to obey Alistair and keep the mission secret, Penny knew she had to go along with this ordeal. Nadine would push her to the brink of her endurance in order to elicit information. Penny must not give that information. She must also give the appearance that she was being pushed beyond pain, even though she was feeling only pleasure. This scenario had been foreseen.

A story had been agreed between her and Alistair. They had surmised that Nadine would want to 'persuade' her first. Penny had to go along with that. She had to act as though some secret was at stake, but not the true one. In the end, of course, she would have to confess, though the confession would be a lie.

It was not hard to respond to Nadine. 'Please don't,' Penny pleaded, her arms already aching from hanging on to the pulley hook, her toes barely reaching the floor.

Nadine laughed as she pulled Penny's shirt up around her shoulders and tied it in a knot above her head. Penny's eyes and hair were covered. Everything from just above her breasts to her waist was naked and exposed to Nadine's smiling face.

She heard the cigar hiss as it was thrown into a nearby drinking trough.

Penny whimpered obligingly as Nadine's hands again bunched her breasts together and pinched her nipples.

'Oh, Nadine, no! Please. I have work to do.'

At the same time as Nadine's strong teeth grated against Penny's breasts, she laughed cruelly but deliciously before she spoke.

'I have things I want to do to you, my darling Penny. You have things you will tell me. First you will tell me whether there is some wonderful secret between you and my brother. Tell me now before your pleasure becomes pain.'

Penny's whimpers slowly turned to sobs. Her muscles felt as though they might snap and her exposed flesh was pimpling in the cold air. It was what Nadine expected her to do – wanted her to do. Penny knew her well. There was no point in giving way and giving the prepared confession just yet.

Blindfolded by her shirt, Penny gasped as Nadine's hands left her breasts and swept over the curve of her ribs. Long fingers eased beneath the waistband of her jeans which were faded but as supple as her body. Penny heard and felt the zip being undone. Briefly, she twisted and swung on the pulley as Nadine pulled down her jeans and her knickers. In response to fierce digs and swift slaps, she lifted each leg as Nadine pulled off both her clothes and her boots.

Regardless of her determination to keep Alistair's

16

secret, Penny relaxed. There was no escaping what Nadine wanted to do to her. But she would rise to the challenge. She knew from experience that endurance must be linked with enjoyment.

Penny gasped as Nadine's sharp nails skirted over her behind. Nadine's bristled hair rubbed softly against her belly. Sensuous lips that knew how to kiss and how to coerce connected with her sex.

Desire crept through Penny's body as Nadine's tongue licked long and languorously over her pubic hair until it lay flat and wet over her mons.

Penny wriggled and squirmed. Small exclamations of pleasure escaped from her lips. This was tantalising, and very pleasurable. Tingles of arousal coursed up from between her thighs. Already taut due to her being stretched as she was, her stomach muscles tightened. Would she ever be able to resist Nadine's bizarre demands? At this moment in time she didn't want to. This event was now for her as well as for Alistair.

Pleasure ran like a tumbling stream over her body. She shivered and undulated beneath Nadine's sweeping caresses and prying tongue.

Nadine sensed her enjoyment. 'Hmmm, my darling Penny,' she purred. 'You sound as if you are enjoying what I am doing to you. Let me see if this is true.'

Penny cried out as Nadine's long fingers slid between her legs. She cried out again as two went further and invaded her vagina.

'Wet,' Nadine exclaimed. 'Too wet. I think I will leave you hanging around a while before we resume this. I want a confession, not an orgasm. You will learn, my darling girl. You will learn. And you will tell me all I need to know. I guarantee that.'

Penny's voice adopted a note of panic. 'Oh, no. Please, Nadine. I can't wait. Finish me off. Don't leave me hanging around here.' She did not add that the insides of her thighs were soaked with the juice of sexual arousal and that she was desperate to experience penetration. That was not her intention.

17

Nadine moved quickly. She folded the blouse away from her victim's face. Her fingernails dug into Penny's cheeks and made her lips pout like a fish.

There was pleading in Penny's eyes as she stared at Nadine. She could see menace in those eyes and a grim determination on that wide mouth. Nadine's lips were very close. Her breath smelt of rich tobacco with a hint of lemon.

'I will do as I please, my dear Penny – as you already know!'

Although her lust was still urgent, shivers of apprehension ran over Penny's body. Nadine was capable of anything. She remembered on first coming here how she had been left suspended over a water trough, a horse collar, leather straps, and an anvil holding her in place. Oh yes, Nadine was a creative creature.

With a swift movement, her own shirt was once again brought around the front of her face. She was again blindfolded. Penny could not see her hands being fastened to the pulley hook, but she could feel the tightness of the bonds biting into her flesh. She also felt the leather harness being passed between her legs and under her breasts. Metal clinked against metal as rings in the end of the leather were fastened to the hook and chains above her head.

'I'll just adjust these,' she heard Nadine say.

Penny yelped as the leather was tightened and pulled upward beneath her breasts so that they were held high and bunched one against the other.

'This too, I think,' Nadine added, as her attention shifted to the leather that ran between Penny's legs.

Penny cried out more loudly this time. She had recognised the unique property of this harness. It had two appendages attached to it, one larger than the other. Seemingly with no care as to Penny's discomfort, Nadine pushed the larger appendage into Penny's vagina. With the aid of lubricant, she pushed the other into her anus.

'Oh, please! Not so tight!' Penny tensed as Nadine pulled on the strap that ran between her legs and held the appendages in place. Once she was satisfied that they were as she wanted them, she buckled the end into the ring that hung from her waist belt.

'Tighter. I think we will have this much tighter!' Nadine cried gleefully.

'No!' cried Penny. But her cry went unheeded. The width of leather that fastened with cold metal buckles at the back of the harness was pulled more tightly so that Penny's buttocks were neatly divided.

Penny had been aware that she glistened with sweat. She groaned and rolled her head from side to side. She did everything to make it appear as if she were trying to escape what Nadine was doing to her. In reality, she had no wish to escape. Things were going exactly how she and Alistair had planned. But Nadine must not know that.

'Now, I'm going to leave you hanging around.' Nadine had pinched her tortured breasts before moving away.

Even before she heard the sound of the pulley chains and the motor starting, Penny had known what Nadine planned to do.

Just as she had suspected, her toes left the ground. How high was Nadine hoisting her? She cried out as the leather harness took her weight. High enough she realised, for the appendages within her to burrow more deeply.

The motor stopped, and Penny, whimpering as Nadine would want her to, swung helplessly between the stable and the hay-loft above, her body writhing, her legs kicking at empty air.

'See you later,' she heard Nadine say cheerfully.

A cool breeze blew through the open double doors and cooled Penny's naked body as she hung there. It had been pleasant. It had also been arousing. There was method in the way she wriggled against the leather that pressed against her sex, divided her buttocks and invaded her body. Tingles of pleasure came into being. Even her arms did not ache so much now that her weight now taken by the harness rather than by her muscles.

In time, Nadine came back.

Penny heard the pulley motor start up. Then she heard it stop again. This time, it left her suspended about a foot above the floor.

'Now tell me,' she heard Nadine say. 'What is this secret between you and my brother?'

Even before Penny heard the hiss of the whip she knew what was coming. Regardless of how much Nadine wanted to know her brother's business, Nadine would take pleasure from inflicting pain.

'I can't tell you.'

Penny spasmed against her bonds as the thin end of a riding whip stung her behind. 'No!' she cried.

'Yes,' said Nadine in a deep, even voice that might just as easily have belonged to a man as a woman. 'Yes, Miss Penny Bennett.' Intermittently, her tongue flicked at Penny's trapped nipples. 'Yes,' her voice hissed. 'I will lace your pretty little backside with pinkness until you tell me what I want to know.'

Each time the whip landed on Penny's backside, she cried out loudly, then whimpered weakly. Each time it stung and lay pink stripes over her creamy flesh, her orgasm took form and rose within her. With mounting excitement, she waited for it to burst into flower and make her limbs tremble, and her belly shiver with delight. It must not happen, she told herself. Not yet. Nadine must believe for a while longer that she was in torment. She was at least glad that the truth in her eyes was hidden behind her blindfold.

'How pink your bottom is, my darling Penny,' purred Nadine. Penny shivered as sharp fingernails ran over her tingling flesh. Knuckles bunched then pushed on the leather strap. The mock penis already deeply embedded in her rectum, went in that much further.

'Does it sting, my pretty?' cooed Nadine. Snake-like, her tongue flicked into Penny's ear. 'Have you had enough, my darling, pretty Penny? Will you tell me what I want to know?'

'No! It's personal!' Penny surprised herself by sounding so strident. 'It's between me and Alistair. It's none of your business!'

Although she was hanging there, naked and exposed to anything Nadine wanted to put her through, Penny sounded as if she was in control. In a way, she was. Uppermost in her mind was what Alistair wanted her to do. In order to protect that, she willed herself to be everything Nadine wanted.

'Then a little more of the same,' Nadine growled. 'Except this time, I shall direct my strokes elsewhere.'

Penny sucked in her breath and prepared herself for what was to come. She yelped pitifully as the fine strand of the whip wound around her belly, her thighs, and over her trapped breasts. Her flesh began to sting.

Soon her cries became whimpers, then her whimpers became gasps. She swung on the pulley hook, and kicked her legs into the air. Nadine grabbed and bound them and secured them to something at floor level.

Penny cried out once more as the whip again laced lightly across her belly and breasts. She twisted this way and that, but there was no escaping the perfectly-aimed strokes. The moment of surrender, she decided, had come.

'No more! No more!'

Nadine came close. 'Shush, my pretty.' Her cool hands held Penny's waist. Her contortions ceased, her body became still.

Penny sighed as the wetness of Nadine's tongue licked at the pink lines that criss-crossed her victim's flesh. 'There now. Let me get you down from here.' Nadine's voice had suddenly turned to honeyed sweetness. 'I will make love to you in the straw and you can tell me all about it.'

Nadine had done exactly that, and Penny had sobbed out a suitable explanation.

In the warmth of the straw, Nadine held Penny close against the slippery latex of her close-fitting outfit. Penny wore nothing except her white shirt which was now crumpled and hung from her shoulders.

'Come,' Nadine murmured between deep kisses. 'Tell me all about it.'

Although her words were carefully rehearsed, Penny sobbed here and there to make them sound more truthful than they were.

'Alistair has tired of me and thinks I should look elsewhere for a new sponsor. He says he is quite willing to continue sponsoring me whilst I look for someone new. He has given me a list of contacts and has sent them details of my skills.'

'Which are considerable,' Nadine interrupted. Her lips were gentle and warm. She sounded genuinely sympathetic as she cupped her hand over one of Penny's stinging buttocks. Her hand felt cool and very pleasant.

Penny's eyelashes fluttered and she managed a blush. 'I didn't want to tell you about it,' she said, sniffing as her sobs faded. 'I thought you would gloat about it – seeing as both keys to Alistair's garment would now go to you. That was why he didn't want to tell you.'

'Because he hates being told "I told you so",' interrupted Nadine again as her hand tensed over Penny's cheek.

'That's why he wanted you to think he was sending me on business,' Penny went on.

Nadine smiled and exposed a mouthful of very white and very even teeth. Penny tried not to shudder as she looked into her eyes. It wasn't easy. Nadine's eyes were smoky grey, yet at times they seemed to be fashioned from steel. Her cheekbones were high and prominent. Her eyebrows were as white as her cropped hair and almost invisible against her equally white skin. Wide nostrils flared above a generous mouth. There was something attractive about Nadine, yet also something quite terrifying.

'How sad for you.' This time Nadine's voice was uncommonly gentle. 'I shall miss you, my darling Penny. Here, take comfort from this.'

Deftly, she undid a star-shaped metal clasp above one

small breast. As she pulled a flap of latex down, her nipple popped into view.

Nadine's hand was not cruel upon Penny's head, but it was firm in guiding her lips to the pouting nipple.

Penny began to suck, and as she sucked, Nadine wriggled against her, then guided Penny's hand to where another star-shaped stud was undone and a flap opened. Penny's fingers met the soft bristles that covered Nadine's sex. Once Penny's fingers were pushing through Nadine's moist labia, Nadine's fingers reciprocated.

Penny sucked more keenly at Nadine's nipple and felt it grow and harden in her mouth. In return, Nadine's fingers toyed pleasurably with her clitoris. Penny ground her hips against the delicious touch so that her arousal, started by the leather hardness, burst into new fruitfulness. Within minutes of sucking Nadine's nipple and fingering the slippery lips of her sex, her own climax washed over her. Penny's cries of delight were smothered by Nadine's breast. Murmuring with satisfaction, she jerked against Nadine's fingers until the last tremor of pleasure had faded away.

Once Penny's climax was over, Nadine had used both hands to clamp Penny's mouth to her breast. She murmured joyfully into Penny's ear as her orgasm caused her hips to jerk and her hands to close around Penny's hand.

'I knew he'd get rid of you eventually,' Nadine stated triumphantly as she played with Penny's breast and pinched her nipple. 'I knew he couldn't really do without me.'

Determined to play her part to the very end, Penny only murmured softly and sadly. Nadine was believing exactly what Alistair wanted her to believe.

Chapter Three

*A*t the racecourse, heads turned and eyes openly appraised the slim, dark-haired young woman whose outfit covered her from top to toe, yet spelt enticement.

Because she knew she was being observed, her body readily responded to the interest in her. Her hips began to sway provocatively and her nipples pushed proudly against the silk lining of her tight-fitting jacket.

To all intents and purposes, Ascot was a racecourse, and racing was the sport of kings. But to her and others, it was more than that. Ascot was fashion, gossip, tradition and intrigue. The horses, gleaming like satin as they snorted and pranced on their oiled hoofs were, to some extent, an optional extra. Jockeys resplendent in silk and satin, perched like folded marionettes on their backs.

Eyes shining with apprehension rather than excitement, Penny surveyed those that had come to see racing, and those that had come to be noticed.

Some of the more traditional gentlemen wore grey morning suits complete with top hat and tails. Old money and old titles, Penny thought to herself. Her eyes turned to men in smart lounge suits and those dressed in blazer and trousers. Like their money, these men looked bright and new; financiers, bankers, industrialists. They are positively oozing money, she concluded, then smiled to herself. They were all the same underneath. All the same as they lay beside, below or on top of her; their members stiff and their words dictated by the thrust of their loins and the progress of their passion.

The women were dressed in their finest: sunlight glinted from earrings and bracelets that were Bond Street and unique rather than High Street and mass produced; watches were Cartier or Rolex. In true Ascot tradition, hats spanned the tasteful to the extreme. Silk suits and dresses were sharply cut and had labels that went with four-digit price tags. Ascot had a look, a smell, and an atmosphere all of its own.

'I want you to meet someone,' said Alistair. He cupped her elbow in his hand and steered her to the owners' lounge and bar.

Heavy doors swished over thick carpets. Well-dressed people infused the atmosphere with a fog of money and power. Looks from men used to getting what they wanted followed her across the room. It was not difficult to imagine what they were thinking.

Hidden by her long skirt, Penny's naked thighs rubbed against her equally naked sex. She breathed deeply as she enjoyed both the sensations it produced and the excitement of Alistair's closeness. What would these people think of her if they knew how little she wore beneath her clothes?

She held her head high, but missed nothing. From men whose wealth was immeasurable, she caught the hint of a smile, a look of lust. Furtive winks came from the jockeys and trainers who had gathered in the owners' bar to take their last instructions.

Alistair guided her on through the crowd and took her to a private room specially hired for the occasion by a company whose name appeared on a placard on the door outside.

'Beaumont,' said Alistair crisply to the man in white gloves who scrutinised his pass. 'I am expected.'

'Yes, sir.' The man, whose shoulders were as wide as the doorway he guarded, moved aside. Penny followed Alistair through the open door which was quickly closed behind them.

The room was full of men. They were laughing, eating, drinking. Some were talking seriously while others were cracking jokes – no doubt lubricated by champagne, ale, or any number of fine, single malt whiskies.

Few could resist looking in her direction. Some regarded her with polite contemplation. Others hid nothing of what they were thinking.

Alistair guided her to where a big man lounged in a wide leather chair holding a cigar. Smoke curled up from between his fingers and formed a dense cloud above him. The man was talking, or rather preaching, to the other men gathered around him. His voice was as he was; big, rich, but from questionable roots.

'What I am saying to you, is that I never got where I am today by being squeamish in thought or action. Him who takes the bull by the horns deserves to win. Him who only tweaks his tail is likely to end up in the shit!'

There was laughter both at the content and the man's rough, regional dialogue.

'Leonard.'

The man in the chair turned quickly at the sound of Alistair's voice and, seeing who it was, got to his feet. Penny was immediately aware of intelligent eyes and rugged features. Leonard Anderson towered above every man there. Penny judged him as being about six foot seven. His smile was broad and, although his gaze appeared to be fixed on Alistair's face, Penny instinctively knew he had noticed every detail about her.

'Alistair. My dear old pal. Glad to see you again.' The man did not adopt a more refined accent just because Alistair was there, and Alistair appeared not to expect one. His hand disappeared in that of Leonard Anderson, the man whose company name appeared on the notice outside the door.

'Leonard. So kind of you to invite me.'

Alistair's voice sounded very refined, almost conde-scending, in comparison to the other man. 'May I present my star rider, Penny Bennett.'

There was little time for Penny to study Leonard Anderson as he took her hand in the roughness of his palm, but she saw enough. His eyes told her everything. Already, her dark-haired good looks had affected him. There was a question in his tawny eyes, the trace of lust on his lips. He smiled down at her; his chin was square, his face bronzed and his skin tight. She smiled back. The warmth of her expression hid the intensity of her thoughts.

She imagined the hugeness of his body crushing her into submission, the hardness of his thighs pressing against hers as he prised open her legs and thrust into her. She also wondered at the size of his penis. Such thoughts made her shift slightly to facilitate the wetness that spread between her legs. He looked like a bull; big, ferocious and padded with muscle. He made her feel small.

'Mr Anderson. I'm very pleased to meet you.' Her eyes shone as she smiled. You're a big, strong man, Leonard Anderson, she thought to herself. But even big men have weaknesses. I shall find yours and I shall pander to it.

'Likewise, Miss Bennett. I've heard a fair bit about you and I must say, it all sounds very interesting.' Leonard's voice became lower and he spoke as though there were some shared secret between them. Penny remembered Alistair telling her that he would make certain her sexual skills became known to the syndicate members.

As planned beforehand, someone came to say that Alistair was wanted in the Royal Enclosure. Alistair made his excuses.

'I have to go, Leonard.' Alistair gave him a friendly slap on the arm. 'I do apologise, but I am sure you understand. Racing business. I have promised to donate a cup for a charity meeting at Chepstow. The governing body there want a word with me.'

'I'm sorry you have to go, Beaumont.' Leonard's face betrayed that he was anything but sorry. He positively beamed before turning quickly to Penny. 'Perhaps Miss Bennett would care to be my guest for the rest of the afternoon.'

Alistair nodded curtly. 'Good. That's if Penny doesn't mind.' His eyes met hers only briefly.

'Of course not.' No, she said to herself. Of course not. Penny is not supposed to mind. Nothing from now on is predictable. All of it must be endured. And all for the sake of Alistair and a thoroughbred horse.

'I'm grateful. Hopefully, I'll see you later.' Alistair turned quickly away from her.

Penny stared at his back. She felt for him, but did not show it. If she was to be of any use in her mission, she had to appear very sexual and very available.

Leonard's arm went round her. 'Never mind, Penny darling. Business is business, you know. Now let me take you to my private box. My company's hired it for the day. I'm sure we'll be very comfortable there. I've ordered champagne and strawberries, and we'll have a right good view of the race. Would you like that, Penny?'

She let herself be led there. The private box was all that Leonard had promised. It was high in the grand-stand and had a good view of the course and the crowds below them.

Leonard's hand was never far from her shoulders. From there it persistently fell to her bottom. Leonard's business acquaintances were supposed to share the box with him but, for the most part, they were not inter-rupted. By their looks, thought Penny, they were men with a definite preference for the bar – where they drank at Leonard Anderson's expense.

His arm drew her closer then his hand fell again to her behind.

'You're not wearing any underwear,' Leonard said softly as his fingers caressed her buttocks.

She smiled sweetly at him, her blue eyes sparkling and her bottom wriggling against his palm. The heat of his breath warmed her face. 'Do you find that exciting?' she asked in her most provocative voice.

'Oh, yes,' he said. 'Yes. I do. I find it tremendously arousing. Your bottom feels very firm, my dear girl. It makes me wonder just how soft your skin is and how warm your sex.'

'Then you should endeavour to find out,' she murmured seductively, and nudged his leg with her hip.

'I will,' he said hotly. 'I most definitely will.'

His hand moved round to her front and rested on her belly. His fingers feathered out to touch her lower down. Two fingers slid beneath her skirt.

Casually, as if nothing was happening at all, Penny raised her binoculars to her eyes and directed them at the track. As she raised her arms, her breasts became more prominent. In addition, she bent one leg further forward than the other. A gap appeared in her skirt. Hesitantly at first, his fingers slid beneath the silky fabric and proceeded to travel down her thigh.

'Go on,' Penny muttered. 'Get going.'

Anyone listening would have assumed she was urging on the horse she had backed. But Leonard knew differently. With one hand he steadied his binoculars. The fingers of the other hand travelled the silky softness of her flesh as he stroked the inside of one leg. Gradually, his fingers climbed higher.

Through her binoculars, Penny could see the horses running. At the same time, she detected an increase in Leonard's breathing. Her flesh began to tingle at his touch.

With long, lazy movements, he drew circles on the softness of her skin. As the circles got bigger, his fingers reached higher. She heard him gasp as he touched the moist hair of her sex.

'That's my beauty,' she said in a husky voice as his fingers slid between her legs. 'Keep going. Not far now. Not far at all.'

She groaned enticingly as his huge fingers divided the lips of her sex. With each passing second, they progressed through her silken folds, dallied over her clitoris and slid enticingly through her wet labia: His palm covered her sex.

'Marvellous,' she exclaimed breathlessly. 'Absolutely marvellous.'

'You're so wet,' he said, his voice half-strangled with his quickening breath. 'If I make you come now, will you come again later?'

'I'm built for stamina. I always get past the winning post.'

Leonard did not falter. As Penny hid her eyes with the binoculars, his thumb did sweet and pleasurable things to her hidden nub.

Wetness lubricated her sexual lips and his finger as he slid it further back and briefly teased the entrance to her vagina. She groaned and licked her lips as he pressed his knuckle against her clitoris while his index finger tickled the nerve ends that clustered around her hidden portal.

Before her eyes, Penny could see the jockeys sliding backwards and forwards over their saddles as they urged their mounts to greater exertion.

Responding to what she was seeing and what she was feeling, Penny too began to slide gently backwards and forwards over Leonard's hand, her hips moving more vigorously as her orgasm approached.

Leonard's perfume, that elegant mix of masculinity and expensive aftershave, filled her senses.

From the efforts of his hand, tingles resembling light electric shocks came into being. Her climax was coming.

Faster and faster went the horses around the race track. Higher and higher climbed her senses. Soft moans came to her throat. Rapture caused her flesh to quiver as if cold, then flush as if hot.

In the crowded stands below their private box, the crowd rose and a roar went up as the first horse passed the post.

Before the roar of the crowd died away, Penny cried out and, as both her cries and her legs weakened, she leant against the broad chest of Leonard Anderson.

'Have dinner with me.' He spoke as if he were in awe of her. 'Please have dinner with me.' He repeated it softly before kissing her lips, then her hair. 'I'll ring Alistair. He won't mind.'

Penny smiled agreeably. 'I'm sure he won't.'

No, she thought to herself, Alistair would not mind. The smell of Leonard, of turf and the sweat of horseflesh brought out her own animal urges. She wanted a man in her. Her triumph of snaring Leonard so easily clouded her eyes to the glint of sunlight on glass.

From lower down in the stand, a curl of blue vapour rose from a half-smoked cigar. Nadine lowered her field glasses and frowned. She had seen what Leonard had been doing to Penny, but why was Penny with him in the first place? Despite what Penny had told her, Nadine could not quite believe that her brother had tired of the raven-haired girl whose sexuality was so excitingly diverse.

'No,' she muttered, her cigar clenched tightly between her teeth. 'No, I do not believe you, my dear brother; nor you, my pretty Penny.'

Chapter Four

*T*he restaurant where Leonard Anderson took Penny was at the bottom of a towering building that vaguely resembled a pyramid. His chest expanded fit to burst as he told her it had been designed and built by his company.

'Anderson Tower.' He said it proudly, one hand flat against his heart as though he were talking about the love of his life.

My word, Penny thought, he worships it. But to be agreeable, she nodded her approval as her eyes scanned the building's height and intriguing dimensions. Aesthetically pleasing, it appeared to be built entirely of chrome scaffolding and sheets of dark blue glass. The glass mirrored the city and sights around it, yet showed no detail of its own interior.

Even the most uninformed could not help but be impressed and wonder at the imagination of the architect who had designed the building and the engineers who had built it. Penny's admiration glowed all over her face. Just as she had intended, Leonard Anderson noticed it.

'Admirable, don't you think? Give me your honest opinion, my darling Penny, and please, don't feel you have to flatter me.'

'I wouldn't dream of flattering you, Leonard. I shall

speak the truth, the whole truth and nothing but the truth. Anderson Tower is a stunning achievement, Leonard. Based on the Egyptian pyramids, I suppose?'

'To a certain extent, yet interpreted with modern materials and the most up-to-date technology.'

Penny pursed her lips with amusement. 'No heavy stones or whipping the slaves to work harder.'

He winced before he smiled and an odd look came to his face. As he took a deep breath, his chest heaved before he spoke. 'Whips are for horses, aren't they?'

Ah! Was Leonard Anderson a devotee of discipline? Was that his sexual weakness? Hopefully it was. This was the opening she had been waiting for. She linked her arm with his. 'Only when they're stubborn,' she retorted a little sharply, and tapped his arm.

His chest heaved again.

And you would like to be one of my horses, Penny thought as she smiled up at him. Now, there's an interesting thing to imagine. His body between my legs, his rump glowing nicely beneath the kiss of my whip.

Twin glass doors opened automatically. The ground floor of Anderson Tower consisted of an enclosed mall of high-class shops and the Michelin recommended restaurant where they were to dine.

The restaurant interior surprised her. It was plush rather than starkly modern and shiny like the glass building that encased it. Penny looked around her as she removed her silk topper.

Leonard reached out and stayed her hand. 'Please don't. I like hats. I like boots too, especially ones with spurs.' It was obvious from his wide blue eyes that he meant it.

Spurs too, Penny thought smugly. She smiled meaningfully at him. 'Then I won't. I will wear whatever you want me to wear.' She put the grey, silk topper back on her head and threw the white chiffon that trailed from it over her shoulder. As he took charge of ordering, she scrutinised the restaurant.

Everything was dark pink, except for the carpet which

was pistachio green. Mirrors shaped like fans decorated the walls at regular intervals. There was a plush 1940s look about the place. It was warm, convivial, she decided, as she attempted to tune in to the conversation that buzzed around her.

She became aware that Leonard was staring at her, his eyes scrutinising her face thoughtfully. When she looked directly at him, he smiled then dropped his gaze to her hands.

'Pretty hands. Strong hands.' His voice trembled. He spoke with feeling as if he were imagining what sensual things those hands could do.

Penny instinctively knew what he was thinking. The light of seduction made her blue eyes sparkle and her lips gleam with the wetness of her tongue. She wound her fingers around the whip handle and whisked it swiftly across the table before returning it to the spare chair on which she had placed it.

Leonard's eyes had followed its progress. He seemed to shiver all over, then licked his lips and blinked before looking her in the face.

'I won't beat about the bush,' he said in a matter-of-fact way. 'You're a beautiful woman, Penny Bennett. I thought that from the minute I saw you. That outfit you've got on hides everything, but at the same time it says a lot. I keep trying to imagine you naked. It makes me weak at the knees just thinking of you with nothing on; so weak that I find it hard to think of what you look like.'

Penny leant forward. 'Is that a proposition, Leonard?'

He flushed. 'Well ... Yes. Yes. As a matter of fact it is.'

He gazed at her questioningly.

Penny took hold of her wine glass and raised it slowly. She took a sip before she answered, her bright eyes flashing seductively over the top of her glass.

She sighed as she put the glass down. 'Can you teach me anything new, Leonard Anderson?'

He smiled slowly. 'Oh yes,' he replied. 'I can certainly do that. I'm not boring when it comes to sex, Penny, and I'm not harsh either. I am sure you will be more than satisfied with my performance.'

'I'm so glad,' Penny responded, then gazed quizzically around her.

Was it purely her imagination or had a sudden silence descended on the restaurant? This was hardly the sort of conversation to have in a place where ears could be more alert than they at first appeared. Eyes had turned their way. Mouths smiled speculatively as if the vaguest shadows of outrageous erotic fantasies had been created in their minds.

'I don't think anyone noticed what we were doing back there at the racetrack. Do you?' asked Penny.

'Would you care if they had?'

She took a while before she answered. She wanted him to think she was giving it serious consideration. 'No.' Her eyes danced merrily as she remembered the many times she had done outrageous things when she knew people were watching. Like with Auberon, for instance, when she had first arrived at Beaumont Place. She had walked him down the path to the stables, her finger firmly embedded in his rectum, his penis stiff before him. Then she had tied him up and used him as he wanted to be used. Eyes had watched from the shadows. The memory made her smile.

'No,' she said again. 'I would not have cared. In fact, I enjoyed the experience.'

Leonard looked pleased. 'So did I.'

She let him do the ordering. She had her own reasons for doing that. She took the whip from the chair. Without even Leonard seeing, she passed it beneath the covering of the table cloth.

Leonard was ordering dinner. 'The warm pigeon with mange tout and orange coulis...' His voice slid to a halt. He stared at her wide eyed.

Penny smiled at him. There was mischief in her eyes. Open-mouthed, Leonard glanced at her arms which

35

appeared to be resting in her lap, out of his vision. But of course, he knew otherwise.

Again he tried to order, but his voice sounded brittle. He swallowed hard. His eyes and mouth remained wide open.

Penny smiled sweetly. Poor Leonard. For a moment he had trouble continuing. But eventually he managed.

'. . . and a bottle of Chateau Talbot. '86.'

Penny continued to smile. Beneath the table, she continued to play the end of the whip over his crotch. It was long enough to do that. The table was big enough to hide what she was doing.

The waiter's eyes were quizzical for barely a moment. Her dazzling smile made him forget that normally Mr Anderson's voice was full of confidence. Tonight it was slightly hesitant – as if he wanted to moan or cry out in pleasure or pain.

Professional discretion overcame curiosity. The waiter bowed curtly, then fussed briefly with the table arrangement before going away.

Once he had gone, Leonard stared at her in delighted surprise.

'You bitch! You delicious, filthy, little bitch.' Leonard's voice was low, and yet there was still great power in it. His eyes glittered with desire.

Still smiling sweetly, Penny pressed the whip end more firmly against what she guessed to be his scrotum. 'Do you like it, my big, beautiful stallion? Do you like what this woman is doing to you?'

'Oh yes.' There was a certain hushed quality to his voice – like the swish of a heavy satin curtain. He was gasping for her, aroused by what she was doing. And she would keep doing it.

Due to needing both hands to use her cutlery, she did give him some respite throughout their meal. But there were times when they talked. During such moments she again caressed his crotch with her whip.

It was easy to assess Leonard's response to her handling of the whip. By looking at his half-closed eyes, his slack jaw, and the continuous swallowing of his very dry throat, Penny ascertained that Leonard was within her grasp. He was the key to the syndicate.

'I'll show you the penthouse suite,' he told her hurriedly once they'd finished dinner. 'It's where I live when I'm in town.'

They left their table and made their way out from the restaurant and into the atrium where scenic lifts rose skywards to the glass roof.

Leonard guided her to a lift that was lined with a yellowish metal. It gave the impression of being gold but, of course, it was nothing quite so expensive. But it did have the appearance of gold and might make some people wonder. Impact, to someone like Leonard, Penny told herself, was everything.

The lift had an attendant who greeted them with a curt nod of his head and a precisely spoken 'Good evening, sir. Madam.' Without needing to be told, the man pressed the correct button.

Penny's eyes followed the closing of the doors until the marble floors of the ground floor mall, its shops and its ostentatious restaurant, had disappeared.

In her mind she assessed what she had achieved with this man and what was yet to be done. As she considered this, her eyes fixed on the light which flashed from one floor number to another as they travelled ever upwards. She was aware that Leonard was looking at her and, sexual creature that she was, she enjoyed the sensations his attention was creating.

She was also aware that his palm was hot against her hip and his fingers were clutching her as if she were something he had recently bought and couldn't wait to get unwrapped. His breathing increased. What he said next surprised her.

'I can't wait to see you naked.'

Although her mouth opened very slightly, she did not blush when she looked at him. Briefly, her gaze transferred to the lift attendant. He gave no sign of having noticed Leonard's pronouncement but continued to concentrate on the rising numbers above the lift door.

Penny flashed Leonard her brightest smile. 'All in good time.' Her voice was little more than a whisper.

Leonard moved closer to her. His palm felt warm upon her hip. His fingers gripped a little more tightly before relaxing.

'Let me see your body,' demanded Leonard suddenly and, despite the presence of the other man, he caught hold of the front edges of her skirt and held them apart. Words of protest came to her lips, but she suppressed them. Protest would achieve nothing. This man wanted her and had to have her. Anyway, the sight of her black triangle reflected in the gold-like glint of the lift walls was highly erotic. Desire was instantly reborn. Already she was enjoying this man's admiration. It was then that she remembered the lift attendant.

Leonard had a wicked smile on his face. It looked as if he had read her mind. 'Don't worry about George, Penny darling. I think he's seen a few pubic hairs in his time, haven't you George?'

George looked round. His face was completely impassive. There was pride in the set of his jaw, the aquiline straightness of his nose and the sensuality of his mouth. His eyes were as soft as velvet and as dark as Africa.

With his hands clasped behind his back, he dutifully studied the patch of pubic hair that thrust so prettily from below Penny's belly.

'Seen plenty, Mr Anderson, sir. Hope to see plenty more before I die.'

Penny felt strangely insulted. She had wanted him to like it and to want it; in fact, to worship it. Why didn't he drool at the mouth? Why couldn't she see a big bulge in his pants?

Leonard pointed at her sexual nest. 'Kiss it goodbye then, George.'

Leonard leant closer to her. 'Be adventurous, Penny.'

Wide-eyed, her mouth parting with surprise, Penny

stared at Leonard, glanced at George, then went back to Leonard.

This isn't happening to me, she told herself as George removed his cap and dropped to his knees before her. But it was happening to her, and what was more, she opened her legs in order to give George better access.

As the wetness of George's tongue slicked her pubic hair into unfamiliar neatness, Leonard opened her blouse and covered each of her breasts with his hands. 'Oh, Penny,' he whispered against her ear. 'What good a time we are going to have.'

Because her desire was coursing like hot metal through her veins, and because words were trapped within gasps of pleasure, she did not speak but only murmured sweet sounds of submission.

As the lift door finally opened, George got to his feet, and Leonard ushered her out and into a private lobby in which there were only two doors. One was a single door marked FIRE EXIT – ROOF ONLY. The other was a double door. On one, etched in black on a polished copper plate, were the words, MR LEONARD J. ANDERSON.

Once the lift door had shut behind them, Leonard drew a remote control from his pocket and pressed it. Soundlessly, the double door opened. Without any prompting, Penny stepped inside.

Chapter Five

Nothing could have prepared Penny for the sheer opulence of the penthouse suite she entered.

'Well, Mr Anderson,' she exclaimed. 'This near to heaven such luxury could well be described as wicked.'

She looked all around her and took in every detail as her feet sank into a white carpet that had hints of turquoise running through it. The furniture was black leather, crisply modern, and extremely tasteful.

'It could be,' Leonard responded. 'But I don't care. I'm proud of it and damned proud of what I've achieved. I started with nothing and I've ended up with a lot. All my life I've strived to get where I am. Now, my dear girl, I intend to enjoy it.' Leonard sounded justifiably proud of his magnificent home and his route to the top.

Penny nodded her head. 'You have every right to be proud of this place. This is the most impressive penthouse apartment I've ever seen.'

Penny meant what she said. She walked slowly across the floor to the one thing that dominated the room. True, the furnishings were impressive enough, but it was the view which gave the room something that paintings, sculptures or antiques could not impart. Huge glass windows took up two walls and made the London skyline look as though it were no more than a decorative

40

mural. Lights from a host of other windows glowed like fireflies through the glass. Even the stars, although muted by the lights of the city, looked like a thousand cut diamonds set into the walls.

'Heaven might not be quite as dramatic as this.' Penny's short statement was delivered in a hushed, awe-struck voice. She knew her tone was right for the occasion. Leonard was a man who would want her to be overawed by what he had, and by what he was. 'So big,' she went on. 'So breathtaking.' She glanced seductively over her shoulder. 'A bit like you, Leonard Anderson.'

Leonard sighed with satisfaction then came up behind her and rested his hands on her shoulders. His palms were hot, his fingers heavy.

'Are you really impressed?' he asked.

She could almost taste his excitement. He was like a small boy waiting for his teacher to voice her approval of his homework.

'How could I not be impressed with a place like this?' She turned her head and rubbed her chin on his fingers. Her eyes flashed with hidden meaning as she looked up at him. 'And are you likely to impress me as much as this apartment?'

His eyes took on a sudden, new brightness. 'I'll do my best.' He smiled and breathed into her hair before his lips gently grazed the nape of her neck and sent shivers down her spine.

'I'm sure you will,' she replied, then undulated seductively against him. Her buttocks rubbed gently against his thighs and the soft warmth where his penis rested. 'That feels so good,' she purred, and lowered her eyelids.

'I want you, Penny.' His voice was low and demanding. Penny sensed his urgency. Just hearing words expressed that way was enough to make her want this man, want whatever sex he wanted.

The smell of a man, a smell she loved so well, was in her nostrils. Desire spread through her body in nerve tingling tendrils. Her limbs felt heavy, her flesh was hot with desire. Closing her eyes, she lay her head back against his chest. 'Here?' She murmured wantonly as she imagined the softness of the carpet against her naked skin and the weight of his body on hers. 'Would you like to make love to me here on the carpet or the sofa? Or do you prefer the comfort of your bed?'

'Here,' he whispered between kisses that he placed on her neck, her ears and her shoulders. 'I want you to ride me here.'

Penny's own vision of their coupling disappeared. Her fingers tightened around the silver topped riding whip that she still held in her hand. She licked her lips.

'So you want me on top. Very well. You will have me on top. I will ride you in any way you want me to ride you.'

'You will?' He sounded surprised. His eyes were open wide and a slight flush had coloured his face.

Penny, keen to play whatever part he wanted her to play, moved away from him, then turned and pointed at him with the whip. 'But I need to get in some practice, Leonard. Surely you can see that.' She tapped his cheek with the length of slick, cured leather. A glazed look came to his eyes.

Ah, thought Penny to herself. Now, my darling Leonard, I most definitely have your measure.

Raising her arm high, she brought the whip down and hit him hard across his chest.

He looked surprised. He gasped sharply before he found his voice. When he spoke it was with respect and a hint of awe. 'Alistair told me you could handle a whip. He said you really know how to handle anything you ride. Is that true, too?'

So, Alistair had told him. Oh yes. The ground was truly laid for this man to be her slave. Alistair had briefed her well. Now it was for her to take advantage of that briefing.

Gently she ran the whip over Leonard's chest. Her eyes glittered. A smile that was almost cruel curved her lips. 'Of course I ride well. I have no trouble mounting. I have no trouble using my legs or my whole body to dictate the pace and what I want from my mount. As the leather of the saddle slides between my legs, I use the cruel hardness of my spurs to elicit the most effort from my mount. To take things to the very apex of perfection, I use my whip. I lay it on any part of the body; any muscle, any limb, any sensitive area that will give me the result I require. Shall I show you how, Leonard Anderson? Shall I show you how good a rider I am?'

As she spoke, she continued to run the whip over his chest. The effect was fantastic.

Leonard stared and licked his lips as he vigorously nodded his head. She guessed his throat was too dry to answer.

With provocative intent she mounted the back of a black leather couch. Smiling and holding her head high, she undid the last fastening at the frilly front of her blouse and let her breasts spill free. Her firm orbs were held rigid by the fact that her jacket remained buttoned beneath them. She still had on her hat and her boots. Her spurs jingled as she moved. Should she take everything else off? she asked herself. Wait, she decided. Wait and see.

Her skirt flared out behind her. She pulled it back further until her furry little patch and her long, satin-skinned limbs were exposed.

As though she were riding a horse, she moved backwards and forwards against the back of the couch. The cool, smooth leather folded and eased its way between her sex lips. Warm juices caused the furniture fabric to bunch into a hard seam that rubbed against her rising clitoris.

'Get going, you beast,' she cried stridently as she whipped the couch and dug into it with her spurs. Tossing her hair as though she were truly galloping, she laughed and took note of Leonard's flushed face.

'Please,' said Leonard, his desire obvious from the faltering of his voice and his wide-eyed stare. 'Please. Take all your things off; everything, that is, except for your hat and your boots. And your spurs of course. And

43

keep your whip. I want you to keep your whip.' His tongue flicked at the film of sweat that glistened on his top lip.

Penny flashed her eyes at him as she did as he required. Her breasts bounced free. Her body glistened in the spangled light that came through the picture window and from the subtle illumination within the room itself.

Inwardly, she congratulated herself. This was her performance, and her audience was captivated.

Leonard Anderson was immobile and staring at the erotic beauty of her near-nudity. She stood there naked except for her grey, silk topper. The flowing chiffon that fell from its brim tickled the small of her back. Of course, she still wore the tightly laced boots with the silver spurs. As she stood before his amazed eyes, she tapped her silver-handled whip against the creamy skin of her naked thigh. She was enjoying what she was doing and relishing the look of lust that was evident in his eyes.

'I hope you will find that my riding is up to standard.' Her words poured like honey and her eyes flashed seductively.

Leonard swallowed hard before he spoke. 'Oh yes! Yes! Alistair was telling the truth. What a rider you are! Such skill. Such subtlety in the way you lay on the whip and dig in the spurs. I tremble at your expertise.'

'Really?' murmured Penny in a low, provocative growl. 'Then how would you like to tremble beneath the exquisite pain of my touch? Would you like me to use my equestrian skill on you?'

'Oh, yes,' Leonard cried, the thick veins standing proud in his bull neck. His whole body seemed to shiver with excitement as he began to undress. The broad shoulders, barrel chest, and huge thighs were soon exposed. They looked hard as iron. But there was far more to Leonard Anderson beneath the well-tailored business suit.

Now it was Penny's turn to be stunned. She had been prepared for the massive muscles a man of his build and stature was sure to have. She had also been pretty confident about predicting the size of his penis which, as it turned out, was of superior size and circumference to what she had imagined. But what she had not been prepared for was the fact that every inch of Leonard Anderson's skin was covered in tattoos.

Excalibur, picked out in red, black and green ink, was etched down each thigh. A tiger snarled across his chest, snakes encircled his arms and, at either side of his fully erect penis, were a pair of what looked like elephants' ears. His penis, too, had been tattooed in alternate bands of colour. It was obviously meant to resemble an elephant's trunk.

Awe-struck by the sheer artistry that covered his body, Penny took time to let her gaze wander over him. What a splendid sight he was! He had the body of a weightlifter, his muscles hard and well defined. Yet instead of glistening with either oil or sweat, he was a walking tapestry of shape, colour and movement.

As his chest muscles rose and fell with his breathing, it was easy to believe that the tiger crouching low and alert across his chest really was waiting to pounce on unseen prey. Each time he clenched and unclenched his arm muscles, the snakes appeared to be writhing up and down his arms, their red eyes glistening with evil intent. Strong and rigid, the hardness of his thighs made the twin swords look to be made from steel.

Penny, despite any previous aversion to such adornment was genuinely impressed. Fascination on her face, eyes shining, she went to him.

'I've never seen anything like it,' she exclaimed. Genuinely amazed, she shook her head. Her eyes were wide with disbelief at this most unusual sight; this most unusual man.

Leonard grinned. He looked to be thoroughly enjoying her amazement.

Tentatively, she reached for him, touched him, and trailed her fingers down over the stripes of the tiger, the sheen of the coiled snakes, and the flared elephant ears.

His pleasure at her admiration was reflected in his face and his voice.

'Look at these,' he proudly proclaimed, and turned round so she could also admire the designs on his back and behind.

A dolphin on the left side of his back rubbed noses with the one on the right side. He had an eagle's wings across his shoulders. The coils of a snake writhed over his behind in splendid detail. A cobra raised its menacing head from between his buttocks and flicked its forked tongue.

Mesmerised by this living art form, Penny ran her fingers over each glistening coil of the sneering cobra. Mixed feelings that she was touching a man and yet, touching a snake, made her shiver deliciously. As if she wanted to see the hole from where it came, she ran her finger between his buttocks, then laughed as he clenched his muscles against her.

Wide-eyed with fascination, she transferred her attention to the curving spines of the leaping dolphins, then reached up, stretched her arms, and attempted to measure the span of the eagle's wings. His muscles tightened beneath her touch and trembled when she kissed his spine, but Leonard endured her curiosity.

As she ran her hands down over his arms, she was aware of him regarding her sidelong. But she did not meet his gaze. She could not drag her eyes from his flesh, and neither could she resist touching him. Shivers of excitement ran over her own body as her hip, her thigh and her breast met the beauty of his painted flesh. She began to want him in the same way a collector might want a fabulous painting or an outstanding sculpture.

Her fingertips flicked wildly over his flesh as if seeking some semblance of skin that was still in its natural state. There was none. Even his feet had not been neglected. A multi-coloured cobweb design covered each foot from ankle to toes. A black head and four legs emerged from between the biggest and the second toe on each foot; a spider emerging from its lair.

It was one particular scene she preferred not to study. Although she shuddered slightly, the feelings of sexual desire did not go away. Still mesmerised, she turned her attention to the more amenable subjects depicted on his flesh.

With genuine pleasure, she licked the open jaws of the tiger that paraded so proudly over his chest. At the same time, she ran her hands down over the tautness of his belly and on to where the elephant's ears flared. As she did all this, her nipples met the warmth of his skin.

Her fingers traced the curving lines and vivid colours of the painted images that surrounded his penis. Then, when she could wait no longer, she wrapped both sets of fingers around it. It was big; engorged with blood and desire as it reared against her belly.

Above her, Leonard's breath came rushing from his nose.

'Do you like that?' she asked him.

'You have strong fingers. A good grip. You're quite a woman, Penny Bennet.'

Penny smiled as her fingers closed more tightly around his stiff member. 'And you, Leonard Anderson, are quite a work of art!'

She looked up at him and again felt the chiffon of her top hat tickle the small of her back. She pressed herself tightly against him.

His lips were hot upon hers as he wrapped his arms around her and folded her to his body. Penny heard and felt the rasp of his palms over her skin as he caressed her back. Success had not softened Leonard's hands. He was a man who had once laboured physically. She admired him for that. He had worked his way to the top. No silver spoon in his mouth at birth. Leonard was a self-made man. That explained his body, the roughness that edged his speech, and the no-nonsense attitude he had towards business.

Penny surmised that in business, he liked to be on top. But in sex? Alistair had given her a vague outline of what he knew. She knew sexual attitudes and habits

47

enough to watch for the right signs, the right directions. Leonard had asked her to ride him, and ride him she would.

With her mouth slightly open, she kissed his skin which was as smooth as it was richly decorated.

She reached up and let the whip fall loosely around his neck.

'Get down on your knees, Mr Anderson.' She did not ask – she ordered.

Leonard looked at her wide-eyed. He gave a little cry. Excitement, Penny decided, and knew instantly she was on the right track.

'Yes, mistress,' he said limply, and dropped to his knees.

Penny paused as she looked down at Leonard's head. She had not realised how quickly he would submit to her. Suddenly, that was all she wanted him to do. To have him there at her feet, this mighty man who had fought his way from the bottom to the top, was strangely arousing. A slight itchiness seemed to manifest itself within the folds of her labia. Even her pubic hairs seemed to move as if an electrical impulse had suddenly rushed through them.

She willed herself not to push him on to the floor and slide herself down on to his penis. Control was important – and that included self-control. She looped the whip around his neck as though he were a dog on a leash. He shook his head briefly – a mere token gesture she decided.

'Keep still!' she ordered, lifting her leg and allowing the sole of her boot to rest upon the painted snake that coiled so seductively over his buttocks. His muscles yielded to her weight. She heard him groan with pleasure.

She looked around the room and found what she was looking for. Alistair, her lover, knew a lot about other peoples' secret lives, their habits, their sins, their fetishes. He had hinted at what she could expect. Riding a man usually meant being on top. Now she knew exactly what

48

Alistair had been hinting at and exactly what Leonard wanted. Beside the chair, coiled up like snakes, was a pile of leather and chrome.

'I see you are all prepared for me, Leonard Anderson,' she said, and saw him shiver.

'I'm always prepared for a good rider, mistress,' he said, in a weak voice that sounded as if it no longer belonged to him. 'I also know a good rider when I meet one. Besides, I'm always prepared for emergencies.'

'Is that what I am? An emergency?' She ground her heel more fiercely into his buttock, and took pleasure at his groan. 'Am I not your mistress? Your rider?'

As she spoke, she dug the tip of her spur into his flank. Of course, she had no intention of hurting him with it. Her actions must only give him pleasure.

'Well, answer, Mr Anderson!'

'Oh, yes! You are indeed my rider, my mistress!' He shuddered deliciously. Penny liked that. It made those tingles that were coursing over her flesh more thrilling and far more intense.

Without letting go of her whip, Penny rummaged among the coils of leather and chrome and retrieved a small bridle that was obviously constructed for a human head.

'First,' she said, as she undid the buckle that held the cheek band, 'I will break you to the bit.'

Leonard's neck muscles tensed as she grabbed a handful of hair, pulled his head back and pushed the cold, metal bit on to his tongue. Metal rings dangled from each side of his mouth. Her fingers clawed into his scalp as she ran the head straps through his pale brown hair.

Penny's hands were trembling. Her urge to throw him down on the floor and have sex there and then was still very strong.

He tossed his head. 'Hold still!' Penny yanked on the reins so that the metal rings dragged at the corners of his mouth and the bit pressed on to his tongue. His jaw dropped open.

49

Once his bridle was in place, she once again reached into the pieces of leather.

'Cute,' she said, as she picked up a small racing-style saddle that looked as if it was fashioned to fit a Shetland pony size. Because it was racing style, it lay flat on his back with no hard edges. Racing saddles were ideal for breaking in purposes. She placed it on his back and ran the girth beneath his belly. The saddle had a crupper strap running from the back of it. Usually a crupper has an opening through which the tail is passed when a stud is undone. Once the tail is through, the stud is refastened. When used on a horse, a crupper strap is designed to stop the saddle sliding forward. But this crupper was designed for Leonard's penis and balls to pass through before being fastened between his body and the girth.

Penny brought the crupper down between his buttocks, the moist strip of leather divided one muscular orb from the other. Once that was done, it was a case of unfastening the circle of leather through which his penis and balls would go. Purposefully, she took her time arranging his cock and his testicles. She smiled as she saw his reaction and contemplated just how much he would ache once his genitals were bound with strips of leather. Beneath her lingering touch, his penis grew and his balls swelled as she fastened the crupper tightly around them. She then fastened the end of the device to the girth.

Both his penis and his balls blushed more hotly, but not hotly enough to suit her or, she guessed, to suit him. He groaned some more as she tightened the buckle that fixed the crupper to the girth.

After examining the severity with which the crupper divided his buttocks and made his sexual organs bulge with the force of their constriction, she stood back and regarded him speculatively. The sight of him filled her eyes; those bulging muscles and that mighty penis were now constricted by her handiwork. It was intriguing to imagine how he was feeling. Shivers ran over her, though not because she was cold. The tendrils were tantalising. It was as if long, iced fingers were caressing her back, her spine and her buttocks. Her breathing became more rapid as she walked around him and gazed upon his heaving body.

There he was, saddled and bridled. And there she was wearing her topper with the chiffon veil, her high boots, her silver spurs, and carrying a silver-topped whip. What a picture they presented! It was hard not to smile or even to laugh out loud. But she couldn't do that. She wouldn't do that. She was playing a part, holding a winning hand, and the stakes in this game were very high indeed. Besides, she was enjoying this, and soon she would get what she truly wanted. But first, she must be what he wanted her to be.

The right words came easily. So did the right tone. 'A painted horse. I've never ridden a painted horse.' Her voice sounded superior – even domineering. She judged it fitted the occasion.

She saw the tip of Leonard's penis jerk and become crowned with a dewdrop of moisture. His erection had grown. She licked her lips in anticipation. What a stallion he was!

'Now stand still while I mount you,' she ordered.

Before mounting him, she ran her hand over his buttocks and felt his bulging scrotum and the jewels within. Like gold ingots, she thought to herself, carried inside a velvet bag. His body trembled at her touch. His muscles tensed as if they were made of iron.

'So, you're still a stallion,' she said, in a low and husky voice. 'Well, you'd better behave yourself or you won't be for long. Two bricks and you could easily become a gelding.' She squeezed his hanging flesh. He cried out. His muscles tensed. But the cry of anguish became a low murmur once Penny was pulling on his penis.

'There, there, my beautiful painted pony,' she said in a soft voice. 'I am merely going to mount you. Then I will dig in my spurs and ride you. But I will be kind.

Am I not being kind now? Are you not enjoying me stroking your rod and making it grow?'

He made a strangled sound that vaguely mimicked the nickering of a contented horse. Obviously he was greatly enjoying her caressing his penis – which seemed to grow each time she touched it.

Penny swung her leg wide and mounted her steed. 'Walk on,' she ordered, and again felt the soft kiss of leather against her sex.

Leonard did not move, but then, she hadn't really expected him to. She smiled. She knew what he was waiting for.

Without regard for how much she was hurting him, she raised her whip and lashed his behind. At the same time, she dug her spurs into his powerful thighs.

Leonard cried out in ecstasy and began to move forward.

Penny rode him all around the room. Power was still playing a part in arousing her. She was enjoying using him like she would a horse. She rode him to one spot where a large mirror reached from the ceiling to the floor.

What a sight! There she was, naked except for her hat and her boots. And there was this man of means, painted with tattoos from head to toe, and wearing a bridle and a saddle. And she was riding him!

The more her sex rubbed against the smooth hardness of the saddle, the more aroused she became. She knew he would not want to hear her moaning with desire, but it was getting harder to hold such sounds back. At last, she could bear it no longer.

'Turn over,' she ordered, once she had dismounted. 'Lie out flat.'

Leonard did just that. The flat saddle cushioned his back. His sexual equipment was still constricted by leather so that it stood hard and purple away from his body. Penny took a deep breath as she eyed its size. Could she deal with such a monster?

She thought of Alistair and her mission. Then she

shoved it to the back of her mind. Her body was responding to what she was doing and she was unable to stop it. No matter that this particular fetish belonged to the man laid out on the floor, she had entered his world and was enjoying what they were doing together.

Now, with eyes wide, she studied the fine penis that stood so proud from its nest of pubic hair. This erection was for her and she wanted it badly.

No longer able to deny herself, she stood astride him so that each foot was level with his hips. Then, slowly, oh so very slowly, she eased herself down on to him.

Her eyes shone as she lowered herself nearer and nearer his body. Her flesh touched his and she felt as though she were on fire.

The tip of his penis nudged gently against her sex. A warm wetness ran from her and trickled down his stem. He was now ready for her, and she was more than ready for him.

As the thickness of his member invaded her moistness, it was her turn to cry out.

Tears of pleasure sprang to her eyes as the first four inches stretched her apart. But such discomfort was short-lived. As her vagina supplied more sexual juices, her discomfort became pleasure. As she took in his full length, her knees sank into the thickness of the carpet. Once she was sure her desire matched his size, she began to bounce up and down on him.

Leonard closed his eyes and began to moan. Penny judged they would have been quite loud if it hadn't been for the bit muffling their intensity.

She knew how he was feeling. She could no longer hold anything back. She had to moan, had to cry out with each breath. This was sex. This was pure pleasure.

Her moans became louder as delicious tremors racked her body.

'Let me play with your breasts,' gasped Leonard in a strangled, distorted voice.

In need of having them touched, Penny leant forward

so that his palms could cup the under curves of her breasts while his fingers rubbed and pinched her nipples.

She closed her eyes as the seeds of her orgasm gathered in her loins. Beneath her, Leonard's hips rose and fell in time with her continued bouncing.

'Not long,' cried Penny. 'Not long!'

It wasn't long.

Her climax was like an explosion of lights, a torrent of water rushing over high rocks. It was powerful, it was beautiful, and it was unforgettable.

Leonard tensed beneath her. His fingers tightened on her breasts as his moment came.

His groans of satisfaction eddied outward from his throat like ripples on a pond after a pebble has been thrown into it.

The first hurdle has been cleared, thought Penny to herself.

She was lying curled up against the painted body of Leonard Anderson, the reins of his bridle held tightly in one hand. She was feeling deeply satisfied, not just that she had seduced the first member of the syndicate, but also because she had thoroughly enjoyed the experience.

It pleased her to think there were more like him to come. On the whole, she thought to herself, this looks like being an interesting mission and there were a lot of air miles between each one.

Never mind, she thought, as she felt Leonard's penis stiffen in her hand. I'll take each one as it comes. If they are all as exciting as this, I can't help but enjoy my mission.

The security guard at Anderson Tower raised his eyebrows as he viewed the low, black car parked across the road. To his mind it had been parked there too long for comfort. How did he know it wasn't some high-class criminal giving the place a look over before doing the job?

He pressed the remote switch that would open the

door, but even before he had reached the top of the steps that would have taken him down to the pavement, the car eased slowly away.

For the briefest of moments the security man's sharp eyes caught a glimpse of the driver. Fair-haired fellow, he thought to himself. Tall, and a bit on the angular side. A thought occurred to him. Had the guy been wearing make-up? He tutted as he shook his head. 'Can't tell bloody men from women nowadays.'

Something was glowing red in the gutter near where the car had been parked.

The guard walked over. 'Filthy habit!' he grumbled, then stamped on a smouldering cigar stub before recrossing the road and disappearing back into the warm luxury of Anderson Tower.

Chapter Six

*L*eonard took great pleasure in taking Penny to another race meeting two days later.

'I'd like to make the most of you while you're still around,' he said cheerily, then checked himself. She noticed a sudden nervousness, but did not question why he assumed she would not be around too long. There were various reasons for that. Firstly, the mission had started well and she was excited about where it might lead. Secondly, another day at the races beckoned. Another day of mixing with the rich, the wicked, and the beautiful.

Peer rubbed shoulders with financier, media mogul, and property tycoon, and Penny rubbed shoulders with them all. They talked, they drank, and they eyed the horses through field binoculars as pounding hoofs sent clods of earth spiralling into the air.

The smell of sweating horses, sweating men, and the rich, cloying smell of damp grass and dark earth heightened Penny's excitement. The distinct aroma of money added a certain piquancy to the whole scene.

Harris Tweed and Burberry mixed with Gucci and Chanel. Colours of rust, green, tan and brown evoked a country casual approach to fashion and was glamorised with the addition of a gold scarf ring, tie pin, or the glint of diamonds in neatly-pierced ears.

Leonard pointed out a strapping chestnut horse with a white blaze that was just about to run in a yearling race.

'One of ours,' he said proudly.

'You and your wife,' she added, as she eyed the handsome beast through her own binoculars.

Leonard quaked as he laughed. It was as though she had merely tickled him. With a twinkle in his eyes, he shook his head and looked at her. She sensed he was about to tell her something. She tried not to look too eager. He leant towards her, his mouth close to her ear.

'By us, I mean a syndicate I belong to. We have mutual interests, mutual tastes. We own several race-horses. Keep a lot of them at a training stable in France, we do.' He arched his eyebrows. The mischief in his smile reminded her of a small boy caught playing with himself. 'We're like-minded in other things too.' She did not tell him she already knew that. Instead she smiled sweetly.

'What other things, Leonard?'

'Things you would enjoy, my dear Penny,' he drawled salaciously. She rubbed her hip against him and laughed as his palm covered, then rubbed, one of her firm, well-rounded buttocks.

Later that night after she had ridden him sore and lay warm against him, she asked him more.

In an effort to weaken any reluctance to be open, she moved her body against him. She kissed his arm, licking the coils of colour that ran over his skin.

'What other things are the syndicate interested in, Leonard? Other rides? Other masculine bodies that need a rider and a whip to bring them true fulfilment?' Her eyes shone and her lips smiled seductively as she eyed him from under her thick, dark lashes. Her nipples brushed against his chest as she nipped gently at his arm, his shoulder, and then his neck. She tasted his flesh, licked at it, sucked on it, and scratched her fingernails long and leisurely down over his belly as he groaned in response.

'Minx,' he groaned, as she pressed herself against him.

57

She mewed with pleasure as he cupped a naked buttock in one great hand and squeezed it. He kissed her, then looked at her speculatively. 'You'd love that, wouldn't you? You would be game for it all whether you rode their bodies or had them running after you, begging you to submit to their most decadent desires. Isn't that true?'

Curving her leg across his, she smiled alluringly and looked up at his rugged face, his dented chin, his boyish eyes, and the coil of golden hair that fell casually to his eyebrows. 'Of course I would,' she purred. 'I am a rider, and they are the runners. I dictate the pace, and they adjust their actions to suit me.'

He laughed at that. There was no doubt in her mind that he appreciated the double meaning in what she had said. For each horse race, the runners and riders are listed in newspapers and on a huge board at the start of the race. The runners are the horses; those ridden, those controlled by whip, voice, and the power of the body riding them. Although the horse is powerful – half a ton of solid muscle, a creature that glories in its speed and its power – it is merely the runner obeying orders. It is the rider who gives it direction.

Leonard did not fully understand that she was indeed the rider, but not just of horses. She had ridden him and, in other ways, she would ride others. They would think they were all powerful, just like the horse, but in order to fulfil her mission and find Superstar, it would be her who would give them direction.

After the race, she stayed on with Leonard at a house that was situated in a Georgian crescent. 'Why here?' she asked. 'I thought your home was at the top of Anderson Tower?'

'It is,' he replied, wine glass in one hand, eyes studying the red liquid he swirled round in it. 'I felt like a change. I thought you would like it here.'

The house was made of dark red brick and had a glass fanlight over the green front door. White-framed windows stared open-eyed on to the crescent.

Inside, the decor was a soft mixture of pale green, grey and peach. Satinwood tables with neo-classical legs, lyre ends, and a high polish, sat alongside brocade-covered settees and chairs.

Chinese and other Oriental carpets covered the wood block floors and soft chintzes fell at either side of the high windows.

There was a smell of freshness and flowers in the house. It was extremely pleasant and could almost be regarded as somewhat feminine.

Leonard took great pride in showing her where everything was.

'Everything you could wish for,' he exclaimed.

'I'd like a bath,' she responded.

He kissed her cheek. 'I'd like to watch,' he added.

'I insist that you watch,' said Penny. 'But first I insist that you run my bath.'

The bathroom was a place of blue and white tiles, dark wood and polished brass.

Leonard did exactly as he was told. Before pouring any bath essence into the steaming water, he took the stopper off each bottle and watched as she sniffed and decided.

Penny undressed slowly before Leonard's ecstatic gaze. With a casual nonchalance, she threw each garment at him and laughed as he pressed her underwear to his cheek then his nose.

She ran her hands through her hair then down over her breasts. Pursing her lips at him, she cupped her breasts as though she were offering them to him; then she ran her hands over her ribs, her waist, and then her hips.

'Do you like my body?' she asked.

Leonard, whose eyes were staring without blinking, nodded, swallowed, then attempted to speak.

'Yes.' It was all he could say.

Penny didn't mind. She was indulging her passion for being watched by sexual men. She was performing for him, but also performing for herself.

After piling her hair up high on her head and securing it with pins, she immersed herself in the warm bath. Soft, white suds covered her as she closed her eyes and lay her head back against a silk-covered cushion.

Leonard watched her from the doorway. He had brought a glass of wine with him. Penny was under the impression that he was searching for the right words. Penny considered this unusual for him. Successful he might be, but basically Leonard was a very unassuming man. He looked down into his glass as he started to speak.

'There's something I have to tell you. It's very important. You see, this house actually belongs to the syndicate, and any member could call in on you at any time. I hope you will give them a hearty welcome if they do, Penny darling. Share and share alike. That's our motto.'

Although his eyes were sparkling, she sensed he was feeling awkward and wondered why. Perhaps he's tired, she told herself. Executive stress and all that, she thought. I must help him.

Raising one soap-covered finger, Penny beckoned him to come to stand at the side of the bath. Once he was there, she signalled for him to bring his face near to hers and, when he did, she kissed him gratefully. 'Leonard, darling. Don't look so embarrassed about this. I shall enjoy staying here and entertaining the other members of the syndicate. And in such a lovely place.'

He looked perplexed. 'I have to tell you this,' he said emphatically. 'Only you see, I have to go away tonight. I have business. But you must understand that if any syndicate member comes here and requires your services, I am obliged to let them get to know you intimately – if you want to that is. You don't have to, but if you don't, it does reflect on me. As I said, we do believe in share and share alike in the syndicate.'

Penny touched his face. She liked the feel of it, the hardness of his jaw, the slight roughness of his skin. It aroused her almost as much as the beautiful paintings that covered his body.

'I will do everything I am expected to do. How could I disappoint you and your friends in the syndicate?' She smiled at him and kissed him again.

'I'll ring you later,' he promised, and sounded sincerely apologetic.

'You don't need to. I'm sure I shall manage perfectly well if someone comes.'

'But you could be lonely if no one turns up. And remember, you can't have personal friends around. Only members of the syndicate are allowed to use this place. You do promise that, don't you?'

'Of course I do,' she lied.

It was nearing midnight when Leonard phoned as promised.

'Are you missing me?' he asked.

'Of course. Are you missing me?' she said. 'If you are in need of my body, let it keep. Store it up. Keep your sex charged up like a heavy-duty battery. Save it for me, Leonard. Save it just for me. Is that the only reason you phoned?'

'No, it's not. I've got something to tell you, baby. I'm taking you on a trip to France to see the stable we keep there. How does that grab you?'

As Leonard went on to tell her what he had arranged, Penny intermittently placed her hand over the receiver. Alistair had come calling and it would not do for Leonard to hear more pleasure in her voice; to hear her sigh as Alistair's fingers held back the lips of her sex while his tongue flicked gently at her inner flesh. After all, Alistair was no longer a member of the syndicate.

It was difficult, but she concentrated enough on what Leonard was saying to know that the first, immense step had been taken.

She lifted her hand away from the receiver. 'That would be wonderful, Leonard darling. Tell me, where is this place in France?'

He appeared not to hear her. 'Oh, Penny, baby,' he gasped, 'I wish I was with you now. I wish your pretty little heels were kicking my sides, and your lovely little hand was using your whip on my wicked flesh.'

His breath sounded as if it was having trouble escaping from his lungs. She could well imagine his adam's apple jerking up and down his throat as he tried to alleviate the dryness of his mouth. In the meantime, Alistair was doing the most delicious things to her body.

'Oh, Leonard, darling,' she purred provocatively. 'Save it. Save it until the morning or until after we've been to this place – wherever it is. You still haven't told me the name of this place in France.'

As Leonard sighed, she bit her own lip. Such beautiful sensations were spreading like a feathered fan over her belly and thighs. Compulsively, she tightened her buttocks, not that it would be strong enough to hold back the avalanche of orgasm that was about to rush through her.

'Angers.'

'Splendid,' she breathed. 'How marvellous.' Penny made a supreme effort to control her voice lest it tremble as much as her loins. It was difficult. Delicious shivers were sweeping over her flesh like ice-cold water. 'Are we staying in a splendid chateau?' she asked, her voice laced with pleasure, her eyes half closed as she regarded Alistair's tousled hair. Besides his tongue lapping up the juices of her desire, his hair was polishing the inside of her thighs.

What Leonard said next captured her immediate attention. 'Sort of. It's near Angers. It's a place where we keep and train our race-horses. The other members of the syndicate will be waiting for us. Won't that be good, baby?'

Penny closed her eyes completely. 'Oh, yes. Yes. That will be good! So, so good!'

Her answer was like a fast flowing breath racing from her body. Once it was spoken, along with polite good-byes, she let the receiver slide from her hand and back on to its slot.

Vaguely, she was aware of Leonard having said that he would see her in the morning.

'Don't stop,' she cried to Alistair. 'That is so good. So very good!'

Lying back against the pillows, she let her limbs become like cotton wool as her climax rushed over her.

'Don't stop, Alistair. Lick every last drop from me. Suck at my orgasm, drink every drop of my climax!'

Spasms made her back arch and her hips heave up into Alistair's face. When his mouth finally left her sex and connected with her lips, she could taste herself on him.

His gaze was slightly serious, enquiring.

'What did he say?'

Penny smiled as though she knew a precious secret. With one finger, she casually traced her lover's hairline. She still enjoyed having Alistair on a hook occasionally. 'I'm flying out with him tomorrow. We're going to Angers in France.'

'To Angers! To the racing stud? I wasn't sure they still owned that particular establishment, but that's not the most important thing,' he went on, after pecking at her cheek. 'What's more important is how quickly you have got yourself invited into their company. I admit to being amazed.'

As she caressed his gleaming hair, she stared spell-bound into his eyes. He looked bemused. She sensed a hint of amusement in his voice and also something resembling triumph.

She frowned and tangled her fingers in his hair. Something about his attitude confused her. 'You seem glad to see me go to lie in the arms of other men. Doesn't it worry you that I shall be opening my legs to them or feeling their hands on my breasts?'

'Of course not, darling.' He kissed her and again she felt that wire of electrical excitement run over her body. 'The quicker you do make it with them, the quicker I get my horse back. Of course, the quicker I get you back, too. That's all there is to it. I know you're up to succeeding on this mission and also to getting pleasure out of it. I know you'll definitely ride them to distraction and run them right into the ground.' He ran his fingers through her hair and looked at her affectionately. His smile disappeared. He looked suddenly serious. 'You can change your mind, you know. I wouldn't hold it against you. If you think you're not seductive enough . . .'

'Alistair!' Penny pouted like a young girl. 'Oh really! How can you say that?'

He wrapped his arms beneath her and lay full out on her naked body. She wrapped her arms around him and caressed his back as though she would pull him into her again.

He was talking between kissing her hair, her lips and her nose. 'I'm sorry, darling.' His lips sucked at hers and his tongue pushed into her mouth and licked at her tongue. 'You are always seductive,' he said, as his fingers played with her hair and her ears. His breath, which was still tinged with a hint of her own female saltiness, warmed her nose and her mouth. She hugged him closer. This was how she always wanted them to be; bodies close, breath melting into one.

The sweetness of the moment was marred suddenly as a frown wrinkled his brow. He looked thoughtful.

'Don't get jealous, darling. Remember, it was you who suggested to Leonard that he might find me interesting. Or are you wondering why he or any of them would risk having me visit a racing stable if there was any chance I might recognise a stolen stallion?'

'What?' Alistair's frown immediately disappeared. 'But you're not there to look for a missing horse. At least, not as far as they are concerned. You are there because you are beautiful, sexual, and your reputation goes before you. I made sure of that. Remember?'

Penny shifted slightly beneath him. The wetness between her legs was turning cold and she wanted it to be warm again. She wanted the hardness of his thighs against hers and the iron firmness of his cock inside her.

'I remember, my darling Alistair. I trust you gave them a good description of my talents. I trust you told them of how I like my body to be invaded in every way possible. How I like to tread lightly the path of pain and more heavily the path of outright pleasure.'

He groaned as she slid her hand down over his belly. Her fingers tapped gently on the head of his penis which was slippery with fluid. She brought her fingers to her face and, with her eyes holding his, she licked long and slow, then sucked each finger in turn until every trace of him had passed on to her tongue.

'I want you,' she moaned. 'I want your cock in me. First I want it in my mouth, then in my sex, then between my buttocks. Will you do that for me, Alistair? Will you do that before I leave for France?'

Alistair half closed his eyes and groaned as though he were in the sharpest yet the sweetest of pain. Hard against her belly, his penis stirred and throbbed.

'Anything you want, Penny my darling. Anything at all!'

Penny's expression was one of pure desire. There was lust in her eyes and demand in the way her body undulated against his.

No matter about Leonard, his leather saddlery and his sexual pleasure. Her pleasure was Alistair – and she meant to have him again before she left for France the following morning.

Following some strident wriggling, she got her legs from beneath him and wound them over his back until she could lock her ankles together.

'Now,' she whispered into his face. 'Take me now!'

'I thought you wanted it in your mouth first?' Alistair managed to ask.

'I didn't stipulate any particular order,' Penny gasped, as the head of his penis nudged into her. Like her, he knew tonight could be their last night together for a long time. Like her, he wanted to make the most of it.

'Then take it, you hot bitch,' he growled, in a masterful style. 'Take it now!'

As he said the last word, he plunged his whole length into her. She cried out. Her pubic lips gripped hungrily. Her fingers clawed his back as if she wanted to leave the scars of her presence upon his flesh. Such action caused him to brace his arms and plunge more fiercely, more angrily, into her, his eyes blazing.

Scratching and yelling, she bucked under him as if to push him away from her body. She knew, of course, that it would not push him away, and that he would only slam more fiercely into her. But she wanted him to do that. Yes, she definitely wanted him to do that.

Bellowing like an enraged bull, he lunged more vigorously into her body; his loins, his belly, slapping wildly against hers.

They were not just having sex, they were sex. Sex was riding her, but also riding him. Alistair was riding her, yet she was determining the force of his stroke and the volume of his climax.

When he came, she came with him. Her nails ran unchecked down his back, and his cry of pain and pleasure echoed around the high ceiling of the peach and cream bedroom. The power of his cry, the strength with which he gripped the satin sheets, exploded at the same time as his climax.

By dawn, he had left. By mutual consent they had agreed that she needed some rest before Leonard came back. By four o'clock she would be at a racing stable in Angers with Leonard Anderson and the other members of the racing syndicate.

Chapter Seven

*I*f they had travelled to France by car, the trip by ferry from Portsmouth and the drive down to Angers, would have wasted most of the day.

But they did not travel entirely by car. They left at two o'clock and, before an hour had elapsed, they were stepping on to Leonard's private helicopter – which sat on a landing pad on top of the Anderson Tower. By four o'clock they would be in France.

As the channel passed like a strip of silver paper beneath them, Leonard poured champagne. He nodded jokingly at the pilot. 'I won't offer the driver one. Anyway, there won't be enough left for us, will there, my darling Penny?' Leonard laughed.

In confirmation of his words, and maybe because the pilot had overheard and taken umbrage, the chopper jerked and a fizz of Krug Brut spurted from the neck of the bottle.

Penny laughed because Leonard expected her to laugh. She drank enough champagne to keep him happy, but not enough to impair the sharpness of her brain. All the same, she was intrigued by a man who had courted success and got it. She was also impressed by the boyish blueness of his eyes and the way he looked at her as though they were sharing some cherished secret.

'Did you truly like my artwork?' he asked her. 'Some women despise tattoos.'

Penny shook her head emphatically. 'Leonard, I can hardly regard the pictures painted on your body as mere tattoos. Works of art would be a more appropriate description.'

Penny meant what she said, and Leonard seemed to recognise that fact. His fingers gripped her thigh as he kissed her.

'I'm glad you like them', he murmured, as his lips came close to hers.

'I'd tell you if I didn't,' she answered.

Penny ran her fingers down his cheeks. There was no fleshiness to his face. Like his body, it had a firmness about it, almost as if it had been sculpted from solid granite.

Incredible, she thought to herself, that this powerful man should want me to ride him as I would a horse. And yet, that knowledge aroused her. It made her want to feel the hard strength of his muscles against her. She felt as though by having his body next to hers, she was somehow blending with him, suffusing his power with her own. Leonard was a man not dissimilar to Alistair – either in business success or sexual habits. Both were powerful. Both liked some sort of restraint put on their sexual prowess.

In Alistair's case it was the wearing of those tightly fitting rubber shorts to which she held the key. In Leonard's case, it was his penchant for being treated, ridden and beaten like a beast of burden.

Penny guessed that, unlike Alistair, Leonard could not perform at all unless he was dominated by a physically attractive woman. It made her wonder what other women did to turn him on.

'You look beautiful,' Leonard whispered. He ran his fingers through her hair and she thrilled to his touch. Here again was that mix of fragility and strength; her hair, his fingers. 'And you have taste, my darling Penny. Brains too, from what little I know of you.'

Penny tossed her hair. She did not intend to appear vain, but she couldn't help feeling a little conceited, and not just with regard to being called beautiful. Without him adding the asides to her taste and her brains, she might not have felt so confident about herself. But he had added those other two comments and so she was content.

Because they were going to a racing stable, Penny wore a white linen suit for the trip. Tan suede ankle boots and a matching Fedora accentuated the whiteness of the suit, the creaminess of her skin, and the midnight darkness of her hair. To match her boots and her hat, she wore a suede dog collar around her neck from which dangled a silver key. Every so often, her fingers played thoughtfully with it. As she played with it, she smiled. It was precious – that key. She wore it with pride, knowing that she would be asked which lock it fitted, but would never dare tell. It was her secret: hers and Alistair's – and Nadine's, of course.

'All gone!' Leonard said suddenly and surprised her from her reverie. His face was somewhat redder than it had been.

Her eyes dropped to the bottle. How many glasses were there in a bottle? Off hand, she wasn't sure. What she did know was that she had only drank one glass. Leonard had knocked back all the rest!

With an air of bravado, Leonard reached for the door of the helicopter and attempted to pull it back. He waved the bottle in his other hand.

'*Non! Monsieur!*' The pilot glanced over his shoulder and tried to reach back with one arm while the other still gripped the controls.

He missed grabbing Leonard's arm.

'Bombs away!' shouted Leonard.

Penny grabbed Leonard's arm before he could despatch the empty bottle on to the patchwork of French fields that now scooted below them.

'Don't be so stupid!' she cried. Her tone was necessarily strident, her grip firm.

Leonard's eyes stared angrily at her. She felt his muscles tense beneath the dark green slipperiness of his Barbour jacket. She checked herself before saying anything else. Despite his sexual habits, Leonard was a man who would not like being called stupid, no matter who by.

'That would be dangerous,' she tempered, and smoothed away his frown with her fingertips. As she kissed him she eased the bottle from his hand and let it fall to the floor where it rolled beneath the seat.

She sighed with relief.

The pilot glanced back once more. His eyes locked with hers before his attention went back to flying the helicopter.

Penny placed her hand around the back of Leonard's head and brought his face close to hers.

'Pleasure me,' she growled, her expression surly and her eyes angry. As she repeated her demand, she began to undo the white pearl buttons of her jacket, then of her trousers.

She cupped one breast in the palm of her hand and squeezed it tightly so that the nipple pouted forward.

At first Leonard stared, then seemed to crumple as he bent his head and sucked loudly on one upright nipple, then the other.

As he sucked, Penny wriggled in her seat and slid her trousers down to her knees.

'That is so good,' she purred. 'But I want more. I want you to do so much more.'

As he sucked at her breasts, she ran her fingers through his hair. It kept its style. It was almost as if that too was as unyielding as his body. Then as the heat of his breath warmed her breasts, she closed her eyes and pretended it was Alistair.

'What else do you want me to do, baby?' Leonard's voice was plaintive. Here was her supplicant now; her slave.

'Pleasure me,' she said as she arched her back, undid the safety belt and slid down further into her seat.

Despite the confining properties of her trousers, she managed to open her legs that much wider though her ankles remained tightly constricted. 'Pleasure me,' she said again, as she caught hold of Leonard's hand and guided it to the waiting warmth between her legs. At the same time, her tongue licked languidly over her lips.

She heard someone gasp. Not Leonard. Not her. Suddenly the whole situation changed. She realised the pilot was taking in every detail of what was happening. The helicopter must have rear view mirrors!

She didn't know. All she did know was that a new facet had most definitely been added to the situation. The pilot, whose hot, smouldering eyes had met hers, was watching with interest and, because he was watching, she was getting excited.

Her flesh began to tingle. She ran her tongue over her lips and her eyes were half closed. Her hips seemed suddenly to undulate up and down, almost as if they had acquired a will of their own.

She wanted Leonard to pleasure her, and she wanted the pilot to watch.

Leonard stared, then smiled. There was no trace now of any anger or childish wilfulness. She was telling him what she wanted him to do to her.

He ran his hand over the superb flatness of her belly. She threw back her head and moaned softly as the roughness of his palms caressed her.

Responsive as ever, her body warmed to the hard bluntness of Leonard's fingers as they went in and out of her. Her breath quickened. Her hips rose to meet them.

'That is so good,' she purred. She was not lying. Leonard was doing a good job. The fingers of one hand were sliding in and out of her, his thumb tapping gently against her clitoris. With the other he played fast and loose with her nipples. He pinched them, pulled them, and flattened each breast in turn with his huge palm, then gripped them with his thick, vice-like fingers.

Although her eyes were half closed, she was aware of

the excitement in his eyes and the rapid exhalation of his breath. But it wasn't just him she was aware of. Somewhere beyond his head, she could see the tableau they presented reflected in the glass of the helicopter windows. Instantly, she knew for sure that the pilot could see them too.

Definitely knowing someone was watching gave new impetus to her yearning loins; new fire to her rushing blood. Just as on so many other occasions, she was the star attraction. She could not help but give a good account of herself. Fired by what was being done to her and by the knowledge that she was being watched like some star turn on a West End stage, she rose to the occasion.

'More, more!' she cried as she thrust her hips up to swallow his fingers. 'Oh, give me more! Please don't keep me waiting! Please make me come!'

The pool of wetness within her overflowed as Leonard's fingers did their sterling work. A warm moisture ran over Leonard's fingers as her labia sucked at his constant motion. It moistened the curls of pubic hair that covered the outer lips of her sex. From there it spread over the satin softness of her inner thighs.

Curious to see the effect she was having on Leonard, she regarded him through half-closed eyes. He was breathing heavily, his gaze fixed on the juicy sex he was so busy manipulating.

A sort of pride came to her; a pride that this big man was regarding her juicy sex with such awe-struck enthusiasm. She could imagine well what he was seeing. The deep pink of her inner flesh would be glistening with the juices of her arousal.

She saw his tongue flick rapidly out between his lips, almost as if he were tasting that fluid, licking it, drawing it in, and running its salt-laden moisture over his tongue.

Knowing this made her moan with a strange, all-consuming urgency.

She sighed as a wave of sensual delight swept over

her. It was as though all her body was moving, shivering, shimmering in anticipation of what was yet to come.

It didn't matter that Leonard would get nothing out of this experience. This experience was for her and her alone. Ripples of sensation spread throughout her body. Her climax was near, and yet she did her best to hold it back, to curb its release in order to make it that much greater. But her time was coming near. Her moment of orgasm would not be denied. Her hips worked more vigorously against his hand. Inside her body, the storm, the eruption that was brewing, began to rise. This time it would not be denied.

Body straining and voice strangled with sensation, her moment came at last. Like thunder in a storm, her climax rolled over her. The clouds she could see through the window tumbling in a vast white and grey cavalcade seemed to be echoing the sensation of her orgasm.

She knew that despite the pilot concentrating on flying the chopper, he had circled the same spot for some time. How convenient, she thought. How considerate to have a pilot willing to postpone landing until she had achieved her orgasm.

Leonard looked a picture of happiness. 'Did I do it well?' he asked her.

'Very well,' she replied. 'It certainly made the journey go more quickly, don't you think?'

'I'm glad,' replied Leonard softly. 'Really glad.' He turned away from her then and proceeded to look out of the small quarter window which he had managed to open.

There was a certain boyish, innocent charm about the way Leonard said that. Penny could not help feeling affectionate towards him. Before pulling up her knickers and zipping up her trousers, she tapped lightly at her clitoris. It leapt beneath her touch, still tingling with residual sexual sensations. She smiled to herself. What a mission this was, and how well exercised her libido had been. Yet there would be more such instances as this. She was sure of it.

She took hold of the back of the flight seat and leant forward so that her chin was almost touching the shoulder of the man who was flying the helicopter.

'How long till we land?' she asked him.

'Just minutes now, *Mademoiselle*.'

'Good.'

'And *Mademoiselle*,' said the pilot softly. 'That was quite a performance you gave. It is something I would like to see again. I must admit, I have never carried a passenger quite like you. I will never forget you.'

'I'll remember you too,' whispered Penny. She glanced briefly at Leonard. He was still occupied gazing out of the window..

Penny turned her attention back to the pilot. Her fingers lightly brushed his neck. It was warm, soft, and covered with a layer of fine hair.

She had only glimpsed that pilot once, yet his details were clear in her mind. There was enough fire in those dark eyes to make any woman smoulder. His chin was strong, his shoulders broad, and he possessed a lean, athletic body.

As Leonard composed himself, Penny made final adjustments to her clothing then refastened her seat belt. They would shortly be coming in to land.

Sky and land seemed to swop places as they banked and sped towards the St Orteus racing stables.

Like a victory roll, Penny thought to herself. It's almost as though the pilot were celebrating my climax; as though he took a far greater part in it than he actually did.

Perhaps, she considered, he would play a greater part in future. But not now, she told herself. This is not the right time. Not yet.

Chapter Eight

Swooping low, the helicopter's nose dipped briefly towards the gateway where they would have entered the racing stable had they been arriving by road. There was a good view of the place at this level. Penny craned her neck to look closer.

There were ivy-covered walls on either side of the gate and a large sign against a screen of deciduous trees. The sign stated the name of the place and the fact that uninvited visitors were not welcome. Luckily, they were expected.

The land around the place was without undulation – like some of the Polder regions of The Netherlands. Flat racers need flat land. There were enough trees around but the expanse of sky equalled that of the land and was unbroken by either hills or mountains.

Buildings were pretty scarce, too, in the surrounding terrain. There were one or two stone farmhouses that looked in need of as much subsidy as the human beings who stared up from small fields at the helicopter swooping overhead.

As usual, in this part of France, the straightness of the road shot like an arrow into the distance. Poplars planted equidistant from each other threw alternating stripes of sun and shadow across the tarmac. Running parallel to the road was the railway line. This took the TGV between Paris, Tours and the South.

Beyond the railway line the River Loire sparkled in the sunshine. It was travelling virtually the same journey as the railway and the road but was less straight, and its traffic travelled much more slowly.

The helicopter circled at Leonard's request before dipping over the signboard and the trees. His voice quick with excitement, he pointed out the direction to Tours, to Le Mans, and struggled with the name of a medieval church tower in the distance.

The helicopter landed on a level piece of grass to one side of a range of stable blocks and a three storey house that had a mansard roof and blue shuttered windows set into its white walls. There were two other helicopters already in the field.

Once the rotor blades had slowed to a relatively safe speed, the pilot let them out.

Whether it was out of fear that Leonard was a little tipsy and might do something stupid, or because he wanted to glance in her direction some more, the pilot insisted on escorting them to a gate that opened into a cobbled yard.

She flashed him a meaningful smile and noted the look in his eyes, the yearning on his lips. The pilot wanted to see her again. He also wanted to see more of her and do far more with her than Leonard had done. She could tell. And she wanted to see him, study the shape of his body beneath the leather jacket and tight blue jeans. But the time had come for him to go. He nodded stiffly before leaving them.

'Enjoy your stay, Mr Anderson, Miss Bennett.'

'Thank you, Sasha,' returned Leonard.

Penny merely smiled. Up in the sky, the dark brown richness of Sasha's voice had been drowned by the noise of the whirling blades. Heard without background noise, the sheer warmth of it, along with the promise of outstanding sensuality, made her heart jump and her legs tremble.

'Nice place, don't you think?'

She roused herself to Leonard's comment and forced herself to gaze in the direction he was indicating. He offered her his arm, and she took it. She did her best to push a growing fantasy about her and the pilot from her mind. It was all about him being dressed in nothing but a leather flying jacket – perhaps with boots – and her in much the same. Their lower bodies would be bare, one pelvis thrusting against the other, his penis pulsating as it sought the opening to her body. They might even be doing it in the helicopter, or they might be . . .

'You do like it, don't you?'

Leonard's voice interrupted her reverie. Her response was immediate.

'I most definitely do. I must admit I'm surprised. It didn't look half as interesting from the air.'

It was a half truth. After all, she hadn't really been looking. Her orgasm had taken priority. But Leonard seemed well satisfied with her answer.

Smells and sounds of the country were all around her. Fresh grass, hay, and even a hint of manure. Bees buzzed from beneath crooked apple trees, and swallows swooped down over the mansard roof before disappearing beneath frowning eaves. They were all part of the scene, and the scene was France. The buildings had survived from before the reign of *Le Roi Soleil* – The Sun King – Louis the Fourteenth. Steep roofs topped white plastered walls. A wide arch seemed cut like an afterthought beneath a trio of shuttered windows.

Beyond the archway was a parking area where chauffeurs leant against shiny cars as they waited for their employers. They glanced briefly in her direction, spoke to each other, then looked again. Without hearing any sound, she knew instinctively what they had said, what they were thinking. She tingled. Admiration from any source was always welcome.

The cobbles were slippery and uneven beneath her feet. Refreshed from her flight and alert to anything of interest, she was glad she had the sense to stick to low-heeled boots. The cobbles would not have been easy to negotiate in high heels. Obviously she had packed higher heels for more suitable occasions.

A youth dressed in a black vest, very tight blue jeans and high black boots was the only person in the yard. He stood smartly to attention when he saw them.

Leonard struggled with his French. '*Où est les gentlemen?*'

Close enough, thought Penny, but did not offer any assistance. School*girl* French could be as acute an embarrassment as school*boy* French. The youth obviously thought so too. He smirked before he answered. '*A l'école, monsieur.*'

In the school. He had pointed to a large double door into which a smaller one had been set.

'This way,' said Leonard and protectively wrapped his arm around her. 'This is where my colleagues will be.'

Penny had a mind to ask him if he wanted to talk with them in private. It would have been convenient if he had, then she could have rooted around outside just in case Superstar was stabled here. Somehow, she doubted it.

The warm mustiness of the indoor school spilled outward as Leonard opened the small door. He let her go in first.

Four men and one woman were grouped at the end of the ring. Their backs were towards Penny and Leonard. Someone was leading a rangy chestnut colt around a viewing ring.

Everyone seemed intent on what they were doing – so intent that Penny wondered whether they were, in fact, expected. A minute seemed like ten before someone acknowledged their presence.

One man looked over his shoulder. 'Leonard. Come and join us.'

That was all it would have remained – a mere glance – a mere looking over his shoulder. But on sighting Penny, the man turned round completely. 'Well, Leonard you old toad, what tasty little filly have you brought us?'

Deep-set eyes with hooded lids assessed Penny as though she were a prime piece of bloodstock. She felt suddenly vulnerable, but also drawn to the strange paleness and dramatic eyes of the man who was looking at her.

'Daz,' said Leonard, his jaw set a little too firm to be friendly. 'As polite as ever, I see.'

The man Leonard had addressed as Daz ignored Leonard's outstretched hand and stood before Penny. He stood with arms akimbo, legs slightly apart. Master of the manor, thought Penny, and wondered more about him.

The smell of leather assaulted her nostrils as the man reached out and gripped her shoulders. His eyes, like chips of black coal, seemed to bore into hers.

'I'm a music artist. Some would say pop star. My name's Daz Dazzler. What's yours?'

His speech was languid, almost lazy. Designer speech, thought Penny. It was meant to be sexually appealing – and it worked!

Penny answered. 'Penny Bennett. I ride horses – amongst other things.' She glanced briefly at Leonard before returning her gaze to the hawk-like features of the man before her. He was wiry, but well formed like all successful pop icons. His shoulders seemed angular, which could have been the result of the padding in the black leather coat he wore. The hem of the coat skimmed the top of his matching boots. Everything about him was black: his trousers, his waistcoat. Even the hairs on his chest which showed above the deep 'v' of his black shirt. The long hair that swept from his head was gathered into a pony tail at the nape of his neck. His eyes matched the rest of him.

His grin was as languid as his speech. 'Penny Bennett. Who rides many things. Ride, ride, ride, baby.' He began to recite the old nursery rhyme, 'Ride a cock horse, to Banbury Cross. To see a fine lady upon a white horse.'

The next two lines he'd amended, however. 'With hands on her nipples, and balls on her nose. She shall have plenty wherever she goes.'

'And I take it you sing?' Penny snapped.

The question was slightly impertinent. After all, she'd seen his gaunt face gazing from coloured posters in the HMV shop. Of course he sang. She'd also seen him on television adverts for pop videos. On all of them he'd been gyrating his hips and thrusting his groin forward as though his penis had somewhere to go.

No offence was taken. Daz actually seemed to lap it up as though it were a compliment.

'I'm your singing, dancing, lovin' man, baby. I sing to them, push it to them, and take their money as I seduce them with my words. Do I turn you on, darling?' he asked as he jerked his hips towards hers. 'Do you like the way I sing?'

The leather of his trousers had barely touched her. Even so, she got the impression that a hard, hot penis was getting ready for action.

But Penny had a game to play. She pouted as she shook her head. 'How can I possibly comment? I've heard very little of your singing. I've seen even less of the way you perform. I would need to experience quite a few performances before forming a considered opinion.'

Her eyes sparkled wickedly and she made no attempt to hide what she was thinking. She looked defiantly into his face. Her tongue rolled provocatively over the lushness of her lips.

Within that gaunt face, above those sharp cheekbones, his black eyes glittered with a magical intensity that left her in no doubt that Daz Dazzler of the Blazing Trail pop group, would be giving her a private performance. Despite his clichéd persona, a thrill of desire travelled through her at the prospect. Daz Dazzler certainly had charisma; his record sales reflected that. So did the stories of his many conquests – unless, of course, they were merely publicity hype.

Now, thought Penny to herself. Will I be one of his conquests, or will he be mine? The question was purely academic. She would do whatever it took to find out about the whereabouts of Superstar, but she would also enjoy her quest, and she would enjoy Daz Dazzler. He aroused her. The black eyes, the height of his forehead, the rich sweep of his waist-length hair. All these things were Daz Dazzler. He'd built his career on being a creature of sexual allure.

Oh, I want him here and now! her desire urged her. Here and now!

Perhaps it would have happened. The moment was there. So was the attraction. She could almost taste it in the air. The smell of him and the way his very presence seemed to pierce her flesh like white hot needles was almost tangible. She tingled, but the moment was lost when someone else spoke.

'Don't hog the lady, Daz. Give her a little air.'

Despite the fact that Daz was standing firmly between her and the speaker, Penny held her chin high and took in what details she could.

Judging by the accent, the man who had spoken was American. Beyond the sweep of hair and the square-cut shoulders that were Daz Dazzler, Penny saw the six-foot man with close-cropped blond hair, baby-blue eyes, and a white-toothed smile. He looked the typical college jock, though nearer thirty than twenty.

As he pushed himself more firmly forward, Penny had a better view of both him and the other members of the syndicate.

The American introduced himself as Aran McKendrick and said he came from Texas. Aran introduced the others before Leonard had a chance to. 'This is Ben Said,' he drawled. Arab eyes beamed from beneath the red and white check of desert headgear that was teamed with a blue silk Armani suit.

'Charmed, my dear lady,' crooned the oil-rich prince.

Ben Said had no hint of an accent – unless you counted Oxford or Cambridge. He took her hand, kissed her fingers, then kissed her palm. His tongue flicked out swiftly within that kiss. 'At your service, my dear lady.' Above sensual lips, she noticed that he had a black moustache that was as thin as a pencil. His skin was as brown as a polished conker.

The next man shook her hand. 'I'm Al.' Green eyes speckled with flecks of some indistinct colour looked down into hers. There was a fierceness about this man, a hint of danger that sent icy shivers down her spine. Al was not as dark as the Arab but his skin was more swarthy, his suit sharply tailored, his shirt crisply white and the dark conservatism of his tie offset by the addition of a gold tie-pin shaped like a dagger. The vivid scar that ran down his left cheek did not make him ugly. On the contrary, Penny found her eyes being drawn to its scarlet cruelty. How had he got it, she wondered, and was that sexual arousal she was feeling, or was it merely fear? Would he notice how clammy her palm had become? He did not appear to notice. His handshake was as curt as his introduction.

The next voice gushed like a mountain spring. Her shoulders were held in a sudden vice-like grip. A generous bosom bounced against hers, and the smell of expensive perfume hit the back of her throat. Penny caught her breath and a sudden fear hit her. For a moment she thought of Nadine. But the woman was not her.

'Babushka! My darling girl. How wonderful to meet you. Leonard has told us all about you.' The woman who addressed Penny in a richly accented voice turned to Leonard and slapped him playfully on the chest. 'He has not enlightened us with the more intimate details of your friendship, but I dare say he will. Won't you, my darling Leonard?'

A proud look appeared across Leonard's features. He took a deep breath which expanded his chest to considerable width. Penny eyed him speculatively. What would he tell them about her?

'This, my darling Penny, is the Countess Lenushka

who is rich, handsome and downri~~~~~
ushka, you wicked woman, this is Pen~~~~
sensuality could well surpass your ow~~~
latest acquisition. She was recommended~~~
old friend, Alistair Beaumont. She is also~~~
horsewoman. I can vouch for it.'

Slow smiles were exchanged. What were t~~~ ~~~k-
ing? Penny asked herself. Judging by their exp~~ssions,
it could well be that they knew of Leonard's favourite
fetish. It did not shame her to think that they would
know what she had done with Leonard. On the contrary,
she took a certain pride in the fact. What was more,
nothing they could throw at her was insurmountable.
She had been warned that there would be many sexual
adventures to experience. But she was ready for them
all. She resolved to throw herself into this set of wealthy
lifetimes heart and soul. She took a deep breath and
listened to what was going on.

The countess confirmed her judgement. There was a
gleam in her dark brown eyes as she tilted her head and
looked from Penny to Leonard. 'And you, my darling
Leonard, do like a woman who rides well, do you not?'

A titter of amusement rose from them all – including
Leonard. A flush came to his cheeks. 'You know I like a
firm hand and strong thighs, Lenushka.'

The woman nodded her beautiful head of ash blonde
hair. Her dark brown eyes seemed round as glass beads
and her red lips opened, smiled, and revealed her ultra
white teeth. Luxurious eyelashes brushed warmly
rouged cheeks as she turned her attention back to Penny.
Red painted finger nails stroked Penny's face: gold
rings, heavy with precious stones, sparkled before her
eyes.

'I am glad to hear you are a rider of merit, my darling
Penny. As that mountain of a man has just told you, I
am Lenushka. Countess Lenushka of Rumania. I am very
pleased to meet you and cannot help but wonder at the
skill and beauty of a woman who has enraptured our
Leonard so. Will you show us this?'

...oke English in that precise way people have ...t they have learnt it as a second language, and then only to be sociable rather than academically brilliant.

However they were spoken, such words were unexpected. Penny blanched and thought rapidly before she answered. She knew instinctively what that answer must be. She made a determined effort to appear confident before this woman who looked so cool and so wealthy in her heavy jewellery and expensive clothes.

Penny took a deep breath and felt instantly braver. 'Certainly. Whenever you're ready to truly appreciate my skills.'

The woman nodded her head slowly. The men beamed.

'I have a suggestion.' It was Aran, the Texan, who spoke. 'Let's look over the last colts and fillies, then we'll look over her. How does that grab everybody?'

Penny noted the twinkle in his eyes. He winked, and she winked back.

'I think that is the most marvellous idea, my darlings,' trilled the countess, her hands as expressive as her voice.

Everyone else looked Penny up and down before nodding their agreement.

Daz took hold of her arm and squeezed her between him and Ben Said. Leonard looked slightly hurt that she had been so swiftly taken from him, but once the colts and fillies were being paraded again, he placed himself next to Aran and was soon talking horseflesh.

Penny asked herself what she had let herself in for. She had a good idea of what Aran had meant by 'looking her over'. Already she was apprehensive, her stomach tightening, her flesh tingling. Her breasts were resting on the top railing that circled the exercise ring. Either side of her were men from very different backgrounds. She could feel the warmth of them both, and hear their breathing as they eyed the horses. But they are not just looking at the horses, she thought to herself. In their minds they are also thinking of me, trying to imagine

84

what my naked flesh might be like. Soon they will know.

As she watched the newly broken yearlings parading around the ring, she felt a hand from each man caressing her buttocks. One of those hands belonged to a pop star and one to an Arabian playboy. Both felt hard, both felt warm, and both were sending delicious shivers throughout her body.

As a bay colt was trotted around the ring, she felt hands run up under her jacket. By the time the colt had slowed to a walk, warm palms were running over her bare back. Prying fingers slid over her flesh and connected with the rise of her breasts. She began to breathe more heavily and, as their fingers followed the curve of her breasts, her nipples hardened and ached for male attention.

'Nicely built,' said Daz, his gaze firmly fixed on a grey filly that was now prancing around the ring. 'Not too big, but well constructed. I should imagine she'll be quick off the mark. Plenty of stamina. Plenty of speed.'

'I agree,' returned Ben Said. He glanced sideways only briefly before he too returned his gaze to the filly before him. She was now bucking playfully – half walking, half trotting. Head proud, neck curved, the filly's dark eyes looked at those who looked at her. Nostrils flared as she snorted with indignation that she could not run, only prance. At least, that was how Penny viewed her.

Penny's flesh was quivering, her breath trembling with pleasure. She gasped as the fingers of Ben Said pinched her nipple. 'Hear that breathing? She is a drinker of the wind, a storm in the desert. She has staying power. Will take on all comers and win.'

'Sure will,' answered Aran, the big Texan. 'She's got a wild look in her eyes, but even the most wild can enjoy pleasing a firm master.'

Through narrowed eyes, Penny watched as the filly was led away. Soon it would be her turn to show off her best paces.

'Come,' said Lenushka, once the ring was empty. 'We

have seen what bloodstock we have available in the equine world. Now let us see what Leonard has acquired in the human one.' The decadent countess patted Penny's face in the same way as she might pat that of a spirited horse. Penny could smell her perfume and hear the rustle of her white silk shirt that was worn with a suede waistcoat of the palest beige, matching pants and white leather boots. She wore a gold brooch at her throat and gold earrings to match. Her hair was just as pale as her outfit and precision-cut to just below her ears. Dark eyes and dark brows gave away the fact that her hair was no longer its natural colour. Perhaps grey had been teased into pale blonde. No matter her age, Lenushka was still a beautiful woman. 'Well my fine gentlemen, it is I, Lenushka, who will show you how best to display prime bloodstock.'

Penny had only the barest inkling of what might be about to take place. The memory of a night in the forest when she had been kitted out like a horse came to her mind. Naked, she had been bridled up in similar leather to that which a pony might have worn. Then she had been encouraged by the use of a whip to take a number of jumps until the sweat was glistening on her body. After that, she had been harnessed to a small cart and a man named Dominic had sat up in the seat and driven her as he might drive a pony. To complete the picture of her being a horse, she had been furnished with a tail. It had been fixed to her by the insertion of its hard end within the confines of her rectum. A false phallus on the harness had been inserted into her vagina.

She trembled as she remembered that night, and even as she followed Lenushka, a tantalising shiver ran down her spine and dug like fine twigs between her buttocks. A weakness came to her legs and a warm moistness erupted between them.

Penny winced as Lenushka's long fingers gripped her upper arm and pulled her into an empty horse stall where fresh straw had been spread on the floor. 'In here, my dear Penny. Now. Let us get you out of these clothes.'

Lenushka gave Penny no time to think about where she was or whether she really wanted to do this. In the close confines of the stall, Lenushka helped her get out of her clothes.

A light chill ran over Penny's skin as her body became exposed. Lenushka reminded her of Nadine and, because of that, she found it impossible to protest.

Anyway, the shame of her nudity would pass. She knew that. Once she was naked, Lenushka would run her eyes over her body, perhaps also her hands. She would admire her, test her flesh, open her mouth and run her fingers through her hair as though she were the most desired of bloodstock.

There was no gentleness or thought of decorum as Lenushka stripped her garments from her. Every so often a sharp nail would graze her skin and leave a burning sensation that in turn led to a more sexual one. Penny yelped because she knew she was expected to. In response, Lenushka slapped first one breast then the other. 'Be still. Let me look at you.'

It was as Penny had assumed it would be. She did as she was told. All her clothes were now stripped from her body. Her breasts were jutting forward, her bottom was jutting behind. There was a proudness to her nakedness. She was revelling in her youth, in her beauty. It would be coveted by Lenushka. She knew it.

Lenushka stepped back as she viewed her. 'Ah, yes. Very nice. Very nice indeed. You have nice breasts,' she said, and her voice was less strident, more lascivious.

Penny stayed completely still as Lenushka's hands covered her breasts and squeezed them quite fiercely. 'You also have a beautiful line to your back,' she added, as her fingers trailed slowly and delicately down Penny's spine. 'And your bottom is very pert,' she said, her soft touch running over the contours of each buttock. 'And see how well they are divided from each other!'

Penny gave a little cry as Lenushka's finger slid

between her smooth, round orbs and, without any consideration for her discomfort, poked fiercely into her anus.

Just as Penny had guessed, Lenushka came to her side. Forcing her fingers into Penny's mouth, she pulled at the corners to the point where it hurt.

'Keep your hands at your sides. Do not move or I will beat you until you cannot stand!'

Penny did as she was told. Of course, she knew she could say no, but at the same time, she did not want to. Now it was not just a case of Alistair's horse. It was also because this was her adventure and, although these people might think they were in control, they were not. They were being controlled by her sensual body, her sexual attraction. And they could not resist her, but in turn, she could and would not resist them.

A hard slap landed on her bottom and made her squeal as its warmth sent currents of desire over her body. How odd it was that pain – gentle pain – could do that; that vulnerability could lead to submission which, in turn, could lead to a breathtaking conclusion.

'Quiet,' cried Lenushka. 'Let me see if you have been broken to the bit.'

Penny allowed her mouth to be opened wide. Not only had this woman's fingers stretched her mouth, her hand had reddened her behind.

'Ah, yes,' Lenushka murmured approvingly. 'You have been broken to the bit and the bridle. What a sensible owner you must have had.'

Penny had a strong urge to tell Lenushka that she had never had an owner. No man had ever owned her. She would have added woman to that, but remembered well that Nadine had caused her to do many things under the threat of the whip. First as last, she had done nothing without having wanted to.

As she slipped a silken lead halter over Penny's head, Lenushka kissed her cheek. 'Be proud, my dear Penny. Let them see how well you can respond to whatever they desire of you. The rewards will be great. You will be able to have anything you want. Anything at all.'

Penny looked at Lenushka sidelong as the words sunk in. Lenushka did not see her looking. She was too busy tightening the silken straps of the halter around Penny's head.

There was no bit for Penny to contend with, but one strap of the halter ran beneath her chin and over her head. She could not open her mouth. Another ran around her forehead. Lenushka fastened her wrists behind her then clipped them to that part of the halter which passed behind her head so that her hands were held high and her breasts thrust forward.

Lenushka stood back again to admire her handiwork. 'There,' she said with great satisfaction, her hands resting on her hips. 'You look stunning, my darling girl. I think my colleagues in the syndicate will like you very much like this. Of course, it does mean that Leonard will no longer have you to himself, but then, by bringing you here he must have known that. Come. Let us go in and show off your paces.'

Lenushka clipped a lead rein on to a silver ring that dangled beneath Penny's chin. She held the end of this rein in her right hand. In the other she held a lunging whip; a long, lean piece of equipment used on a circling horse when going through training, or more readily recognised as being used by a circus ringmaster.

All eyes turned in their direction as they re-entered the ring. Penny could almost feel their thoughts as their eyes swept over her proud breasts, her flat stomach, and the long, leanness of her legs.

'Gentlemen,' called Lenushka. 'See what I have here. A filly of the best bloodlines. Guaranteed to be anything you want her to be. Quick to please, fast to go. See how well she is constructed. See how well she can move.'

Penny felt the lead rein being let out and the whip lightly touching her buttocks. Without any further instruction, she knew exactly what she was expected to do.

The distance between her and Lenushka became greater as the circle was extended. Now she was walking around the countess, arms at her sides, head high, legs striding out.

'Trot on!' Lenushka's voice was loud and demanding. The lunging whip bit that much more sharply. Penny gasped through clenched teeth. The strap beneath her chin prevented her doing anything else. Instantly obedient, she broke into a trot. As she trotted, her breasts bounced and she imagined how pretty they must look.

'Raise your knees higher!' The whip tapped the firm cheeks of Penny's behind even though she had instantly obeyed.

Penny was again reminded of Nadine. Nadine had liked using the whip and any other form of punishment she could think of no matter how much someone had pleased her. However, she had liked inflicting pain on some poor young man even more than she had on a young woman.

Aware that her body was being closely studied as she trotted swiftly around the ring, Penny made a great effort for them to see it at its best. No matter that her skin was glistening with sweat and her hair was flying free, she was determined she would become a close companion to all of them, in turn or all together. Thinking of Nadine had made her think of Alistair. Thinking of Alistair had made her think of why she was here and what she had to do. The first step had been to acquire the trust of one member of the syndicate. That had been achieved. Now she had to acquire the trust of all of them.

'Canter!' This time the whip seemed to burn into Penny's flesh as Lenushka barked out her order. Swiftly, her trot became a slow run. Her stride was long and her heels kicked out behind her. Now her arms were bent at her sides as she strained to keep up the pace. Her breasts bounced more readily. Friction was working its wicked way on the moist flesh between her legs. Her pubic lips were sliding over her hidden treasure, rubbing against each other and against her hardening clitoris that was trapped between them. Soon her legs would begin to tremble, her stomach to tighten. Those around her were suddenly of no consequence. Her own body was responding to this treatment. Threads of arousal were spreading through her.

'Gallop!'

This sounded impossible. Penny was already running, but Lenushka's command and the sting of the whip had to be obeyed.

Her pace quickened, however, as the whip kissed her buttocks. How its kiss stung, how her legs became more motivated as she sped around the ring.

Trickles of sweat were now running down her spine, between her breasts, and over her belly. Her heart was pounding in her chest, her hair was awry and flying out behind her. Because her speed had increased, her breasts were bouncing more rapidly, her nipples hardening as they pierced the air before her.

Moisture began to seep from her sex. She could feel it seeping out from between her pubic lips, sliding through her pubic hair and smearing itself over her inner thighs.

'Stop!'

As she came to an immediate halt, Penny trembled. Her breasts heaved rapidly and her nostrils flared as she fought for breath.

Delicious shivers spread up from her loins. She was reminded of the feel of a small electrical current or the faint vibration of something hard and humming pressed tightly between her legs.

Her hair was now damp with sweat. Even the thick, dark bush that usually thrust far forward of her belly, was wet with both perspiration and the still seeping juice of arousal.

It was true to say that no one spoke as they looked at her heaving body. Even so, it was easy to assess what they were thinking. Their breathing was clearly audible. Penny could almost feel what they were feeling. Their throats would be dry, their stomach muscles contracted. In the warm darkness of their trousers, their penises would be filling with blood and thrusting hard against their zips. And all because of her. It made her feel powerful.

'So,' said Lenushka, as she wound in the lead rein and rested her whip and her hand on Penny's behind. 'Who will first be host to our dear little girl? Who will give her some good riding and take her to the places she needs to be seen?'

Everyone seemed to speak at once. It was no more or less than Penny had expected. Each one of them had a glint in his eyes, and an open-mouthed expression.

'Gentlemen, gentlemen. Please.' Aran raised his arms and called for order. 'Please, gentlemen. Let us not argue about this, and first, let us thank Leonard Anderson for bringing such a prime performer to our attention.'

There were nods of assent. In turn, each person gave Leonard genuine thanks.

It was Aran who spoke again. 'And now, gentlemen. Let us settle this problem in the way that sporting gentlemen – and women,' he added with a polite nod at Lenushka, 'should settle it. Let us draw lots.'

Where there had been discord, there was now laughter. Racing and betting were bread and water to these people; things they had to have.

'Very well. That is what we will do.' Aran beamed with pleasure as he surveyed them all. His broad shoulders seemed less heavy, and his square jaw less like the blunt end of an anvil. Amusement gave added light to his bright blue eyes. 'I shall call an unbiased party to cut the straw.'

'No need,' said a female voice.

It was Lenushka whose hand was so pleasantly cooling the heat that criss-crossed Penny's buttocks. 'I will cut the straws. I am quite willing – as the only woman here – to go last. I have no immediate erection to worry about.'

As she smiled, Penny felt Lenushka's hand caress one

buttock and squeeze it gently. She had the sudden notion that Lenushka wished to go last and that she had her own reasons for doing so.

'I would still like to be considered even though it was me who introduced her,' piped up a slightly subdued Leonard.

'Of course,' said Ben Said. 'It is only right you should have the chance to hold on to your protégée a little longer.'

Leonard beamed then handed Lenushka a bundle of straw. She turned her back on the men and cut them to length. Then she turned back round and, to Penny's surprise, thrust the bundle of straw between her naked legs.

'Hold them there, Penny. They have to draw for you from that jewel between your legs. After all, that is what they are after.'

There was more laughter as Leonard got a pack of cards out of his pocket in order to assess who was going first. It turned out to be him.

He smiled as he bent forward. Penny felt his breath upon her belly as he deliberated. She felt his fingers pulling playfully at her pubic hairs before he made his selection. She wanted to giggle, but the strap beneath her chin would not allow that. Then he straightened up, looked at it, and sighed hopefully.

Daz was next. He glanced up at her as he made up his mind which straw to draw, but first he tangled her pubic hair around his finger and ran it downward until it nudged into the beginning of her divide.

Having made his selection, he straightened up and stared her in the face. Then he smiled and without giving away its length, he ran it under his nose and sniffed.

'Nice smell, baby,' he chuckled, and the straws between Penny's legs became damper than they had been.

The others selected their straw, then each of them held it up in turn. Daz was smiling and his eyes were raking her body. 'My win, I think.'

Heart racing with excitement, Penny stared. Daz was her choice. What would she learn from this man, and what could she learn from a brief tour of these stables?

Lenushka went back with her to where her clothes had been left. 'Let me help you out of this,' she said, as she began to undo the head halter.

'That's a relief!' Penny stretched her jaw and rubbed at her cheeks once the silken web of straps had left her head and her hands were free. Privately she was as much relieved at having infiltrated the syndicate as she was at her freed jaw. It was obvious they viewed her as a plaything and little more. If they were guilty of stealing Alistair's horse, they wouldn't be allowing her such intimacy.

'I am so sorry, my dear,' said Lenushka, her brows furrowed. She was talking in a rather motherly voice. 'But you did give a very good account of yourself. You have them all eating out of your hand.' Her face came nearer. 'They are mere men and are easily dominated. You can ride them with as much ease as you can ride a horse. Just remember that.' Bejewelled fingers held Penny's chin as red lipstick left its mark on her cheek. Penny felt justifiably proud of herself. Her nakedness had cast its awesome spell over them all.

'Now,' Lenushka, continued. 'Get dressed in your old clothes for now. You can have a shower in your room. The chateau is old, but well equipped. We all intended staying overnight, but will not do so now. We will respect your privacy – unless Daz should invite us to stay – which he won't. So, my darling girl, you will have him all to yourself.'

Good, thought Penny, with a smug sigh. That is exactly what I was hoping for.

Chapter Nine

*S*asha burned with desire as he flew from Angers and headed for the south and the marshlands of the Camargue.

Once he had reached the land he loved, he smiled down at it as he would a lover who had waited patiently for his return.

As he manoeuvred the helicopter to where he usually landed, the black bulls of the region circled noisily in their pens and the white horses in the paddock snorted, threw up their heads, and galloped madly around the perimeter fence.

'I'm home,' he said softly, yet there was something missing. He wished the woman who had indulged in such unusual sex with Leonard Anderson was with him. But she wasn't, so he sighed and considered getting rid of his erection and his desire in a very cold shower.

He wiped the sweat from around his neck with the end of his scarf and pushed his sunglasses up amongst his thick, curly hair.

Cool air came out to meet him as he stepped inside the low-ceilinged farmhouse that was home. The sound of a telephone echoed off the rough plaster walls before he had gone more than half a dozen steps. He stopped abruptly and turned to answer it.

'Sasha Amele, Saint Denis Maison.' It was his habit to offer his name followed closely by the name of the place he lived in. He took the view that the caller would remember it when there was piloting work available.

'Ah, my darling Sasha!'

Sasha froze. 'Nadine!'

As though she were there, whip in hand, he clenched his buttocks. He thought of her chiselled face, the cold greyness of her eyes, the spiked whiteness of her hair.

'Sasha.'

'Nadine! To what do I owe this pleasure?'

Nadine's voice seemed to darken. 'Pleasure? I'll give you no pleasure, my dear little Frenchie. I'll give you pain. I'll give you the sting of my whip across your naked backside if you don't give me a truthful answer.'

Half closing his eyes, Sasha threw back his head. Nadine was cruel as well as domineering. He should tell her to leave him alone, to go to hell, but he could not. Nadine fascinated him. She was his mistress and he was her slave. He could not help but worship her. Would he ever escape her clutches?

'Answer me, Sasha, my pretty boy!'

Her voice was louder now and much more menacing.

Sasha's lips trembled before he answered. 'Yes, Nadine. I will answer you truthfully.'

'Good,' she murmured. 'Good, my little Frenchie. Now just to prove that you are still my own pretty little plaything, I want you to undo your zip and release your penis from your trousers. Tell me the moment you have done it.'

As if neither his hands nor his will were his own, Sasha did as she ordered.

He stared at the hardness of his member; its brazen response to the purring, growling voice on the other end of the telephone. It weighed heavy and felt hot in his hand. Still staring at his own flesh, he swallowed hard before he found his voice.

'I have taken it out for you,' he said, and his rod jerked in his hand. He gulped, half closing his eyes.

'Good,' purred Nadine. 'Now I want you to squeeze it. Squeeze it very hard; imagine that your hand is my hand. Right?'

'Yes.'

'Then do it.'

Sasha winced then gritted his teeth as he squeezed his penis as hard as he could. A harsh gasp escaped his mouth as the head of his weapon glistened with the first seep of sexual fluid.

'I am doing it,' he groaned. 'I am doing it!'

'Good, my beautiful young man. That is good, is it not?'

'Yes. It is good,' replied Sasha.

'Too good,' Nadine growled. 'Too pleasurable. Now we will have pain. Dig your nails into yourself, my darling boy. Make yourself jerk, make yourself throb.'

Unable to stop himself, Sasha did exactly as she asked. He cried out as his penis responded to the digging fingernails by jerking against his palm.

'Such exquisite pain!' he cried.

'Exactly as I wish,' purred Nadine. 'Now, my darling Sasha. This is what I want you to do next. Wind the telephone cord around your hanging fruit. Wind it tightly around your balls.'

Sasha, his breathing fast and almost painful in his chest, did as she ordered. After completing his task he found he was bending forward somewhat.

'It's not long enough,' he said. 'I can only just do it. I have to lean over.'

'No!' responded Nadine. 'Stand up straight. I command it!'

Telephone held tightly against his ear, Sasha slowly straightened.

'It's uncomfortable,' he muttered, yet still his erection persisted.

'It's meant to be!' exclaimed the strident voice on the other end of the telephone. 'Now, my darling. As the wire of the telephone cuts into your scrotal sac, I want

97

you to pull on yourself for all you are worth. As you pull, you will answer my questions. Is that clear?'

'Yes. Yes. It is clear!'

There was a pause. Sasha knew she was doing it deliberately, holding him in suspense, checking him in with her voice just as easily as a rider might check a horse with the use of the reins and the bit.

Sasha allowed himself the luxury of thinking about Penny, the girl in the helicopter. Nadine was cruel, yet he loved what she did to him. But thinking about the dark-haired girl with Leonard Anderson also made his erection that much harder, that much more intense.

'Start pulling.' Nadine's voice was deep and even.

Sasha obeyed her willingly. In his mind it was not his hand doing this, but Penny, a creamy-skinned young woman with long dark hair and bright blue eyes.

'Are you obeying me?' Nadine's voice interrupted his thoughts.

'Yes. I am pulling on myself, and I am digging at my flesh. Is that what you want?'

'Yes, my darling boy. It is indeed what I want. Now tell me what Penny Bennett was doing with Leonard Anderson at Angers.'

Penny! She had mentioned Penny.

'I don't know,' he replied.

'Pull harder!'

Whimpers of pain came from his mouth. Oh, what a mistress Nadine was, he thought to himself. Initially he had been grateful for her patronage. But somehow he did not want to divulge anything of what had happened in the helicopter. Penny Bennett, he decided, was a find he wanted to keep to himself.

'I do not know anything about this woman,' he murmured and was careful to sound convincing. There was a chance she would not believe him, though he prayed she would – for Penny's sake and his own! A change had come over him. Slowly but surely, Penny Bennett was infiltrating his affections, burrowing beneath his skin, and yet, he told himself, you have only met her once.

And why was Nadine so keen to find her? What was more, how could he escape Nadine's clutches, and when would he see Penny again?

'Who else was at Angers?'

'Mr Anderson, Countess Lenushka, Daz Dazzler – and others.'

'And?'

'Prince Ben Said, some Texan guy named Aran, and a New Yorker named Al Puteri.'

'And what did they have her do?'

'Parade. They had her parade.'

Sasha should not have known this if he had gone about his business on the day Penny had been led around the selling ring like a piece of bloodstock to be auctioned to the highest bidder. But he had been there watching from the shadows. He had seen her naked flesh, her breasts bouncing to a healthy tempo as she walked, jogged, then ran around the ring.

He had seen her body being examined by them all – so say for blemishes – but in reality purely for pleasure. He groaned in an attempt to stay silent, but the force of Nadine's will was too much for him. Bit by bit, he recounted what had gone on. As he spoke, his penis pulsated and his testicles felt as though they were about to burst.

Nadine fell to silence as she imagined the creamy body she knew so well being examined by rough palms and probing fingers.

'It sounds as if I schooled her well,' purred Nadine. 'Obedience is such a precious commodity. I like the sound of the halter. I also like the sound of the whip lacing over her firm little behind. Did you enjoy watching her, Sasha? Did you enjoy watching her breasts being squeezed, her sex and bottom being examined by so many different hands?'

'Yes . . .' replied Sasha, the word almost painful as it wrenched from his throat. 'Oh, yes. It was incredibly arousing.'

'Then think of it now, Sasha. Think of it now. Imagine

her groaning as they pinch her nipples and explore her vagina and anus with their coarse, thick fingers. Just imagine it. Can you see it? Can you imagine it?'

'Oh yes!' It was an exclamation, yet came out as little more than a whimper.

'Then use it. Finish it. Jerk yourself off,' she suddenly ordered.

'I will, my mistress. I will start doing it right away.' Faster and faster, Sasha's hand moved up and down his penis. He was ashamed of himself, yet he was also pleased with himself. Sasha had never tried to resist Nadine since the day he had met her. He didn't try now. She aroused him. He enjoyed being used by her.

At the sound of her voice, he pulled more vigorously on his erect penis. But it was another woman he was imagining behind his closed eyelids.

There she was, her body creamy white, her dark hair falling over her bare shoulders, and her complexion as natural and as perfect as when he had last seen her. Her eyes were closed, her head thrown back in ecstasy. He licked his lips and wished his tongue was touching her breasts.

And it was her hand, her fingers, pulling on his trapped penis. It was her that was encouraging the fluid to rush up his stem.

Her face was vivid. The warmth of her body a mere memory. Yet he was coming because of her, and he was coming fast.

The sound that came from his throat had no words. It sallied forth like the semen that spurted from his penis as he climaxed. He cried out in pleasure and in pain for the telephone wire was still tight around his testicles.

'So, you are come, young man,' murmured Nadine. 'I enjoyed hearing you come. Perhaps I enjoyed it more than you did. And now it is all over – for the time being. Now, I understand you will be required by the syndicate again to accompany Miss Bennett. This is what I want you to do. No matter where she is, I want you to be near her and to report back to me. Is that clear?'

'Yes,' he said softly, his heart still pounding in his chest even though his orgasm was over. 'That's no problem. I already know they want me to do some more flying for them. If it's not the helicopter, it will be the aircraft. I will keep close to her. Very close.'

Again, a pause. He leant his head back against the coolness of the wall, closed his eyes and bit his lip. He was aware of sweat trickling down his spine as he waited for Nadine to say something. When she did finally speak, he could clearly hear the menace in her voice. 'I bet you will, Sasha Amele,' she snarled. 'You always did have an eye for a pretty face and a cock for a choice piece of pussy. Report to me when you find out what she's up to.'

Sasha told her he would. Normally, it would have been no problem. He would have coughed up every little bit of information he had been able to collate in order to have her reward him with the feel of her body and the touch of her whip.

But things had changed. He had met Penny Bennett and he couldn't get her out of his mind.

Chapter Ten

*P*enny was of the opinion that once she and the gaunt pop star were left alone, they would really 'get it together'. It occurred to her that sex with Daz would be as wild and eccentric as he appeared to be. The truth surprised her.

After the travelling and the events that had occurred so far, Penny was hungry. She dressed carefully for dinner in a slinky satin dress that clung to her body and swooped downwards from her shoulders so that her back was left bare. Her nipples showed through the creamy white like two pale rubies. Her jewellery was minimal; plain pearl earrings with a leafy gold surround, a bracelet of gold leaves, and small pearl clusters around one wrist. Underwear was completely absent beneath such a clinging dress.

The eyes of Daz Dazzler opened wide with amazement and, Penny assumed, desire. Her assumption proved wrong.

Daz, with eyes averted almost bashfully, told her he had a headache and anyway, he never dined in company. 'Sorry, hon,' he stammered a little apologetically, 'but I gotta leave you to take to the nosebag alone.' He chuckled nervously at his own joke, then kissed her on the cheek – as if such a gesture would be was enough to placate her.

Angry at first, Penny soon recovered. Her host's absence might give her time to take a look out in the stables. After all, that was what she was here for.

So she smiled sweetly and then took on a suitably downcast expression. 'Then *I'll* take a rain check while *you* take an aspirin,' Penny said.

'Sure will,' he replied with a chuckle, and nodded.

I wonder what he would have done if I'd ran my hand over his forehead then took a quick grope of his crotch? she thought to herself as she watched him go.

She frowned. Daz, she decided, was not quite the sex idol he was made out to be. No matter. An evening to herself would be very useful. She was hungry so, despite dining alone, she would enjoy her food. Afterwards she would turn the situation to her advantage. Tonight would be the best time to make her way to the stables and inspect the horses kept there.

Despite being by herself, she still swept into the dining room as though a fine-looking man or an audience awaited her.

Satin, she thought to herself, was a sensual fabric. As she walked into the stone-vaulted dining room her breasts jiggled slightly so that the satin rubbed deliciously against her nipples. It swept on further to delicately caress her ribs, her hips, her thighs. From there it rasped gently over her nest of dark and curly pubic hair.

Her hair hung loose down her back, its silkiness continuously caressing her bare skin.

A butler wished her good evening and told her in an intriguing accent that his name was Paul. An elegant man, she thought to herself, as he pulled back a Baroque chair of gold brocade and serpentine legs. The table before her was just as elegant and could easily have taken 24 people at one sitting.

Paul, she decided, was a sensual man. The butler's fingers were just inches from her shoulders. His hands were trembling.

Once she was seated, he pushed the chair in for her,

103

his chest almost brushing her hair. His breath gently warmed the back of her head. Its warmth and intensity increased. She instinctively knew he was taking in her looks and her smell as much as she was taking in his.

She looked up at him and smiled as their eyes met. 'Thank you, Paul. That's very kind of you. I hope we will have a good dinner this evening – just the two of us.' Her black lashes fluttered provocatively as she eyed him over her shoulder.

'*Enchanté, Mademoiselle.*' So far his voice did not echo the trembling of his hands. Yet it would, she told herself. It most certainly would.

There was a tingling in her that she had hoped to placate by feeling the heat of Daz Dazzler against her. That had not transpired, but the tingling had not gone away.

As the butler busied himself uncorking wine and fetching the first course, she studied him, her bright blue eyes hidden by the thickness of her lashes. Even so, she knew he was aware of her interest.

Besides being an elegant man, Paul had sculptured features, a straight nose, dark almond-shaped eyes and cropped hair. Immaculate in black and white with gold buttons on his cuffs, he served her politely as though to be of service was a religion rather than a mere profession.

Just occasionally as he bent over her left shoulder and breast to serve her food or pour her wine, his hand trembled and his breathing increased. Each time he served, she said 'Thank you' and he bowed his head politely.

Penny ate a little of everything. What was life for if not to indulge in the things you like? To Penny's mind eating and drinking were as pleasurable as sex and, she mused thoughtfully, they were easily combined.

As she watched Paul busy himself with the dishes or stand waiting while she finished her course, she made plans as to how to make the meal that much more interesting and how to get Paul to become more involved in partaking rather than serving.

She fidgeted in her seat. Her own nakedness was getting to her. She had prepared herself for this evening so carefully. Her body was ready for far more than just eating. It was alive with passion and with lust.

As she watched the butler, she imagined what his body was like beneath the trim black and white of his uniform. Hard, she decided, and lightly covered with silky dark hair.

She inhaled deeply and imagined what he might smell like. A subtle mix, she decided, of lavender and masculinity. She stifled the moan of longing that came to her lips. Instead she sipped at the ruby red wine that Paul had just poured into her glass. But her eyes still followed him.

Paul, she surmised, was a man who would never overstep the mark unless asked to do so. He would do his utmost to give no sign of his inner turmoil – not if he could help it. And yet she could see that vein throbbing just beneath his jaw. She lowered her eyes. His trousers seemed tighter than they had been, but of course, they were not. It was what they contained that had grown in size, and what they contained was something she wanted.

Her fork, missing a piece of broccoli that went rolling off her plate, gave her an instant idea. She decided to wait for the dessert course to put it into operation.

At last it came.

'Strawberry Pavlova, *Mademoiselle*? Or we do have some fine Camembert or Cheddar.'

Penny's eyes opened wide when she saw the size and texture of the dessert from which she would normally have had only a small portion. Meringue base, thick with layers of strawberries and cream. It was a work of sheer artistry.

'Oh, yes please, Paul. A large piece please. I would like a very large one.' She measured her words carefully, delivered them huskily and looked meaningfully into his eyes.

A hint of a blush seeped over the butler's cheeks, but

neither his eyes nor his mouth suggested he had understood the meaning of her words.

Paul moved the serving knife over the circular pile of white and pink until she nodded her agreement. He looked surprised that so slender a woman with such a very clear complexion would ever contemplate such a large slice of confectionery. But of course, he didn't know then that it wasn't her who was going to eat it.

He placed the plate in front of her and asked her if she would like cream. Silver cream-jug in hand, he awaited her command.

Now is the time, Penny thought to herself. Desire in her eyes, she looked up at him and rested her hand on his.

'Do you like cream, Paul?' She said it very softly and in a voice that hinted at something other than eating.

He blinked his dark eyes. Penny felt his hand tremble beneath hers. Her plan was working.

'Yes, *Mademoiselle*. I do.'

She licked her lips provocatively and felt his hand shake enough to drop the jug. 'Then pour,' she said, her voice pouring out as thickly as the cream from the jug. She kept up the pressure of her hand on his until the pavlova was surrounded by a pond of thick whiteness.

Once all this was done, he made movements to leave her. She held his arm.

'Don't go, Paul. I want you to stay.'

Paul bowed politely. 'Yes *Mademoiselle*.'

'Put down your jug.'

'Yes, *Mademoiselle*.'

'Now, Paul. You told me you like cream. Do you also like pavlova?'

She saw him swallow quickly. His eyes never left hers. She let her gaze travel down over his body until she could see the stirring at the front of his trousers.

'Yes, *Mademoiselle*.'

'This is too big a portion for me. Would you like to eat it for me?'

She saw his throat contract as he swallowed again.

'Yes, *Mademoiselle*. If that is what *Mademoiselle* truly wishes me to do.'

She smiled her slow, seductive smile. 'That, my dear Paul, is exactly what I wish you to do. Now, I want you to get down on your knees.'

Paul's eyes opened wide. 'On my knees?'

'Yes, Paul. Yes! On your knees.' She spoke to him firmly, though not with the same force that she had used on Leonard. 'Put the jug on the table and get down on your knees.'

Carefully, hand still shaking, Paul put the jug on the table and then dropped to his knees.

Penny turned her chair round to face him, then slowly, very slowly, she lifted her skirt up until it was folded in a shiny, satin heap around her thighs, her bottom bare against the rich brocade of the seat.

Paul gasped but could not drag his gaze away from the sight of her black bush as she opened her legs. He licked his lips as the pinkness of her clitoris erected from within her frills of moist flesh.

'Would you like to eat this?' she asked huskily.

Paul's eyes opened wide as he stared at her hair clustered treasure. He nodded avidly. 'Oh, yes. If that is what *Mademoiselle* truly wishes.' His chest heaved. His breath cascaded from his mouth.

Penny felt triumphant. Daz had not seduced her yet, and she was in need of seduction. In the meantime, this butler could prove to be a most willing and pleasurable substitute.

'Fine,' she said, and reached for the plate of pavlova. 'Then eat this first.' She placed the plate so that half of it was beneath her body. Her sex was immediately behind the pavlova and swimming in cream.

Paul moaned as though in pain. He looked up at her, his eyes liquid with longing. Then he licked his lips and ducked his head towards the magnificent offering.

As he bent to his task, Penny ran her hands over his closely cropped hair. It had a lovely, silky electrical feel. Her pussy felt good too. Although Paul's mouth was busy on the pavlova, his nose was immersed in her pubic curls.

This, she told herself as she listened to Paul lapping at his dish of cream, is a pleasurable experience.

The creamy dish moved ever nearer to her sex, and so did Paul's mouth. Eventually, the plate was beneath his chin and the remains of the pavlova were cool against her hot sex.

Moaning with pleasure, she threw back her head so that her hair tickled the base of her spine. Caressing her cheek with her shoulder, she purred with satisfaction. Paul's lips were now sucking with increased vigour on her pubic hair. His tongue was exploring her cream-covered sex.

Warm with sensation, Penny wondered how something as small as a tongue had the strength to push aside her pubic lips and the delicacy to softly tap and arouse her clitoris. Tongues, she thought, can be as exciting as penises – given the right moment – the right scenario.

But this was no time to dwell on such things. Desire was taking her mind as well as her body. She licked her lips, moaned deliciously, and slid her straps from her shoulders. Once her breasts were exposed, she held them high and played with her nipples. Then she bent her head and licked her own, sweet flesh.

Like food, she decided, my flesh has a taste all of its own. That is why eating and having sex have so much in common. We hunger for both.

Paul's mouth and breath were as hot and moist as her sex. His hands clasped her thighs and he was almost whining. It was as if he could not get enough of her.

Penny's hands left her breasts, closed on either side of his head and jerked it back so he had no option but to look up into her eyes.

'Have you finished, Paul? Have you eaten enough of what I have given you?'

He made a strange noise like a gasp and a moan combined. His eyes were wide, almost fearful. At last he found his voice which seemed to be steeped in adoration. 'Oh no, *Mademoiselle*. I could go on eating you forever. I would have you smeared with more cream, have your pussy filled with wine and drink from it as I would from a crystal goblet. I would place oysters between the lips of your sex, kneel between your legs, suck them out and let them slide down my throat one by one as if it were you I was swallowing.'

Now it was Penny's turn to stare. The way he had spoken was almost like a prayer of adoration. He was worshipping her, or rather, he was worshipping the treasure she had between her legs.

'Food and sex,' she said excitedly. 'What a brilliant idea, my dear Paul. And you would like to suck oysters from my body?'

He nodded. 'Oh yes, *Mademoiselle*. Oh, yes!'

As excitement ran through her veins, Penny smiled, her eyes as bright with enthusiasm as his were. 'Then you shall!' she exclaimed. The dress that had lain in rumpled silkiness around her thighs, now fell to the floor along with her shoes.

The shiny wood of the dining table was cool and smooth beneath her behind. She stretched out in the middle of it, arms behind her head, legs wide.

'Use me,' she mewed with desire. 'Use me as you would a plate or a wine glass.'

Paul's eyes were still wide and his breathing was quick. 'My clothes . . .?'

'Keep them on.'

He looked surprised.

'Think of it,' she purred in her most beguiling voice. 'Me here naked and covered with whatever you wish to eat. A mere platter. And you dressed for dinner and dining like you have never dined before.'

His face shone with immediate understanding. With professional aplomb, he draped a white towel over his right arm then with careful consideration he selected the food he wished to devour.

First he ladled cream on to her breasts then sprinkled them with brown sugar.

The cream was cool and soft. Penny had trouble

containing the movements of her body. Too much movement and his chosen dish would have ran in sugared streams over her ribs or under her arms.

'*Très bien!*' he exclaimed, and stood back to admire her, his tongue running hungrily over his bottom lip.

She watched as he went to the fruit bowl, removed and peeled the rind from a large pineapple, took one slice and lay it on her belly so it formed a ring around her navel.

Again he stepped back to admire his creation, before adding a cherry to the middle of it.

'*Voilà!*' he said triumphantly. 'That is very good.'

Penny clenched her stomach muscles. The pineapple was cold against her flesh and its juice was ticklish as it ran over her skin.

She wanted to groan, wanted to tremble, but she dare not. Instead she stored up all the sensations she was feeling. She would keep them to herself until she could hold them in no longer.

'And now,' Paul said, turning his eyes toward her. 'The *fait accompli.*'

She closed her eyes as he removed the oysters from their shells, then gasped as she felt their cold saltiness pressing between her labia and into her vulva.

'Hmmm,' she heard him say. 'In this instance, I will eat dessert first, main course last.'

'*Bon appetit,*' she said softly. Shivers of excitement ran down her spine as she waited for him to taste the food and then taste her desire.

He was as good as his word. His tongue licked long and slow over her breasts before he sucked noisily at the last of the sugar and cream that clung stubbornly to her nipples.

Desire throbbed in her and raced out in tremulous waves all over her body. She was dizzy with delight, her eyes half closed as she tried to hold her more physical responses in check.

'Eat me,' she said between rushed breaths. 'Please eat me.'

She arched her back as his lips and hands skirted the pineapple ring and its crowning cherry. His mouth went down to that deep 'v' between her legs. Gripping her hips, he sucked and licked at her pubic hair.

At last she had to respond. She cried out in those guttural tones of abandonment so well-used at such moments – tones that use no words but are so easily understood.

Slowly and carefully, she let him slide his hands beneath her buttocks so he could more easily suck the oysters from her sex.

They're supposed to be aphrodisiacs aren't they? That was the thought that ran through her mind. Was it because they resembled a woman's sex in appeareance and aroma? She was vaguely aware of having read this somewhere. It was of no consequence. Such thoughts, she pondered, only drift through one's mind when the senses have over-ruled logic. And at this moment in time, her senses were on fire.

She cried out with delight as his mouth sucked on her and the first oyster left her body and slid down his throat. She mewed like a pampered cat as he licked the residue of its juice from her body before turning his attention to the second oyster.

The second was not so easy to get at as the first but with a little determination, his mouth was soon around her, his tongue probing inside so he might better remove the oyster's alien presence. She felt the force of his sucking, the odd, vacuum-like effect as the once living thing inched toward his lips. Then, as though it were indeed part of her body, perhaps even part of her soul, she felt the last oyster slip from her.

His mouth left her in order to swallow this most fêted of shellfish, but then he was back, his tongue probing deep inside her to lick away the juices left by the salty sea creatures.

Threads of desire were emanating from his tongue, his mouth, and the pressure of his nose against her clitoris. Could he tell which was the smell of her and which of the oyster? The thought amused her, but amusement was overcome by libido.

No longer could Penny control her urge to move, to undulate against the pressure of his face and tongue. She had a need to replicate the incredible sensations erupting between her legs.

Paul had eaten everything off her body. No, she suddenly thought. Not quite everything. The pineapple ring and its cherry remained.

'The cherry,' she said breathlessly, but her words were lost on the cry that accompanied her climax.

Her climax racked her body with quick jerks of sensation. With shivers of delight, with a soft, cool feeling that sent tingles of pleasure over her skin, made her mouth dry, and her cheeks hot. Her hips jerked again and again against Paul's face, and his tongue licked her clean until the last tremor had disappeared.

Penny got herself up on to her hands. 'What about those?' she said, nodding her head towards the pineapple and the cherry that still sat on and around her navel.

Paul smiled. His face looked softer now, his eyes twinkled. 'That is for you, *Mademoiselle*.'

She understood instantly.

She gave him no resistance as he pulled her to the edge of the table so that her legs dangled over it. Whatever he had in mind was sure to be interesting. She just knew it.

Affectionately, his hand stroked her hair. 'Now it is your turn to kneel down.'

Smiling, she slipped to her knees and, as she did so, Paul retrieved the pineapple and the cherry. He had already opened his trousers and his penis was in his hand.

'This is for you,' he said. Before her mesmerised gaze, he slid the pineapple ring down over his member and pressed the cherry on to its end.

Her eyes widened as Paul's penis, so prettily decorated with the colourful fruit, came towards her mouth.

'Hmmmm,' she said breathlessly. 'I've never eaten fruit like this before.'

Closing her eyes, she opened her mouth. His penis slipped in, the cherry adding a rich sweetness to the salty taste of his skin.

Lost in the pure delight of it all, the ripe fruit was soon in her throat, and once Paul's cock was completely in, the pineapple pressed against her mouth and its sweet juice seeped through her lips and down over her chin.

From there, it trickled down her neck and between her breasts. Like a soft caress, it pleased her, even soothed her; just like the warm penis that was sliding back and forth over her tongue.

He gripped her head as she sucked on him, and she closed her eyes.

Although it was he who used her head to suit himself, it was her tongue that made sweeping gestures over his penis as it pulsated in her mouth.

Pearl drops of salty essence seeped on to her taste buds. She licked them off and sent them into her throat. With her tongue she also felt the swelling of his channel as his seminal tide surged upwards.

When he came, the taste of his semen cascaded over the cherry and complemented its sweetness.

She ate of it, drank of him, and afterwards she licked the sweetness of the pineapple from his softening member and from around her lips.

Then, with alarming speed, they returned to being the house guest and the servant; Penny in her satin dress, and Paul, face serene, dress impeccable.

'Give my compliments to the chef,' she said as she dressed. 'A most splendid meal. One I shall always remember.'

'Yes, *Mademoiselle*,' he replied, as he returned to being the respectful servant.

As if I could ever forget such a dinner! she thought, as she left the dining room and made her way up to her room.

Chapter Eleven

*E*verything had gone better than planned for Daz Dazzler. From behind a silk screen that looked to be part of the wall, he had watched the most uncommon coupling he had ever seen in his life. Only now had his hand-held erection subsided. It had been a long time since he had experienced such a momentous rising and hardening of his piston.

Of course, he had watched other couples have sex in very many ways, but he likened Penny's imaginative use of food and man to a great art. In its own way, it was every bit as accomplished as a painting by Botticelli, as sensual as a sculpture by Rodin or as skilful as a ballet performed by Dame Margot Fonteyn.

Some nights Daz woke up from a nightmare in which his adoring fans had found out that he was not the stud they assumed him to be. Imagine, he thought with cold dread, if they ever found out the truth about the solitary nature of his sexuality.

'Heaven forbid!' he muttered as he wiped away the sudden sweat on his forehead. Thinking about his failings in a negative light was something he tried to avoid. He had his sex symbol image to think about as well as his bank account. It must never be revealed that despite the jerking of his pelvis on stage, his performance in bed was somewhat lacking. In fact, he was a non-starter.

On a more personal level, it was a failing he had got used to years ago. In lieu of physical contact with a woman, he watched men and women copulating and brought himself off that way. Anyway, actually doing it would make him breathless and his lungs were not up to it.

'Fags! That's what caused it,' he'd told that guy Beaumont who used to be a member of the syndicate.

'Liar,' Beaumont had replied. 'You like watching. Admit it, Darren. Besides which you're a hypochondriac. You're terrified someone else might touch it and give you some nasty disease. Go on, admit it.'

Daz had stomped off. Firstly, he hated being called Darren which was his real name, and, secondly, Beaumont was pretty near the truth.

Of course, it wouldn't do to publicise such a failing. No one must know that far from feeling aroused by the screaming fans around him, his hip jerking was aided by thinking about those he had watched do it for him – by proxy, so to speak.

Daz was happy to go alone to his vast, cold bed after such a splendid ejaculation. But before he actually climbed into it, he stripped off all his clothes, placed them in a plastic bag, then put them in the laundry bin.

After taking care of that, he stepped into the shower and, with the assistance of a nail brush and a bar of non-perfumed, antiseptic soap, he washed the smell and the feel of sex from his body.

Wrapping a pure white bathrobe around him, he made his way to his favourite chair – which was as white as the rest of the room.

He read a few music articles, listened to some pre-recorded ideas through his headphones, then got up, stretched, and went to use the lavatory.

After he'd finished, he placed the white robe in a plastic bag, put that too in the laundry bin, and again

115

stepped into the shower to scrub yet another bodily fluid down the drain.

Once dinner was over, Penny too had gone to her room to shower, and to change into her jeans, boots and a dark blue sweater.

Before venturing out, she opened the blue-framed casement windows and looked out at a scene of darkening silence.

The light was fading fast now. A bat flew past the window, up over the roof, and beyond. There was a smell of wood smoke in the air, and the crumpled clouds in the far west had changed from salmon pink to dark mauve.

A feeling of satisfaction crept over her and made her smile. Her clothes would blend well with the descending darkness. Unseen, she could examine each stable block in the hope of discovering some secret stall where Superstar might be munching on his hay net or tucking into the last feed of the day.

Carefully closing the bedroom door behind her, she made her way on tip-toe along the creaking landing, down the back stairs and out in the direction of the stables.

Everything seemed quiet except for a few roosting doves cooing in unison from a cote set into the stone apex at the end of the château.

A flitting bat – perhaps a relative of the one she had seen earlier, or even the same one – flashed past her. She started, but refrained from making any noise – not even a gasp. Nervousness was something she must banish on this mission.

A sudden sound made her start. A door had opened at the far end of the yard and a stable lad came out and then walked off towards the place where earlier, the cars had been parked.

Until his footsteps had died away to nothing, she pressed herself against the chipped, grey stone of a wall. Trailing ivy clung to her hair and scratched at her shoulders. She took a deep breath, then counted to ten. After this, she checked to see if the coast was clear.

It was. The stable lad had gone. The yard returned to her, the bats and the doves.

Unlike the château, the barn and some other adjacent buildings, the stable block was modern. Each animal was housed in its own separate stall which had a double door entry system. As usual, the top part of the first door was left open.

Glancing furtively to either side, Penny undid the remaining half of the door and let herself into a subsidiary area that served one stable alone. There was another door after that, an exact match to the outer one.

'Admirable,' she said softly as she slid in beside the big bay that was housed in the first stable. The flanks of the horse quivered beneath her touch and his eyeballs rolled backwards so he could see her better.

'Now, now, my pet. Be still. It's only me, Penny Bennett. I've come to check you really are who you say you are. Or at least, I've come to find out if you really are a bay and not a chestnut in disguise. Now you won't mind me doing that, will you?'

She spoke softly and in a whistling kind of way that horses always seemed to like. This animal was no exception. He turned his head away from her and snorted approvingly into his hay.

'I didn't think you would,' she whispered, and proceeded to do what she'd intended doing.

The first thing she did was to go to his mouth and check that the regulation tattoo inside his upper lip did not belong to a chestnut named Superstar. It did not.

Penny ran her hand along his spine, then wetted her fingers and rubbed vigorously at the spot where the black tail joined the animal's quarters. Peering closely in order to detect the colour of any root growth, she parted the hair she had wetted. There was just enough light to see that this animal was naturally bay and his tail black. There was no tell-tale chestnut showing through.

'No colouring job for you, darling,' she said, patting his rump before letting herself out.

Changing the colour of a horse was a possibility that had occurred to her. Even changing the tattoo was not impossible.

She checked the other horses in the same way as she had the first. Obviously, she left out the mares, the geldings, and the young stock. She also left out the greys. It would not be possible for chestnut to be lightened, only darkened.

Just as she closed the last door, she heard footsteps.

Quickly, she glanced from side to side, sucked in her breath, and did her best to melt into the shadows.

Uneven stonework grazed her hands as she felt her way into one of the older buildings. A door gave way behind her and she found herself in darkness.

But still the footsteps came. They only stopped once. They too were in the old barn and not far from her.

Her heart thumped against her ribs. She knew at once that whoever they belonged to must have seen her. All the same, she was adamant that they would speak first.

'Please, Miss Bennett. Do not be afraid. It is me. Sasha. The pilot. Remember? I have only just got back. I was hoping to see you.'

Her heart calmed its hectic dance as she recalled the warm eyes, the dark hair and the smile that said they would meet again.

'Here,' she said, and stepped into a pool of light thrown by an ancient lantern that swung high on a metal bracket above them.

Even before she saw him, she smelt his absolute maleness – a pulsating, glorious smell that made her feel she wanted to touch him, to fuse with him, to have his naked flesh against hers.

As he stepped forward, the lamplight turned the warmth of his eyes to fire. His mouth opened slightly as he smiled.

Penny's legs seemed to turn to jelly and a familiar warmth spread quickly over her body.

'I had to see you,' he whispered, his voice betraying the same desire as his eyes. 'I had to know if you want my body as much as I want yours.' He raised his arms and held them out to her.

'Oh, yes!' It was all she said and all she needed to say. She did not hesitate to go to him, to fall against his chest and feel his hardness and his warmth before his lips covered hers.

As she tasted his mouth and his probing tongue, her nose rubbed against the grainy feel of his cheek. The smell of him was like a match to a flame. Her body burned with desire, her stomach tightened. She rubbed her sex provocatively against the mound that grew ever harder at the front of his jeans.

'Oh, *chérie*,' he moaned, once his mouth had left hers. 'When I saw what Mr Anderson did to you in the helicopter, I so wanted to make love to you the way it should be. She is wasted on him, I thought. Wasted!'

His breath was warm as he moaned into her hair. Penny could not help responding to him. Dinner was not that long past, and neither was Paul and the splendid sex they had enjoyed together. But an early supper would not come amiss, she told herself as her ardour mounted. Anyway, I am hungry again. I will eat this man and have him eat me; I will have his tongue lapping at my flesh, sucking at my breasts like a hungry, suckling babe. Such thoughts made her writhe against him, made her fingers rake his back and dig demandingly into his buttocks.

'Then make love to me, Sasha,' she said, in a hushed but urgent way. 'Make love to me over and over again until you can do so no more.'

The muscles of his back tensed as he looked down into her face. His cheeks were flushed, his eyes bright, and his breath was quickening in time with his desire.

She felt the firmness of his chest, his stomach, his penis and his thighs against her. This is no Daz Dazzler, she told herself. This is no man who pretends that he is a sexy stud. This is the genuine article!

Drunk with desire, they explored each other with fast, furtive movements. It was almost as if they feared missing one inch, one sensation. It was also as if each feared the other might disappear before they had enjoyed the ultimate delight.

Clothes were removed with no regard to the fact that they were expensive items and deserved to be treated with respect. They were flung into the shadows like the flimsy paper from a surprise present.

It was the item within that each wanted; the giving of one body to another, the coming together of two halves.

Naked in the straw of an ancient barn their bodies met, their legs entwined and their breathing warmed the chill air.

Their bodies were rampant with the heat of sexual desire.

Strands of dark hair fell across Penny's face as Sasha licked delicious circles of pleasure around her nipples. The touch of his tongue made her cry out with need. So hot was their lust, so fluid their movements, they seemed almost to blend as one.

'Suck them!' exclaimed Penny suddenly. 'Suck my nipples as if I am feeding you and you were dreadfully hungry.'

She heard him groan with ecstasy as he carried out her suggestion.

With eyes half closed Penny opened her mouth and tasted the saltiness of his hair, then nuzzled her nose into its sleekness.

She arched her back as he transferred his hungry sucking from one breast to the other. She felt the hardness of his penis throbbing against her sex as if it were trying to slice through her rather than take the more usual route.

It is demanding entry, she thought to herself, her mind dizzy with the intensity of it all. It is knocking at the door and I will have to let it in. I want to let it in!

While the heat of his hands and his lips explored her body, Penny wrapped her legs around him, crushed his pelvis on to her belly, and enclosed his thighs with hers. Now it was her turn to moan, to turn giddy with desire as the pleasurable hardness of his penis almost turned to pain.

Soon she could resist no longer. 'Put it in me, my darling Sasha. Please put it in me.'

Pleasure replaced the ache in her loins. His entry was urgent, though not brutal.

Penny, her mouth dry as toast, gasped loudly, grasped his buttocks and pressed them more tightly against her, It was as if she had an urge to pull him into her, to have him make love to every organ in her body.

In turn, he groped beneath her so that her buttocks were in his hands, and his fingers were sliding between her cheeks and making her muscles clamp over them. One finger sought and gained entry into her anus which made her cry out and clamp herself more tightly to him. They moved as one.

The straw beneath and around them rustled in time with their movements. It was like an accompanying song, a sweet harmony for their coupling. They rolled in the straw, first him on top, then her, then him again.

Penny mewed like a kitten each time he withdrew, then cried out in ecstasy each time he thrust forward.

Her senses were reeling, her body and her mind were lost in the sweet pleasure of the moment.

The vigour of his thrusts lessened. He was grinding against her now, his pubic bone rubbing against her clitoris, coaxing it from its hood.

Penny uttered sweet sounds as the first tremors of orgasm gathered around her clitoris and ran like warm rain through her labia.

She so wanted to prolong this thing that was happening to her with this man. She was desperate to control it, and did her best, but her orgasm would not be controlled. It broke away from her, then rose like a swift flurry of snow: cool and completely overpowering.

Sasha was not far behind her. 'A first time!' he cried. 'A christening!'

People say strange things at such times. Penny did not surmise the true meaning of what he had said until he withdrew his penis and let its fluid spray over her belly in sticky white trickles. Then he lay his body flat upon hers. Then she understood. It was a symbol. His sperm was a christening of their first sex together.

They lay facing each other on their sides afterwards as they talked and caressed each others' bodies.

Alistair crept into Penny's thoughts and made her feel guilty. She told herself not to be. Wasn't it just possible that Sasha might know something about the stolen racehorse?

She chose her words carefully but sounded almost casual. 'How long have you worked for the syndicate?'

'About five months. Why do you ask?'

She shrugged and trailed her fingers over his sleeping penis which jerked slightly. She smiled down at it and wondered how long it would be before it was ready to go back into her.

'Purely out of interest. How did you get the job – if you don't mind me asking?'

He dropped his eyes to her breast and proceeded to run his finger around her nipple as he spoke. 'I have a place where the syndicate keep their horses sometimes. The salt marshes of the Camargue are good for lameness.'

No, thought Penny, it could not be that simple. She could not accept that Superstar might be in some isolated farmhouse in the south of France – a place of black bulls, white horses and the incessant wailing of the Mistral, the wind from the sea. But she had to probe further.

'I have heard the Camargue is very beautiful.' Her voice was enticing and so was the finger that traced patterns across his chest.

His nostrils flared as he sighed. 'It is not all as it was. Rice fields have taken over much of the area near the Rhone delta now. But my land is as it ever was. It is still wild, still astonishingly beautiful.' He took her chin between finger and thumb and kissed her affectionately. 'Like you, Miss Penny Bennett.'

She raised her eyebrows. 'Am I wild?' She tried her best to sound serious but knew she could not possibly be convincing. She wanted him to pour sweet words in her ear. She also wanted him in her body again.

'And beautiful.' A faraway look came to his eyes as if he were making mental comparisons. 'As beautiful as the land I love and the people I grew up with.'

His voice and the caress of his hands made Penny tingle. It was as though someone had attached electrodes to her big toes and the current had been switched on and was coursing all over her body.

She trembled with pleasure and, although she continued her line of questioning, she did her best to disguise the intensity of her interest. 'And these people who you work for . . . How do you feel about them?'

He shook his head and shrugged at the same time in that nonchalant way that only the French can do. 'I do not envy them. They have many houses, more than me, much more land – and many more stables full of fine horses. But no, I do not envy them.'

She let her hand rest on the nape of his neck as his mouth met hers. She wanted to eat him, to drown in him. She wanted her body to melt into his so that they could make love forever.

His hands now ran down her spine, divided her behind, and probed unashamedly at the puckered orifice within. She pushed herself back on to it, then groaned deliciously as she felt its intrusion.

'We have so much more to do,' he murmured breathlessly.

'Then we must do it,' she replied, in exactly the same tone.

The sound of three o'clock being rung from a church tower echoed across the Loire.

Just as furtively as they had made love that first time, they kissed and caressed once more before departing the stone barn where the smell of hay gave the air an added sweetness, and the rustling of owls, bats and other small creatures added natural background music.

'I will see you again,' said Sasha before departing.

Penny echoed his wish, then watched him go. Although regretful at seeing him leave, she could not give him any definite time when she could see him again.

He'd asked her to go with him, to leave the syndicate and fly with him to his home in the Camargue where they could make love from dawn till dusk. But she could not do that. She had promised Alistair that she would do her best to infiltrate the syndicate and find Superstar. Much as her loins ached for Sasha, she had to keep her promise. Inadvertently, Sasha had given her information that she could not possibly ignore. After their bouts of vigorous lovemaking, Sasha told her that each member of the syndicate had their own racing stable – except for Leonard who kept his horses at this one near Angers. This one belonged to Daz. The others had theirs in other countries with the probable exception of the countess who was basically just a very wealthy gambler. Once he had told her that, Penny thought it her duty to visit each one. Superstar could not have vanished. Someone must have him or must know who did have him.

After dressing, and before going back to her room, Penny made one last search of the stables inspecting each horse in turn. There was no sign of the chestnut Superstar.

'So,' she said softly to herself, 'he's not in this stable, but perhaps he is in one of the others, which means I have some travelling to do.'

There was a loud rustling of something scurrying through the straw. Penny froze and peered in that direction. Dawn was fast approaching, but although it was still too dark to see what had disturbed the scurrying creature, she was convinced that something had.

'Sasha?' she called questioningly, but was sure he had already left. Hadn't she heard the engine scream and the rotor blades whirl into life?

Yet something did move. Something fibrous, transparent and floating on the air. Smoke! It was smoke!

'Oh no! Please don't let it be a fire!'

Fire once aflame among hay and straw is almost unstoppable, and horses are terrified of it. Penny's heart thumped fiercely in her chest as she considered the fastest and most effective action to take. The smoke drifted until its smell betrayed its true source. Suddenly, her panic melted as quickly as it had arisen.

'Nadine!' Her voice was thick, her eyes staring.

The tall, lean figure she knew so well, stepped confidently from the shadows.

'Well, well, my pretty pussy. Now what little game are you playing at?'

Penny swallowed hard as Alistair's sister drew on her cigar. The resulting red glow lit up Nadine's features and gave a chiselled hardness to her brows and her cheekbones, a grim firmness to her mouth, and a hint of crimson to the paleness of her eyes.

Lie, Penny told herself. You must lie rather than betray Alistair's trust. At the same time, you must go along with all that she wants. Your mission depends on it.

Penny betrayed nothing of what she was thinking. Smiling, as though she was truly pleased to see Nadine, she stepped forward, stood on tiptoe and kissed Nadine's cheek – which was as cold as the supple leather jerkin and jodhpurs she was wearing. 'Nadine. How sweet it is to see you. What are you doing here?'

As she looked up into the dispassionate face, she saw the hooded eyelids lower and was reminded of a bird – an owl, or a falcon – before it falls on its prey.

'Sweet?' Nadine's stone-like features seemed to crack as she laughed. The cigar was suddenly extinguished and flung into the nearest bucket of sand. Long, powerful arms reached out, and Penny shrieked softly as Nadine's fingers gripped her as if they were talons. 'Me being sweet has sod all to do with it!'

Nadine's face was inches from her own. The smell of

125

cigar tobacco made Penny feel suddenly queasy, but she dared not complain.

She summoned up as much fortitude as she could muster, yet spoke as sweetly as she knew how. 'Then why are you here, Nadine?'

Nadine's deep-set eyes narrowed as though she were looking straight through Penny's flesh and into her soul. The wide, sensual mouth smiled. There was no warmth in the smile, only a hint of the decadent nature of the person to whom the smile belonged.

'I want answers, my pretty. You see, I know my brother very well. Too well. I know how you inflamed him, how infatuated he became with your body and your sexuality. He responded to you as he has never responded to any other woman.'

'But we parted . . .' Penny began.

Nadine pressed one of her fingers firmly against Penny's mouth. 'Silence! You told me he had tired of you, yet I see him looking too thoughtful as he talks to your horses or moons around your old room. He even keeps some of your underwear – stuff you left to be laundered. Of course, it never has been laundered. He keeps it in his room. I've seen him take it out and moan as he inhales its scent and licks at it as though you were still in it.'

He thinks of me, thought Penny, and his face came to her mind. With the image of him nuzzling his nose in her underwear came the new stirrings of desire. What joy to think he missed her so much to make him retrieve it from the laundry bin!

Alistair, unfortunately, was not here, but Nadine was.

Penny tensed a little as Nadine wrapped her arms around her and held her tight to her chest. Nadine's soft, wide mouth kissed her forehead. 'So don't lie to me. Tell Nadine the truth before she has to beat it out of you.'

Penny shivered slightly as she recalled the abuse she had endured and Nadine had so obviously enjoyed. Not that such treatment had caused her undue suffering. Taken as part of the whole of her stay at Beaumont Place, delight and enlightenment had come to her as a result of meeting Nadine. Nadine knew how to elicit the most delightful responses from a body that should only be feeling pain. Nadine knew how to balance pain and pleasure, knew and exploited the darkest secrets of the human psyche.

In this particular instance, Penny knew that no matter what happened and what Nadine did, she must say nothing. Alistair had told her it was vital to tell no one, especially Nadine.

'I am telling the truth,' Penny said at last. 'Really I am.'

'*Really* you are?' Nadine's voice was full of mockery. Suddenly it changed and her expression clouded, her eyebrows diving into a deep 'v' above her nose. 'Well *really* I just do not believe you. It looks as if I shall have to beat it out of you regardless!'

Nadine was tall, angular, and very strong. Penny offered little resistance as she was pulled into a tack room. Nadine switched the light on.

'Now,' said Nadine, her hands still gripping Penny tightly. 'Now what encouragement can I give you to tell me the truth?'

She did not need to look far. One particular item dominated the room. It was a western saddle created from black leather and decorated with intricate carvings and bright silver studs. It was a monster of a thing – at least twice the size of an English saddle. Because of its weight, it was not stored on one of the wall mounted saddle racks like the rest, but had been placed astride a free-standing item in the middle of the floor which reached roughly to waist height.

Penny knew immediately that Nadine's busy imagination would choose this particular object on which to execute her threat.

Just as Penny had surmised, Nadine's eyes grew wide with admiration as she gazed on the saddle. 'Splendid,' she said with a thoughtful growl. 'Just splendid.' She turned back to face Penny. Her eyes were cruel.

Penny winced as she felt Nadine's hands pinch her arms that much more tightly.

Smiling, Nadine held her very close, then swayed her body from the waist upwards so that her own breasts rubbed against Penny's.

'Let's get you saddled up, shall we Penny, my darling? Come on. You know how you like a good ride.'

Nadine transferred one hand to Penny's hair and screwed it around her fingers so Penny could not move. With the other she pulled Penny's sweater off over her head.

Penny squirmed and cried out as Nadine gripped her hair that much tighter.

'Take the rest off,' Nadine growled. 'You were quick enough to get it off for that helicopter pilot. Now you can do the same for me!'

Her head locked at an odd angle, Penny felt for the button and zip of her jeans. Gingerly, afraid that Nadine might pull out her hair, Penny groped down her leg to the top of her boot.

'Wait,' cried Nadine. 'Leave the boots. I want you naked, but you can leave the boots on. Now straighten up.'

The pressure on Penny's head lessened as she obeyed. She did not look at Nadine but knew that the cool, grey eyes would be sweeping over her bare breasts, her flat belly, and the frizzy hair that sprouted so vigorously from between her thighs.

Nadine chuckled as she appraised Penny's body. 'I like that. I like you having nothing on except your riding boots. Strange that it makes you look more naked than if your feet were as bare as your behind.' Suddenly, her tone changed just as Penny had expected it to. 'Now mount up!'

With Nadine's fingers still in her hair, Penny slid her booted foot into the huge metal stirrup that hung from one side of the western saddle. Then she swung herself astride, her sex open and sucking warmly on the smooth leather.

'Lean forward,' ordered Nadine.

Penny leant as far forward as she could until her breasts were divided like saddle bags over the rear of the saddle, and the pommel was pushing into her vagina thus thrusting her bottom high into the air.

Nadine ran her fingers down the cleft between her buttocks, dipped into the wetness of her sex, and returned to her behind, her fingers wet with sexual juices. Penny imagined how shiny her sex would be, how exposed her most secret place would look to Nadine. The thought of it excited her. Moisture was trickling out from her and wetting the saddle.

I should not be enjoying this, she told herself. But she was. With Sasha she had enjoyed sex on a mutual level. With Nadine those levels were changed. Nadine controlled the proceedings. Penny merely submitted to her will.

Nadine came round and bent down so that she looked directly into her face. Her eyes glittered and her white teeth shone as she spoke. 'I don't like secrets, Penny. I don't like being told silly stories that have no bearing whatsoever on the truth. Now! Are you going to tell me what the truth is immediately or do I have to make you scream and squirm until you beg to tell me?'

Penny cried out as Nadine squeezed her breasts and pinched her nipples. Penny gasped as a light sweat broke out over her body and gave her skin a beautifully translucent sheen. 'Please . . .' she moaned, aware that although her breasts were smarting, the pommel of the saddle was giving her pleasure as it gradually entered her vagina.

'Please . . . I have told you the truth. Truly I have.'

Again Nadine tangled her fingers in Penny's black hair which fell like a veil before her face. Nadine jerked her head back so that their eyes met.

'My, my,' Nadine said, that blood-curdling smile still etched sharply on her face. 'You, my darling Penny, are either telling the truth, or otherwise you have something naughty to hide from me. Now, which one is it?'

Penny groaned as Nadine licked slowly and seductively over her eyelids, around her nose, and then her lips. Finally, her tongue pushed into her mouth.

Eventually, she spoke. 'I can see I am going to have to use force to get you to tell me what I want to know. Is that not so?'

Penny gasped, then bit her lip as Nadine tied the ends of her hair beneath her chin so she could not see. Helpless and unwilling to protest, she stayed silent as Nadine bound her wrists to the crossbar arrangement of the saddle rack.

Leather straps cut into her breasts as Nadine fastened them to the rear flaps of the saddle. There was no way she could jerk up from this position. She could only squeeze her eyes more tightly and tense her backside as Nadine's quick fingers fastened her leather boots into the stirrups.

'Very nice, my darling Penny.' Nadine spoke in a low, slow voice bordering somewhere between a purr and a growl. 'Very nice indeed,' she repeated as she trailed her fingers languorously down Penny's spine and over each buttock.

As Penny cried out, Nadine pulled her sex lips apart so that the pommel of the saddle could nudge more positively at the entrance to her vagina. Nadine then used her own weight to press down on her buttocks so that the pommel could finally invade her. It wasn't too great in length, but it was thick and very, very hard.

Penny groaned. This rod within her was not as delightful as Sasha's, but it was hard and it was pleasurable.

Nadine laughed, then ran her fingernails over Penny's bare behind. 'What fine skin you have. Come. Would you really want me to mark such pretty flesh? Think how a young man might view it. Think about that young man with whom you have lain half the night. Do you think he might like you more with a striped behind, or less?' She laughed. 'Yes, I was watching, and no, you don't need to answer my question.' Her mouth came close to Penny's ear. 'It doesn't matter whether you wish to tell me the truth or not. Either way, I will still whip your pretty little backside and slide something hard and brutal into your pert little bum. You see, my darling, I enjoy making you squirm. I enjoy using you as a plaything for my own enjoyment more so than for yours. Do you understand that? No?' said Nadine. A smile broke into a chuckle. 'Never mind. Let me find some implements to suit my task. Wait here, my darling.'

The heat of Nadine's kiss burned through Penny's hair. The sound of her jackboots echoed around the tiny room and out in the passage outside.

She was quick in returning. 'This is for you, my darling Penny,' said Nadine. Her breath came in short gasps as Nadine pushed something into her anus. Once it was in, she felt something very light and very fragile caressing her buttocks and her thighs. It reminded her of the false tail she had worn on the night in the woods with Nadine, Dominic and the others when they had used her as they would a pony. But this was something different.

Whatever it was tickled and caused Penny to wriggle her bottom.

Nadine laughed. 'You're wondering what it is aren't you, Penny? Well I'll tell you. It's a carrot. A nice, fresh, juicy carrot that still has its foliage. Delicious, don't you think?'

She laughed again. 'And this is my old stand by,' Nadine went on. 'This is my crop; my favourite one, the one with the silver handle, and you're going to savour it.'

Penny wriggled as though she was trying to escape her bonds and also dislodge the carrot from her behind and the saddle pommel from her sex. But there was pleasure in these things. Nadine knew best how to blend pleasure with shame.

Penny did not see the whip rise and fall, yet she cried out each time she felt it. Again and again Nadine laid it across her bottom and each time it landed the carrot went in further. In response, Penny flattened herself against the saddle so that the pommel began to do delicious things to her sex.

She groaned between strokes and cried out each time the whip landed on her behind.

After every six strokes or so, Nadine turned her attention to Penny's nipples. First she tweaked each one. At the same time she kissed Penny's back and murmured affectionate words. In turn, she rested a breast in her palm and landed a few strokes of the whip on that.

Even without Nadine landing more blows on her bottom, Penny could not stop jerking herself against the saddle and enjoying the hardness inside her. Why was it so easy to respond to Nadine? What was it in her cruel torments that gave such pleasure? There was no turning back: her orgasm had started and there was no way she could stop it.

With each blow, her hips jerked and the first ripples of orgasm grew larger and larger until, at last, it became a huge wave of release that washed over her, flooding her senses and making her body tremble.

'You've come!' cried Nadine. 'You've come and you've told me nothing!'

Penny hid her smile. At last she sighed and found her voice. 'I can tell you nothing, but as you well know, I can make you come too.'

Nadine stopped pacing up and down the room.

'Oh, yes, my darling Penny. So you can. And you will, my darling, you most certainly will.'

Nadine left Penny bound as she was, but lifted Penny's head.

She was wearing black suede leggings that were festooned with gleaming steel studs. Two zips ran up in a deep 'v' from her crotch. She unzipped both of them and a triangle of suede fell away to reveal her hairless sex.

'Lick me,' she ordered, and again grabbed hold of Penny's hair.

Infused with the smell of Nadine's sex, Penny slid out

her tongue and licked the slash of pink flesh that gleamed from within the white lips.

There was moistness in the pink flesh, and a certain abrasiveness to the white where bristles of hair were only just beginning to grow.

Nadine began to moan as she jerked her hips backwards and forwards to Penny's mouth.

Penny's tongue flicked in and out at Nadine's clitoris. Every so often, she brought it back into her mouth and tasted the salty crispness of Nadine's moistness.

'Keep going,' ordered Nadine, as she thrust her hips more vigorously. 'Lick at my clitoris. Tap it with your tongue.'

Penny did exactly that. She did it quickly, she did it slowly. She licked Nadine's labia and brought the taste back into her mouth.

Nadine's murmurs of pleasure became more rapturous, and because she was giving pleasure, Penny took pleasure from hearing those sounds.

At last, Nadine's hips spasmed against Penny's face and as though loath to have Nadine's sex leave her, Penny plunged her tongue more forcefully and flicked her tongue more deeply.

'Delicious,' murmured Nadine, the word released on a long drawn-out sigh.

Afterwards they lay together and, as Nadine caressed her hair, Penny asked whether anyone else knew she was there.

'No one,' Nadine replied, 'and you must tell no one that you have seen me. Is that clear?'

'Very clear,' Penny replied and congratulated herself on coming through this intrusion without giving anything away.

Chapter Twelve

*P*enny stayed two more days in the company of Daz Dazzler. His only sexual demand occurred on a day when they drove to Tours, a medieval town further down the Loire valley.

Penny dressed very carefully in the hope that something might come of it. Her dress was of white linen and, although classic in design, it reached only to mid thigh. Besides its length accentuating the firmness of her legs, its whiteness made her skin look more tanned and more silky.

Because they would be doing some sightseeing while they were in Tours, she wore low-heeled shoes that were a dull gold in colour. She plaited her hair and let it hang in one girlish braid down her back. Continuing the girlishness, she wore white cotton knickers beneath her simple dress, but left her breasts unfettered.

The city of Tours seemed to smile on them as they drove through its narrow streets and parked near its ancient square.

Surrounded by houses with pointed roofs and the bustle and chatter of the famous square, they enjoyed a light salad lunch served with crisp bread and salt free butter. To complement their meal, they drank a cold Chardonnay, then nibbled at a few local cheeses before consuming coffee.

Daz was back to being his flamboyant self. He was also extremely attentive; in fact, he could hardly keep his eyes off Penny.

He leant closer. 'I bet you've had some unbelievable sexual experiences,' he whispered to her, his chin resting on one hand as he gazed into her eyes. 'Why don't you tell me about them?'

Penny looked back at him in a quizzical manner. To those watching he must seem a besotted lover, sexuality oozing from every pore. So far he had done nothing to confirm the impression.

'Of course I will Daz, darling, but only on condition you tell me about yours.'

She saw him glance swiftly around. Some people were looking his way as though they had recognised him.

His audience, Penny thought to herself. What an actor.

After imparting a few smiles here and there, he laughed nervously, leant closer to her, and took her hands between his.

'Oh, my dear Penny. I wouldn't want to shock you. You know what sort of a reputation I have got. I'm a sex symbol, darling, so I have to work at what I am. I have to delve really deep and push my body to the limit in order to please my fans. After all, baby, they have to believe in me. They have to feel my sexuality coming over to them in my songs.

Penny could see his eyes flickering as he caught the admiring glances from some of those around them. She smiled sweetly and let her voice rise above a whisper. 'But Daz, darling, do you feel any sexuality yourself? Be honest, do you ever fuck anyone? Man or woman?'

'Honey – keep your voice down,' Daz muttered, as a slight flush came to his cheeks.

'But darling,' Penny went on, 'do tell me the reason you have not seduced me. Is it because you're gay, or merely because you have no libido at all. Or perhaps it's because you are so ashamed of the size of your penis, you don't want any hot-blooded woman even looking at it?'

135

Daz turned puce. His eyes stared as he let her hands drop and sat back in his chair. Like her, he heard the giggles from those who had understood what Penny had said.

'Are you satisfied?' he muttered through clenched teeth. 'Have you finished embarrassing me?'

'Have you finished embarrassing me? Is there no shred of sexual action in you? Make me feel as though I have some sexual purpose, Daz. Make use of me. Make my body tingle.'

'Make use of you? What do you mean by that?'

Penny leant forward and covered his hand with hers. 'Inspire some sexual reaction in me and in yourself. You don't have to have straightforward sex or even kinky sex. There are other ways in which to make me respond to you as a woman and for you to respond to me as a man. You're a star, an enigma, so you must have some imagination. So . . . be imaginative!'

He stared at her for a moment and blinked before he spoke.

'OK. OK. Let's take a walk by the river while I give it some thought.'

'It's a start. Let's do it.'

She got to her feet and he called for the bill.

As gravel the colour of butter scrunched beneath her feet, Penny decided to give it one last shot. Perhaps there might be something from his youth that might trigger him off, she thought to herself.

That, she decided, was a valid point. Today she had dressed in a girlish way; the plaits, the white cotton knickers etc.

She bit her bottom lip as she thought, then looked sidelong at Daz. She decided it was worth the chance.

Penny knew a lot more than her legs would flash into view as she bent over to sniff at a clutch of purple dahlias. She knew he had noticed her innocent-looking cotton knickers the moment she heard his sharp intake of breath.

With the flower held deftly between her teeth, she

136

turned round and kissed him. '*Voilà*,' she said provocatively. 'How do you like me now?'

Daz cleared his throat and stammered some unintelli-
gible comment before he recovered his cool. 'So, you're
holding a flower between your teeth. How about holding
it . . .'

In a sudden moment of self-consciousness, he glanced
around him, then leant forward to whisper more closely
into her ear.

'Hold it between your other lips,' he said, 'and keep it
there until we get back to Angers.'

Penny smiled at him before looking around her. There
were few people about, but enough to warrant her taking
his arm and guiding him behind a crop of purple
flowering shrubs.

'Just watch me,' she said, as she lifted her skirt. With
that, she slid the crotch of her knickers to one side, then
opened the lips of her sex with her fingers. Bending the
stem of the flower, she inserted half of it into her vagina.
Her pubic lips folded over the rest of the stem so that
the bloom itself appeared to be growing from between
her thighs. The crotch of her knickers held it in place.

'Is that what you wanted?' she asked him, her finger
toying delicately with the brightly coloured petals.

'Right on, baby,' he said, his eyes glued on her thighs
and his voice falling like rain. 'Right on.' Daz took a
deep breath as though some terrible weight had been
lifted from his shoulders. He was suddenly aglow with
confidence. 'Let's see if you can keep it *in situ*, as they
say, until we get back.'

'I will,' she said with the utmost confidence. 'My
muscles are well used to holding things in place.'

On the journey back, Daz ordered the driver to stop
the car on three separate occasions. Each time they
stopped, he asked Penny to raise her skirt so he could let
his gaze dwell on the sight of such a perfect flower
blooming from between her thighs.

On each occasion a dreamy look came to his eyes and

he hummed a snatch of a tune and muttered a few softly-spoken words that seemed to have no meaning.

On the last occasion they stopped, the tune and the words seemed to roll together and the meaning became more obvious.

'My latest song,' he explained beaming brightly. 'Once I get back, I'm going to bash it into place. It's gonna be great. I tell you this for sure.' He narrowed his eyes, frowned thoughtfully and looked upwards. 'I'm going to call it Penny Dahlia – the album too. How do you like that?'

The suggestion made her smile, and perhaps some of his enthusiasm rubbed off on her. 'I'm flattered. I'll be even more flattered once I've heard it properly.'

Daz smiled happily. 'Then I'll sing it to you!' And he did just that, his voice full of a raw rhythm; the sign of a song not quite yet licked into shape. All the same, the words lay easy in Penny's mind.

'Satin smooth and dark your hair, your eyes are like no other.

Let me kiss your petalled mouth, oh let me be your lover.'

But of course, Daz would never be her lover. She knew that now, knew that all his energies went into creating his songs. She could see that by the excitement in his eyes, his flushed cheeks and his animated arm movements as he went on with his song, taking bits out here and sticking them in elsewhere to make the music and the lyrics lie more easily together.

When they got back to Angers, he told her he would have to leave her and head for his recording studio. Although he apologised and told her that Ben Said would be entertaining her in his absence, she could see he was in an enormous hurry to be on his way.

'I'll be seeing you,' he said, his face wreathed in smiles. 'And thanks – for the day and the song.'

Chapter Thirteen

*B*en Said sent Sasha to collect Penny in his helicopter with instructions to take her to Charles De Gaulle Airport where his private jet was waiting. Unfortunately, on this occasion, Sasha would not be piloting the aircraft that would take her into the presence of Ben Said.

Penny looked longingly at Sasha as he helped her aboard his helicopter. He looked just as longingly back, then whispered close to her ear once they were both seated, 'I wish I could have you now.'

Penny undid the top button of her pink satin shirt. 'I'm hot,' she whispered, her words urgent with longing. 'Have you heard of the mile high club?'

His answer was half drowned by the scream of the rotor blades as he prepared for takeoff, but she knew what his answer had been.

'You do have an automatic pilot?' she asked, as they rose gently into the air.

She saw him nod his head.

Flying at several thousand feet, Penny found herself with her feet hooked over the two front seats. Her clothes were tossed to one side and Sasha had removed his trousers. His penis rose from his thatch of pubic hair hot and ready for her.

As they cruised the skies, he gripped the backs of the

pilot and navigator seats. As he did this, the gleaming head of his penis nosed between her glistening flesh and slid smoothly into her.

Their coupling was by necessity rather brief. It was too short a flight from Angers to Paris for anything too adventurous. But their last kiss was sweet, and their words even sweeter.

'To the next time,' whispered Penny as Sasha escorted her beneath the slowing blades of their craft.

'To having you on the cool tiles of my house,' murmured Sasha, his voice as low as possible. 'To riding naked at sunset on my white horses, and making love among the shifting dunes of the Camargue.'

'To riding horses,' Penny responded, her voice as low and furtive as his. 'To you riding me and me riding you.'

She left him and felt she had left behind a part of herself.

Ben Said's private plane came fully equipped with a pilot, navigator, and two stewardesses, one of whom handed her a cool lime and soda once she was seated.

She drank thirstily and thought of Sasha and his body. She thought of the tumbling darkness of his hair, the contours of his muscles, the polish of his skin. She thought of them lying together, of him pumping himself into her. Just thinking was enough for her to miss him, to miss what he had given her. Her lust for him had not been satiated. I hunger for him, she thought to herself. I thirst for him. Sex, she concluded, could be a thirst as well as a hunger.

Once she'd finished her drink, Penny took more notice of her surroundings. There were only about twelve seats in the whole lounge of the sumptuous craft, and lounge was the right word. This craft was not fitted like a scheduled or chartered flight where as many seats as possible are crammed in consecutive rows. This really was fitted as though it were a lounge on some sea-going liner or a plush hotel.

The seats were covered in soft white leather and the

same leather had been used to cover the whole interior except for the carpet – which was pale blue.

Drinks were served in crystal glasses, and an intermittent spray filled the air with perfumed moisture.

No chance, she thought, of becoming dehydrated on this flight.

The two stewardesses wore knee-length tunics of cobalt blue over loose fitting trousers of a paler hue that were banded with threads of gold. They wore sandals of gold. There was gold in their ears and gold collars around their necks.

In flight, the tunics were removed and the full sensuality of their outfits became apparent. Penny was stunned.

Slim straps of blue satin ran under and around their breasts and over their shoulders. In effect, they formed a brassière, the cups of which were non-existent. Plump pink nipples and brown breasts jutted proudly outwards, ably assisted, of course, by the tightness of their garment.

The legs of their trousers were fastened with satin to a band which ran around their waist. Their bellies and sex were completely exposed and blue stones – the size of pigeons' eggs – hung on gold chains from some device which seemed to clamp their pubic lips together.

Penny could not help staring at her surroundings and also at the firm breasts so blatantly displayed, the subtle roll of the brown buttocks, and the gentle swing and lucid tinkle of the jewels that hung between the legs of these girls.

A pair of dark eyes gazed into hers as one of the stewardesses leant over her. 'Would you like to shower and change, Miss Bennett?'

Penny blinked and felt suddenly weak. She took a deep breath before she answered. The sweet smell of sandalwood wafted from the girl and filled her senses. The plump nipples and firm breasts hung like ripe mangoes.

'Yes. I'd like that very much,' she answered, swiftly

aware that her neat suit, despite its non-crinkle guarantee, was now a little crumpled after her session with Sasha.

'Incredible!' she exclaimed as they entered the bathroom which was towards the tail of the plane. 'Definitely not tourist class!' she added in a more hushed voice.

'Prince Ben Said has much taste for beautiful things,' said one of the girls, her voice lilting as she rolled her tongue around an alien language.

'And much money!' exclaimed the other with a light laugh.

The bathroom was on an aircraft, so the marble was not real but a lightweight imitation. Swirling patterns of blue, white and gold swept over the floor, the walls and even the ceiling. Moorish pillars topped with gilt-leaved diadems stood either side of the steps that led up to a sunken bath. A pale gold cashmere rug sat on the bottom step.

From where she stood, Penny could see gleaming taps of gold and knew immediately that even the plug would be made of the same metal.

She saw one of the girls press a button and heard water cascading from a hidden outlet. Steam began to rise and mist the pillars and some of the phantom marble.

'Fabulous,' she said, and raised her hands to the buttons of her jacket.

'We will do that for you.' Brown fingers with gold painted nails pushed her own hands to one side.

It had occurred to Penny that these two women were not likely to leave her to bathe alone. She had experienced enough of sex to know when people were dressed to play a part. She instinctively knew what part they were likely to play.

As the first girl removed Penny's jacket, the other undid her skirt and slid it to her ankles. She kicked off her shoes herself.

Penny gasped as the first girl cupped her breasts and studied them admiringly.

'They are very well shaped.' Her white teeth flashed brilliantly as she squeezed Penny's breasts and flicked her thumbs at her nipples. 'Very firm. Very responsive.'

Penny sucked in her breath. She could not help enjoying what was happening to her. All the same, she had a need to treat this lightly. She managed to laugh. 'I'm glad you like them.' She was suddenly aware that another pair of hands was being very familiar with her bottom.

These were two women, and she was having no trouble responding to them.

The girl who was holding her breasts smiled. 'Let us see the quality of the rest of your body. Clasp your hands behind your neck.'

Penny did not hesitate to obey. A fantastic feeling of total relaxation was permeating her body.

Soft fingers rolled down her stockings and pulled them from her toes. Once both girls were kneeling before her, they turned their eyes to the thick hair that covered her sex.

'It is very copious,' said the first one. 'Look, Sharana. Feel how silky it is.'

Penny stared as their soft brown fingers investigated her body. One removed her suspender belt as the other tapped the inside of her thighs. Penny opened her legs that bit wider. She murmured a wordless sound as a single finger slid along her slippery lips, gently probing from side to side as it did so. Suddenly, she felt no more than an object – an object made to be used solely for sex.

'Terisha, my dear friend, she is already wet. See?' Sharana, the first stewardess, sounded very excited.

This is delightful, Penny decided, her inner thighs trembling as a result of the sensations erupting along her vulva.

Another finger joined the first. 'My friend, Sharana. You are quite right. Miss Bennett is indeed very moist. She is in need I think, and it is our duty to do something about it.'

Penny wanted to shout out that the bath might overflow with water. Not that it overly concerned her. It was just that she didn't want them to leave her body alone while they went to turn off the water supply.

But there was no sound now of running water. Automatic, she said silently to herself, and sighed contentedly at the prospect of enjoying their uninterrupted attention.

Their fingers probed her, each entering her in turn and the women chatted excitedly to each other about the rapidity of her response, the trickles of fluid that ran down over their fingers.

Penny just closed her eyes and let them do what they wanted. This was too precious to end.

'Enough,' said the one called Sharana.

'Oh, no!' Penny sighed with regret. 'Why not go on with this?'

The stewardess named Terisha smiled and her eyes twinkled. 'We are going to continue. Please,' she said with a sweeping wave of one arm. 'Please come to the bath. You will see it is a very special one.'

Adamant she would not relinquish the volume of arousal already ignited, Penny sashayed to the bath in such a way that her sex lips brushed lightly against her clitoris.

Penny climbed the steps and looked into the bath. Something about this bath was very different to any other.

'Get in.' A cool hand, wet with Penny's bodily fluid, pushed her gently forward. Penny stepped into the bath as directed. The water was very soft. It was also blue and smelt like a host of violets at early dawn.

She spread out her arms. The water came to her waist.

'Lie down,' she was ordered. 'There. At the end.'

She lay where they directed. She found that one end of the bath was higher than the other. There were seats built against its side. Once she was sitting down, her legs began to float.

The two girls took off their diaphanous uniforms and joined her. They also took off the odd looking ornaments that clamped their sexual lips so firmly together. Each took one of her ankles on their shoulder and hoisted some sort of platform beneath her behind.

The water ran off her pelvis as she was lifted out of the water.

From her shoulders to waist she was immersed in the blue, warm water. From there on she was exposed, her legs wide, and her sex open to exploration.

Penny closed her eyes and half dozed as they circled her flesh with their fingers and then with their tongues. Each took it in turns and excitedly exchanged comments.

'Here it is,' said one. Penny couldn't tell who was speaking and didn't really care. But she did know what they were talking about.

Her clitoris was throbbing. She knew it would be jutting forward, begging for attention. Around it the rest of her sexual divide would be wet and slippery, aching with arousal.

'Ah, yes,' said the other. 'See? Her little pink rosebud is swelling with passion, and soon it will climax and go back to sleep.'

They've found my clitoris, thought Penny. And they're doing lovely things to it.

Penny's thoughts seemed to separate from her body. She was now not only floating on water, but floating on the most decadent, most lustful sensations. Shivers of pleasure were spreading over her flesh as each girl took it in turn to lick at her clitoris, to toy with it, play with it.

She closed her eyes and let herself float away on a wave of desire. This was the gentlest arousal she had ever experienced. The touch of their tongues and their fingers was as fragile as butterfly wings. And yet, gentle as it was, the result was the same. Silky soft sensations were intensifying around her sex and spreading like gossamer up and over her belly.

Like silk winding on to spools, desire gathered and spread over her body until, at last, all the sensations aroused burst in a final explosion.

'Now we will help you wash,' said one.

'And dress,' said the other.

They helped her select a yellow outfit she had brought with her.

'Do you think Ben Said will like it?' asked Penny.

'Most suitable,' the attendants said in unison.

It was merely a plain silk tunic and wide-legged pants, but the cleverness of the cut made it outstanding.

The neckline was slit to her waist and when she moved, her breasts were glimpsed rather than over exposed. Like all good silk, it sang its own tune when she moved, the material rustling gently as it caressed her naked skin.

Something of the Middle East and the way the stewardesses were dressed made her decide to wear gold slippers with her yellow silk. With their help, she tied her hair up in a high knot with yellow and gold silk scarves interwoven among it. Gold earrings swung from her ears.

'I look good,' she said confidently to her two accomplices, and reached for their hands. 'I hope Ben Said likes what this aircraft will bring.' She smiled like a very young girl. Her smile froze as a sudden thought struck her. 'By the way, where exactly are we going?'

'Sri Lanka,' Sharana replied, with a wide smile.

Chapter Fourteen

*P*eacocks shrieked and spread their tails as they stalked the lawns in front of the palace of Prince Ben Said. The prince had chosen to live in fertile Sri Lanka rather than the arid Middle East.

Sharana explained the history of the place and, looking suitably impressed, Penny took in the details.

The palace dated from colonial times and was said to have been the unofficial residence of some past Viceroy when the country had still been called Ceylon. The official residence had been the one in which he did his imperial duties and lived with his equally imperial wife. This palace was one given to him by an Indian prince along with half his harem.

It was not stated in British historical records where the honourable viceroy spent most of his time but in Sri Lankan history, given verbally from one generation to another, the truth was that he hardly strayed from the place. He serviced the Sri Lankan people – the female ones – in an entirely different way than his orders obliged him to do.

Penny could well understand why. This was opulence, this was the fabled luxury outlined in a tale like Aladdin or one of the other stories from the Arabian Nights, but with a few modern improvements such as electricity, a swimming pool and a helicopter landing pad.

Beyond the great expanse of lawn on which the peacocks strutted, were box-like hedges and marble steps leading to the white-walled residence which was built in a Florentine fashion.

The windows on the lower floor were larger than those on the next, and those at the top of the building were that much smaller again.

Blue shutters sat beside each window or were drawn across where the sun had already reached. At one end, on the ground floor, a blue and gold awning had been erected.

'Welcome,' exclaimed Sharana and Terisha. Each kissed Penny's cheek, then took hold of her hands and led her up the marble steps.

They entered a cool atrium of blue-tiled floors, tinkling fountains and tall green palms. The plants grew in outsize pots that Penny assumed to be brass but could just as easily have been gold.

Whirring fans with blades of ornate fretwork hummed overhead. Modern air conditioning ducts augmented the more traditional means of cooling the air.

Accompanied by the two stewardesses, her luggage carried behind her by two house servants, Penny really felt as though she had entered another world.

'This way,' said the sweet Sharana, bowing her dark head as, with a sweep of her gracious arm, she indicated a wide marble staircase. 'Your room is ready.'

Each stair took Penny upwards and somehow further away from Sasha. Even thoughts of Alistair seemed out of place here.

She was here for a purpose, and yet that purpose was set aside for the moment as she took in the smells of sandalwood and a host of other perfumes that made her feel she had entered a garden rather than the palace of a playboy. And how big was this place? If the missing racehorse was here, how did she go about finding him? Where were the stables?

Her room, like everything else connected with Ben Said, was a mix of soft blues and bright gold. White curtains that only hinted at blue billowed in from the open windows. A gold fringe dangled from the hems.

The dark ebony floor was scattered with Turkish rugs of dark red and rich blue. Fretwork screens gilded with gold and lustrous strands of lapis lazuli were folded back to reveal hidden cupboards where the male servants were hanging her clothes.

Behind rich silks in blues that ranged from the colour of the sky at the brightest time of day, to the darkest indigo when the stars came out, was a bed fashioned from scrolled iron. Gilt leaves sprouted from iron stems, and flowers of lapis lazuli, onyx, amethyst, and other stones burst from gilt buds.

I'm in a fairy tale, thought Penny. I've walked from reality and have woken up in a story book. Her musings were quickly interrupted.

'See,' said one of the stewardesses. 'There is a balcony out here. From here you can see almost the whole layout of the grounds – even to the stables.'

Penny immediately followed the attendant out on to the balcony. She had been thinking of taking a bath and a nap until the stables were mentioned.

Resting her hands on the warm balustrade, Penny leant forward. 'It's splendid,' she exclaimed with a hint of triumph. Her gaze was needfully quick. This was a large palace and she needed to get her bearings. Now, she thought, where might the stables be?

'What is that building over there?' She pointed to a long, low roof of red tiles.

'The stables. You see, they run either side of the clock.'

Penny did see. A clock tower broke the clean line of the roof at around the halfway stage. Strange as it might seem, Penny was reminded of a Constable painting. The clock could have easily slipped into an English county landscape, its black hands – probably smelted in Birmingham sometime in the last century – forever reminding the human ants that scurried around it that time always marched onward.

Time was beginning to trouble her. So far she had found out little about the whereabouts of Superstar except that he could be in any one of the stables owned by the syndicate members.

As she pondered, she gazed at the far horizon. Away in the distance she discerned a yellow haze rising from the city. How cool this house was in comparison to that, she thought.

'Are the stables air-conditioned?' she asked, then could have bitten her tongue.

Sharana was frowning. 'That is a very strange question to ask, Miss Penny. I had thought you would be more likely to ask the name of this place and what manners will be expected of you during your stay. I certainly did not expect you to ask after the health of the masters' horses!'

'My profession makes me think that way,' explained Penny with a light laugh. 'Being a horsewoman does make you look at things very strangely. But you are quite right. I do wish to know the name of this place.'

Sharana's frown slowly melted. 'This is the Bibbighar. The house of women. The only true man here will be the Honourable Prince Ben Said although he does invite guests from time to time.'

'His racing friends?' asked Penny.

Sharana nodded and told her it was so. As she nodded, the gold chain which ran from the stud in her nose to the one in her ear, jangled with the heavy note that only gold can produce.

Penny left the warmth of the balcony and followed Sharana back into the bedroom.

It was hard not to smile to herself as she wondered what the stewardess thought of her. She probably thinks I'm just a batty Englishwoman, thought Penny. A left-over from the days of the Raj when men were men, the natives were trampled on, and white women were either frustrated or eccentric.

All such thoughts flew from her mind when she saw

150

the young man who was supervising those entrusted with putting her clothes away.

With agile movements and expressive waves of his arms, he pointed and gestured as to whether he was pleased with them or otherwise.

He wore the tunic and loose fitting trousers more common among the Moslems of Northern India than Sri Lanka. His skin was a soft shade of brown and had the same silky sheen as his clothes. His long, black hair was caught up in a spiral band of blue and gold that left a pony tail trailing down and reaching his shoulders.

His height, his form, and the dramatic effect of black hair on blue silk was enough to set her pulse racing. When he turned round and she saw his face, her pulse raced that much more.

'This is Chasek – your personal body servant whilst you are a guest here.'

Penny heard the words but didn't know or care who had spoken them. Before her was the most beautiful face, the most dramatic countenance, she had ever seen in her life. His face was oval, his cheekbones prominent – almost as if God had pasted them on as an afterthought. Dark eyebrows slanted deeply over large, almond-shaped eyes. Although his pupils were as black as the blackest night, there was a gleam in them, a regal shine that was both passionate and dreamlike.

'Chasek,' she repeated and nodded politely at him.

He bowed in return, his expression inscrutable except for his eyes. At first, Penny told herself she was only imagining things, or perhaps, *wanted* to imagine such a thing. But Penny had always been a perceptive girl. It had only been the most fleeting of looks in those coal black eyes, yet she had recognised passion and also something else. His look, she decided, hinted at sadness.

Chasek lowered his eyelids and the look was gone. 'I trust I will please my mistress whilst she is here.'

His voice confused her. It alternated between soft and strong, flitting like a bird from one to the other. She managed to collect herself, to smile pleasantly and wonder at the body beneath the shimmering silk. Strong, she told herself, hard and completely hairless. Desire followed her thoughts, but she managed to control her voice. 'I hope we will get on very well together.' She couldn't resist adding, 'And I hope you will be happy with me.'

'Of course, my mistress. How could I fail to be happy to serve one as beautiful as you.' His eyes fluttered. He bowed. 'Please excuse me.'

He went back to overseeing the unpacking of her things. She also noticed that new clothes were being added to her own. Some looked dramatic more than sensible, and she couldn't help wondering what sort of occasions they were meant for. So engrossed was she in studying this beautiful man, that she almost forgot the stewardesses who had accompanied her on her journey.

They were looking at her with bemused smiles on their faces.

'Chasek is very beautiful. He gives rise to many thoughts, does he not?' Terisha was speaking, her hand gently caressing Penny's back as she did so.

'Oh yes. He does indeed give rise to many thoughts.' Penny's eyes went back to the slender, masculine form as the last item of silk was put away. His body was in her mind, pressing her on to the hard ground, his belly slapping loudly against hers as he pumped in and out of her. Oh what joy, she thought to herself, and tingled all over. Yet how could one so beautiful, such a mix of all the races the Orient had to offer, have such a look of sadness in his eyes?

Terisha must have seen her look. 'You have a question?' Her voice was high-pitched like a small child.

'Nothing much,' Penny answered casually. 'I just wondered why Chasek has such a sad look in his eyes.'

Terisha stopped rubbing her back. She blinked nervously. 'The steppes,' she spluttered in a mixture of surprise and panic. 'I expect he is missing the vast expanse of plains between Samarkand and Tashkent. He is descended from the Tartars and the Cossacks, those people who roamed that great empty place.'

Instinctively Penny knew that she was lying. So why was she lying and why did the beautiful Chasek look so sad?

Chapter Fifteen

Chasek had drawn the blinds so that Penny could take a rest after her journey. Originally, her intention had been only to pretend to rest, then to sneak out, find the stables, and hopefully find Superstar. But her body was more tired than she had thought. She slept until the light was gone and the sound of running water was echoing from the bathroom.

Although she had only just woken up, Penny eyed the darkly-muscled Chasek alluringly. To her great chagrin he appeared not to notice. What was wrong with the man? she asked herself. Or was there something wrong with her?

'The master has arrived,' cried Chasek with a flourish of his arms as the fretwork doors of the wardrobes flew open. 'He will be hoping you are dressed to his taste and ready for him.'

Penny, the bedclothes tumbled around her, blinked as Chasek switched on a number of lamps that swung on black chains. She stretched as she swung her long legs to the dark wood of the floor which was warm beneath the soles of her feet.

Because the lampshades were made of soft, blue glass, they threw a cold light. And yet their coldness did not give rise to a reciprocal sensation. On the contrary, her naked flesh was very warm and tingled in its subtle glow. It was as though it were touching her with the smallest but most intense electrical current.

Furtively, she glanced to where Chasek was spreading out a garment of royal blue silk. His shoulder and back muscles seemed to ripple beneath the light silk garment that flowed over him like the surface of the sea. She had a yearning to see beneath that surface and to touch the hidden flesh the deepness within.

In an effort to entice him, she sat on the edge of the bed and, on opening her legs, smelt the sweetness of her own sex, her own honey.

Eyes narrowed and, looking at him sidelong, she ran her tongue over her lips fully expecting him to be aware of her nudity and the subtle shades of cool light that were playing over her body.

If he had noticed, he gave no sign of doing so. Even when she stood up and stretched, he did not look her way. It peeved her – so, with eyes blazing, she ran her hands down over the firmness of her breasts, that concave sweep beneath her ribs and the undulating curve of her hips. Still there was no response.

'I have run a bath for you,' he said, as he fussed with a pair of golden slippers that had curving toes and high heels.

Slightly disconcerted, Penny went to her bath. She looked over her shoulder to see if he was following her as Gregory had done on the very first occasion at Beaumont Place. How swiftly had he stirred her desires as his hands had soaped her willing body. But Chasek did not follow her, so she entered the bathroom alone.

As befits a beautiful house, this was a beautiful room. Chips of dark blue and gold mosaic edged an arched doorway. Mosaic pictures and patterns, picked out in many shades of blue and interspersed with gold, decorated the bathroom. Perfume filled the air and water streamed down over mosaic sea-horses, voluptuous mermaids and a wildly priapic Neptune. She wondered vaguely as to how an aroused Neptune could possibly

155

seduce a fish-tailed mermaid but couldn't think of any reasonable answer.

'Never mind,' she said softly to herself. 'That's his problem.'

As she breathed in the aromatic odours of her bath water, Penny closed her eyes and returned to fondling her breasts.

These are not my hands, she said to herself. These belong to a man who pretends not to want me, yet lies to me and to himself.

Sighing somewhat regretfully, Penny rubbed one thigh against the other as she rolled her breasts in her palms, traced lines around her areolae, then pulled at her nipples until she whimpered with desire.

'See how I pleasure you, my love,' she whispered to herself. Her whisper rasped over the mosaic walls where the sweat of her bath ran in silver rivulets.

'Oh, yes,' she murmured as though she were responding to an invisible lover. 'Oh, pleasure me, my love. Rub my breasts until I dissolve in my own desire. Squeeze my nipples until the threshold of pain recedes and only pleasure remains. Let me fall, breathless, beneath the torrent of passion that is washing over us.'

She took a deep breath; exhaled it as a sigh. One hand remained on her breast. The other travelled over the flatness of her belly until her fingers tangled in the black forest of hair that grew so vigorously on her sex. One finger nudged gingerly in between its warm lips.

'Oh, my mistress,' she said in as hushed a voice as before. 'Warm honey seeps from your treasure and coats your flesh with its sweetness. Let me lick it from you; let me taste you before I divide one half of you from the other. Before I breach your ramparts and run my weapon into your hidden courtyard.'

She sighed more loudly, more intently, as shivers of desire ran over her. She could have gone on until the shivers had turned into spasms and her hips jerked against her hand, but she was suddenly aware that she was no longer alone.

Slowly, as her breasts heaved and her hand movements lessened, she opened her eyes.

Chasek looked as though he could kill her. His black eyes were aflame. His jaw was set like cast iron.

Suddenly, Penny's desire was displaced by fear.

'This is not the time for doing that,' he said coldly. 'It is not good manners to do that here. You are here as my master's guest. While you are here you will dress as he wishes and be what he wants you to be!'

For some odd reason, Penny had the urge to cover her breasts and her sex as best she could. Even so, there was some spark of rebellion still left in her. 'And if I don't?' she said hotly.

He was on her in a minute. 'Then,' he said as he grabbed a handful of her hair and forced her head back, 'you will be chastised.'

She cried out and raised her hands to her hair in an effort to force him to let go of her.

'Obey!' he cried.

Still she squirmed. The hand lowered. Her heart thumped and her throat had become very dry.

Slowly, oh so very slowly, she saw his hand go to her breast. At last he was going to touch her. He gripped her nipple. At first there was only pleasure, but he pinched her and she cried out.

'Chastisement,' growled Chasek through gritted teeth. 'That is what you get for giving yourself pleasure when my lord, your master, is not around. While you are a guest in this house, the pleasures of the flesh are reserved solely for my lord. You do not indulge in such pleasures without his permission. Is that clear, my mistress?'

Penny winced then nodded. 'It is clear, Chasek. It is very clear.'

'Now, continue your bath,' he said.

He let her go and she slumped into the warm water. Suddenly it was a fit but fragile barrier between them. All the same, she was still aroused, still wondering about Chasek, and still in need of achieving an orgasm.

Curiosity bubbled in her mind, but she hid that and her naturally defiant spirit beneath a veneer of submission. No matter what pleasures, what perversions she might indulge in, she still had a horse to find.

Chasek helped her from the bath when he deemed fit. He also helped her dry herself.

He was close to her now, but something about him was strange. Although she was aware of his masculine odour, she could not locate any sign of an erection. As he rubbed the softness of a Turkish towel down her back, his belly brushed against her behind. She felt no rise of his member, no ramrod hardness beating a gentle tempo against her buttocks.

What was it the stewardesses had said? There were no real men in this place. It was a place of women. But Chasek was a man surely?

As he massaged her flesh she wondered about what he was. Although she could not help her eyes following his every move as he rubbed perfumed oils into her skin, he never once returned her ardent glances.

Why doesn't he throw me down on the floor or the bed? she wondered. Why doesn't he thrust himself into me, or even turn me over and take me from behind? Failing that, why doesn't he order me to kneel and take his member in my mouth?

But he did none of those things. He went on giving her pleasure simply by anointing her skin.

Arousing this man seemed almost impossible, so perhaps, thought Penny, he might be useful in other ways.

'Do you always do everything your lord asks you to?' she ventured.

'Yes, my mistress.'

'Have you been with him long?'

'Quite long.'

He wasn't saying much, but at least, thought Penny, he is speaking.

'This is a very beautiful place. Are the peacocks the only creatures allowed in this place?'

Chasek slowed slightly as though he were thinking

about it. 'No,' he said at last. 'They are not the only ones. Horses are here too.'

Horses! The subject I want. Penny congratulated herself before she asked the next question.

'Does Ben Said have a lot of horses?'

'Very many, mistress,' returned Chasek as his hands did delicious things to her breasts. A certain warmth came to his voice. 'In fact, they are the most important thing in his life. Horses affect everything he does. As you have seen, the uniforms of his staff are based on the harness that horses wear.'

'That never occurred to me.' Penny's voice was barely above a whisper. She was suitably surprised. I should have realised, she thought, as she remembered the tight constraints that had made their bosoms stick out and the straps that had ran through their legs and emphasised their pubes.

Chasek's voice stirred her from her reverie. 'And now you will wear the attire chosen for you by my lord.'

She eyed the blue silk he held out for her. Traces of gold thread ran through it and caught the light. What did she care if no underwear was offered? The sheer blue robe fell to her ankles. Its touch cooled her flesh, though she was somewhat surprised at the way it covered her from head to toe and reached her wrists.

Nothing could have surprised her more than what happened next.

Chasek tore open the front of her robe which was fastened by a simple device that stuck one side to the other. There was a device next to the gold slippers on the floor that he began to fasten above one knee. It appeared to be rigid with a leather strap at each end.

'Hold your knees apart!' His order was accompanied by a slap to her inside leg.

Intrigued, she did as he ordered. The device he strapped on to her legs would keep her knees firmly parted. It also subtly parted the lips of her sex so that her inner flesh was more exposed than it would normally be.

'You can open your legs wider if the master wishes,' Chasek explained. 'See,' he added, as he opened her legs wider. 'The ends of the device are flexible. It is only the middle of the device which is solid. This, of course, means you cannot possibly close your legs.'

She was going to make a comment, but something in Chasek's dark eyes told her the time was not right. Instead, she watched as he produced two more devices that might humiliate her but arouse Ben Said.

They resembled thimbles. 'Goodness,' she said with a smile. 'Am I going to sew for him?'

Chasek's chiselled countenance showed no amusement. His fingers placed the first thimble on her nipple. It was cold, but not unpleasant. Then he turned it.

Penny gasped as something inside the nipple thimble pinched her flesh.

'No, my dear mistress. You will not sew for my lord, you will mate for him.'

Penny cried out again as the other thimble was fastened to her breast. She made a small, high-pitched sound like a cat would when someone has sat on its tail.

Chasek's comment had not gone unnoticed.

'Mate?' It was all she had time to say before Chasek's strong hands were on her shoulders and forcing her downwards.

'Bend over,' he ordered.

She did as he asked and felt the silk robe being raised to her waist.

It was a strange sensation to have her head covered by her hair and the silk robe and her behind exposed. She wondered how he might be affected by the view of her twin orbs and the pink slash of sex that shone from between her legs.

She felt his hands run over her as though testing the softness of her skin and the firmness of her flesh.

You'll find they're very firm, and my skin is very soft. Of course, she only thought this. She did not say it. Chasek, despite his dramatic countenance and the sheer lust she felt for him, still appeared unapproachable. Even so, she could not help but wonder how his penis might feel trapped in her womanly muscles, or held tightly between her youthful buttocks.

It was because she was thinking these thoughts at the same time as his fingers were folding her buttocks away from her anus, that she made a mournful noise as if she were not getting enough exploration, or indeed, enough pleasure.

Suddenly, her groan was more prevalent and her legs gave way slightly as his finger entered her.

Surprised by his intrusion and unable to control her reaction, she cried out loudly.

'Be still,' he said, and slapped her behind with his free hand. 'I have to ensure that you are able to adhere to my lord's code of manners. I will insert a suitable plug that will prepare you for him.'

Penny clenched her fists as she felt something cold and smooth being inserted into her anus. In that single moment she remembered exactly what Alistair had said to her when he had first asked her to infiltrate the syndicate: 'I am asking a lot of you.' You can say that again, she thought to herself.

After her bodywear was in place and she was standing up straight, the gold shoes with the turned-up toes were slid on to her feet. They had gold silk fronds hanging from them which Chasek criss-crossed around her legs until they almost met her knees. 'That is good,' he said without the trace of a smile. 'Your calves are taut, your breasts are thrusting forward as they should, and your bottom sits pertly above the stretched muscles of your thighs.'

'I'm glad you like it.' She spoke in a resigned way and without any trace of sarcasm.

'Never mind what I like. My master will like it even more. It is for him you are dressed like this. Not for you and not for me. It is an homage he is paying by having you look like this; an homage to his horses and an homage to your sex.'

The tone of his voice was not exactly sharp, but did

convey to her that non-compliance would not be toler-
ated. But she would comply. She still had a mission to
accomplish. Was it possible that Ben Said, a man utterly
obsessed with horseflesh, might have Superstar here, in
his stables?

It was possible. In fact, anything was possible.

He brushed her hair so it fell in glossy waves around
her shoulders and she delighted in the gentle touch of
his hands. Although a pleasant calmness swept over her,
her flesh tingled as she anticipated the demands of Ben
Said.

Chasek's voice entered her thoughts. 'Your hair is like
a horse's mane,' he said, in a faraway voice. 'Just like the
mane of a little desert mare – the creature you are to be
for this night and this night alone.'

He paused. Penny sensed he wanted to say something
but remained silent. Best not to put him off, she decided.
Best to listen, not to talk. Perhaps then she might find
out what was in store for her.

His lips came close to her ear. 'Be good, my mistress.
If you play your part well, my lord will be everything to
you, will do anything for you; as long as you are what
he wants you to be.' His breath stirred her hair as he
spoke.

His sloe eyes met hers as though she would know
exactly what he meant by her being everything Ben Said
would want her to be. She did not know, and not
knowing was making her fearful.

'Come this way,' said Chasek. He held open the door.

'Like this?' She spread her hands and sounded helpless. Her legs were trembling. 'How can I walk properly
with this thing keeping my legs apart?'

Chasek glanced at her briefly before leading her out
on to the indoor landing where a stone balustrade looked
down upon a cool courtyard below, where fountains
played and lemon trees whispered in the breeze.

It wasn't easy to walk, but with jerky steps and the
awkward look of her legs hidden by her full length robe,

162

she managed to get as far as the balcony, but her progress was obviously slow.

'You see?' She shrugged her shoulders and tottered as she began to lose her balance. Chasek checked her fall and shook his head. 'Put your arms around my neck, please,' he said.

He scooped her up in his arms. No look or comment passed between them. But Penny, one leg in definite danger of slipping from his grasp by virtue of the device, took pleasure from the scent of him. Man of the steppes he might be, but his smell was reminiscent of pine forests and mountain torrents.

In response to his masculinity, beads of love juice seeped along her sexual valley and trickled between her buttocks.

Penny had expected Chasek to take her to the dining room, the library, or some other comfortable room where Ben Said would play his sexual games and use her to ignite his libido. To be placed on the back seat of a car and driven to some outer precinct of the great palace, was something of a surprise.

Still, she thought to herself, think how difficult it would have been if he'd asked me to walk all the way!

The journey was short and did not go outside the perimeter walls of the main establishment. In the descending darkness, she might not have recognised that she was in the stable yard if it had not been for the clock. There it was, just as she had seen it from her balcony, boldly upright and striking loudly as the big hand hit half past.

Chasek led her into a low building at the end of the stable yard. The smell of horses was in the air. So was the scent of well-soaped leather and fresh hay.

Penny was still afraid of what might be about to happen to her.

A horse whinnied from some place beyond the building and the clock that surmounted it. An answering whinny came from the fields beyond the main stable block.

'This,' said Chasek as he set her down inside the purpose-built structure, 'is the covering yard. The mating place.'

Penny stared. 'And a mare waiting to be covered,' she said softly, and was suddenly relieved.

The mare's head was held by two men. Her legs by thick, leather restraints. The mare had been eased into the box-like affair that would prevent her lashing out at the stallion who would come shortly to mount her.

As she watched the sturdy little mare, Penny became more acutely aware of the device between her ankles and the metal tips that gripped her nipples. I feel like her, she thought to herself. I feel like that mare awaiting her stallion. Was that what Chasek had meant?

The mare snorted. Although her head was restrained, the mare was trying to look behind her, the whites of her eyes flashing, her flanks quivering.

Penny saw Ben Said watching from the other side of the covering box. A serious expression seemed to have turned his face to stone. The scar on his face looked more scarlet than she remembered. His eyes were shining. Only once did he look across at her. He only gave her the briefest acknowledgement. She wondered why and gave herself suitable excuses. Perhaps he too can feel the trepidation of the mare, she concluded, or perhaps he is surmising just how the stallion must feel. It didn't matter. His presence meant nothing to her at this moment in time. Her eyes were full of the mare and wondering exactly when her suitor would be brought to her chamber. She did not have too long to wait.

Two more men brought forth a black stallion of Arabian ancestry. His nostrils flared and he snorted impatiently as he tried to shake off his handlers. His flanks glistened and the veins standing proud in his neck moved as his blood and his excitement pumped through his body.

The stallion spotted the mare almost immediately. He shook his head fiercely, his eyes wild and his hoofs pounding, raising dust from the shavings that covered the floor.

A feeling of fearful anticipation made Penny breathe more quickly. This mare was about to be mated, yet it might just as well have been her waiting for some fine figure of a man to push himself into her.

But why am I thinking this? Penny asked herself. Is this mare telepathic or something? Don't be stupid. You are just affected by the sight of this, by the fear she is feeling and the excitement engendered in the stallion. That was Penny's excuse, yet somehow she knew it was not entirely so.

The tableau evolved before her eyes. One of the men lifted the mighty penis protruding nearly three feet from below the stallion's stomach. As the mare twitched her tail over her quarters and braced her back legs, the stallion reared, his legs splaying over the mare as he came down on her. Below his belly, the man who had restrained him now put the tip of the stallion's penis into the mare.

A few aggressive thrusts and the mating was over. Both animals were led away. It was then that Chasek jerked Penny forward.

'The stallion has mated the mare. Now it is the turn of the man to mate the woman.'

Penny went cold. Her legs trembled as Chasek pulled her forward into the fenced-off box that had so recently housed the mare.

The trembling did not stop as Penny was placed where Chasek wanted her to be. Was that sex she could smell? she wondered. Was it that primeval instinct to survive, to continue the species, that she still perceived among the hay in the mating box?

And now her. Now for a man to mate the woman. That was what Chasek had said. She was the woman. There was no doubt about that. But who was the man? Ben Said? Chasek?

The question was unanswerable. She shook her head like the mare had and her hair flew wildly around like a horse's mane. She knew her eyes must be as full of fear as the mare's had been. Her flesh trembled just like hers had done.

In an effort to know her fate, she tried to look in the direction of Ben Said to see if he was making a move to come for her, to mount her, but Chasek was already fastening a leather head collar around her neck. A chain ran from the collar and was fastened to the front of the covering box which was about four feet by ten.

Once the collar was in place, Chasek ripped the blue robe from her body.

As though she were some frightened virgin, Penny brought up her hands in a vain attempt to hide her nakedness. Chasek hit them away, then grabbed her wrists and, with the aid of the same pieces of chain and leather that had bound the mare, he fastened her hands to the wall.

'Back,' he said, while tapping his rod against her thighs. 'Your feet are not where I want them.'

She did as he ordered until she heard the sound of chains being clipped to her ankle straps.

Now she was bent slightly, her hands clinging to the pole she had been fastened to. Knees bent, legs out behind her, bottom tilted and feet wide apart. Her breasts hung gently downwards.

Like the mare, she tried to look through her mane of hair to see what was in store for her. Apprehension made her breathe more deeply. As she breathed, she sucked in her hair then blew it out again until it sounded as if she were snorting just like the mare had done.

'Be calm. Indulge all your natural instincts. Submit to the one who will mount you. Submit and please my lord, but also please yourself.' Chasek's voice was unusually soothing – almost hypnotic.

He's right, thought Penny to herself. Never mind about pleasing Ben Said, what about pleasing me?

As her imagination began to stir, so did her body. Who was this chosen man? She still imagined it might be Ben Said or even Chasek, but nothing was predictable about this place and these men.

The image of each man flashed through her mind; Ben Said, dark, suave and as sharp as his silk shirts and silk suits. Chasek? The thought of his sloping, almond-shaped eyes made her quiver.

Either man, she guessed, had a hard body, a strong pelvis, and hopefully, a firm erection.

Her braced legs trembled at the thought of what she was about to receive.

Straw rustled behind her and she tried again to peer through her hair in an effort to see the man who was about to mount her. Like the mare, she tossed her hair and caught a glimpse of flesh that gleamed like satin and was the colour of midnight. Like the stallion, fine veins stood proud of hard, black flesh. Sweat glistened as desire tensed those muscles so that each and every one looked entirely separate from the other.

The smell of him came to her, that rich, masculine smell that is not clouded by anything superficial, by anything applied from a bottle.

Straw, sweat and leather made her head reel and give in to the animal passion that was rising inside her. She let it swim over her, mewed and wriggled her bottom as smooth, huge palms cupped her buttocks before moving to her thighs.

Dizzy with need, she tossed her hair again and looked along her body. Black fingers, strong and demanding, were digging into her creamy flesh. Like the stallion, she thought, he is just like the stallion. And I am, indeed, just like the mare.

Suddenly, she gasped. Not only was the tip of his penis nudging at her sex lips, but fingers were helping him guide it in. And not *his* fingers! She knew they could not possibly be his. Hadn't she just seen them clinging to her flesh? Couldn't she still feel them?

Chasek! It was Chasek helping him in just as the other men had helped the stallion take the mare.

As the first inches of a large penis entered Penny's

body, her legs trembled and buckled slightly. Again she snorted, breathed in and blew out her own mane of dark, glossy hair.

She closed her eyes and moaned approvingly as more of the rock hard penis entered her body. There was no way she could close her legs against this invader. The device that kept her legs apart was firmly in place. So was the bridle and the chain that kept her facing the wall, and the straps around her ankles. Because of the size of this intruder, Penny opened her legs that bit more. This penis, she decided, must belong to a big man.

Sweat had broken out all over her body and was trickling down her back. She was still shivering, her stomach tight against her spine, her nipples throbbing against the thimble clamps that contained them.

She began to cry out. They were small, apprehensive noises.

But the initial fearful cries turned to soft purrs of contentment as the heat of her stallion's thighs at last connected with hers. The crisp curliness of his pubic hair rasped her behind and his balls, along with Chasek's fingers, slapped rhythmically against the tops of her legs.

As her stallion, her stud, began to thrust back and forth, her legs continued to tremble and she continued to moan.

This man had a penis to be proud of. It was a feast of a penis, a giant among the mundane. For the first time ever, she could not meet a man's thrusts. Such was his power, such was his size, that she was swept away on the thrill of it all.

So lost was she on these waves of delight, she did not at first notice that Chasek's fingers were no longer manipulating the stud's black rod.

She opened her eyes, and through her hair she could see his slanting, almond-shaped eyes staring down at her. His mouth hung open. There was lust in those eyes: it was unmistakable. Yet there was also the sadness she had seen before.

But she did not dwell on such things. Chasek suddenly

became of no consequence. The man slamming into her was causing beautiful, thrilling sensations to travel all over her body. They were indescribable sensations, dramatic sensations, that were difficult to put into words. It was as though they were rushing along some undefined layer between her skin and her flesh.

The world melted as she closed her eyes. Chasek was blocked out from her vision and her thoughts.

Without her knowing, his eyes blazed because she was no longer looking at him.

He glanced briefly at his master. Ben Said did not see him look. His eyes were fixed on the sight of the magnificent Sudanese who did everything his master wanted him to do.

Chasek turned his gaze back to the woman who appeared so submissive to the masculine onslaught. He instinctively knew that this was not a weak woman. She was a woman he could desire, and he did desire. But what else had he to offer? Nothing, he told himself. Absolutely nothing.

Passionate thoughts of what he might have been capable of flashed through his mind. He watched her breasts tremble each time Osman, the man from Khartoum, slammed into her. If only he – Chasek – could do that. Pangs of regret circled his heart as he wished for what might have been. As he wished his thoughts and dreamed his dreams, it seemed his own body was trembling in time with hers; trembling so much in fact, that he could no longer resist touching her.

No matter that his lord and master, Prince Ben Said, was watching him and looking angry, he reached out and cupped her breasts. She made a soft, pretty noise that reminded him of the moan of the wind as it caressed the Russian steppes.

Because of the angle of her head and the fact that her hair hid her face, he could not see her expression, but he could imagine it. Oh yes, he could imagine it all right. She was in ecstasy. He knew enough of a woman to know that. Her cries were those of a woman willing to

169

submit, yet not necessarily to a man. This was a woman, he had decided, who submitted to her own sexual urges, her own instincts.

Feelings he tried to contain raged through him as his eyes met those of Osman – who was absorbed in his own ecstasy. His mouth was open and his eyes were wide with lust. Oh how Chasek envied this man – this whole man!

Lost in his own imaginings, Chasek did what he wanted to do with Penny's breasts. He squeezed them, rolled them in his hands, and twiddled at the nipple thimbles until she squealed.

But why use such things, he thought to himself, when my fingers can do a better job than mere metal?

Once her nipples were released, he took each one between forefinger and thumb. Gently, he rubbed them until any numbness she might have felt was completely gone.

'They must be a little tender,' he said softly.

Penny heard him. No, they did not feel tender, but she did not want to say anything. Desire dried her throat and blocked her speech. The feel of flesh upon her nipples was far more arousing than the feel of metal.

She made agreeable sounds. Osman, the big Sudanese, was causing the most incredible feelings to throb and spread out from her well-filled sex. And Chasek. Here was Chasek, knelt now before her, gently fondling one nipple whilst he kissed and licked at the other.

Kissing was not enough. Suddenly, he was sucking at each breast as if it were feeding him some delicate ambrosia, some sweet nectar that might be gone if he did not swallow it quickly.

Behind her curtain of hair, Penny closed her eyes. She had no need of seeing what was happening to her. The most sensitive organ of her body – her skin – was tingling as though it were icy cold, and yet it was hot, flushed and sizzling with desire. Two men were giving her pleasure. One was sucking her nipples, tapping and licking around them with the tip of his tongue. The other man was ramming himself into her, his pubic hairs cushioning the violent thrust of his pelvis. Mannish smells, earthy, hot and intoxicating, drifted beneath her veil of hair.

The mouth that had so pleasured her breasts now moved down over her belly. Chasek had joined her beneath her hair. He was kneeling before her open thighs. He kissed her pubes then licked at the delicate petals of flesh that nestled between her pubic lips.

Rising like a pink rosebud from amongst leaves, her clitoris responded. Delicate tremors of pleasure radiated from her very core and streamed like hot lava over her loins.

'Chasek, Chasek,' she murmured as her climax spread over her body.

Chasek pressed his face against her sex, his tongue licking up the last of her climax, his nose nestling in her pubic hair and inhaling the essence of woman.

He would go on doing that, he told himself. He would press his face against her until Osman had hit his peak and he himself, Chasek, had cried the last of his tears.

With one last, powerful jerk of his hips Osman, the man whose skin had been burned to a bluish black by the African sun, yelled in a language Penny did not understand and did not need to.

Chapter Sixteen

*I*t had been Penny's intention to creep around the stables of Prince Ben Said after everyone else had gone to bed. She ended up being taken on a guided tour.

'I love horses,' Ben Said admitted to her, 'That is why I watched them copulate first and you and my slave second. I also love women – and sex – of course! That is why I try to integrate the two, you understand. My love of horses is reflected in my love for women, my beautiful lady.'

Ben Said, prince and playboy, held her hand gently as he walked her around his gardens. The smell of roses was in the air and a myriad night insects provided an accompanying chorus. Nature had added an extra inducement to lustful liaison by scattering the sky with a thousand stars and a sliver of moon. Penny sighed with satisfaction. She glanced sidelong at her escort and a shiver of excitement ran through her. His features were dark, his nose slightly hooked, and his smile was sardonic but wonderfully disarming. Strangely enough, the scar that ran in a livid line down his cheek did not detract from his wild good looks.

As they walked, the silk of his tailored suit brushed pleasurably against her naked flesh. Her robe had been taken from her earlier along with the device that had held her legs apart. She still wore the golden slippers with the silk fronds and the turned-up toes. Only the device in her anus still remained in place. She was aware of its presence as she walked with Ben Said, her buttocks adding pressure to it as they rolled from side to side. She was not discomforted. Indeed, it only served to heighten the threads of sexuality that remained after her climax.

Soft strands of pubic hair fluttered around the tops of her thighs and the hair on her head blew unrestrained across her face and neck.

They stopped beneath a blossoming almond tree. Petals fell on and around them as a roosting bird took flight.

Ben Said's dark brown eyes looked intently down on her as he raised her hand and held it against his heart. Concern came to his eyes and a frown to his forehead. 'I hope my little charade did not upset you, but you see, the only way I can truly be aroused by a woman is to watch her being mounted by another man. But what gives me the greatest pleasure is to watch my horses first. That is a great joy indeed!'

Smiling engagingly he gripped her hand in both of his, raised it to his mouth, and kissed her palm. His lips felt like damp silk. A thrill ran through Penny's body.

'I think I can understand that,' she said as she remembered the smell that had come to her in the covering stall. 'Nature crosses all boundaries and sex is just a part of it.'

'A wise woman. A treasure indeed. Tonight, my dear lady, I am yours. All yours.'

She allowed herself to melt into his arms, allowed his lips to kiss her and elicit all manner of hot sensations from her body.

At the back of her mind, the one true mission again raised its head. Would it be possible to escape from Ben Said's bed after he had fallen asleep and go to the stables? She could only try.

As his lips crushed her mouth and his tongue slid on

top of hers, she rubbed her breasts and belly against him.

A lone mynah bird cried into the night. Leaves rustled and so did Penny's pubic hair as it rasped across the front of Ben Said's silk trousers.

'I love horses as much as you do,' she murmured as their lips parted. 'I might say I love them even more than you do.'

'Impossible!' There was a seriousness in Ben Said's voice, but amusement in his eyes. 'But never mind. I refuse to be offended by such a comment, but as one horse lover to another, I will take you around my stables and show you my greatest prizes.' He grimaced suddenly. 'I will also show you one who has offended me. I will also show you how I punish those who offend me.'

There was no amusement in the look that followed, and neither was there mere severity. Darts of crow's-feet struck out from the corner of each of his eyes and a hard, grimness came to his mouth.

Cruelty, thought Penny, but did not voice the word. She smiled at him as their lips parted yet again. She had no wish to cause him offence. 'I would enjoy that,' she said.

As she responded with pleasant sighs to the way his hands caressed her breasts, she became aware of his erection pressing against her. Soon, she thought to herself, that erection will be mine.

His hand eased down over her back and came to rest on one of her firm buttocks as he led her around the stables.

Never had she seen such splendid horses kept in such superior surroundings. Fly mesh covered the openings at the top of each stable door. Each stall had its own water tap, its own chute from the food bins and hay loft.

Every animal there gleamed with good health, eyes bright, hoofs oiled.

Penny made the right noises as he showed her each stallion, each mare, each filly and each leggy colt.

'And as you may have guessed,' he said stopping

before a big, black stallion. 'This is my favourite. He never fails to perform. Never fails to father another like himself.'

Regardless of his recent performance, the horse, who Ben told her was named Azrael, was still bright-eyed, still snorting, one hoof pawing at his bedding.

'All Arabian?' Penny posed her observation as a question.

Ben Said nodded and clapped his hands together. 'Indeed yes. These are my loves, my beauties. If the camel is the ship of the desert, then the Arabian horse is the racing yacht. He is the demon of the desert, the drinker of the wind. I have devoted my life, my money, and this place to the pursuit of excellence in the breed. That is why there are only pure-bred Arabian horses in this place.'

'Only Arabians,' echoed Penny. 'So where do you keep your racehorses?' She asked the question as casually as possible.

'Kentucky,' he answered, his eyes still glued to his prize stallion. 'With my friend Aran McKendrick who you have already met.'

Penny leant forward onto the stable door. She must not allow Ben Said to see the disappointment on her face. As she did so, the dry wood of the stable door scratched her naked breasts. She felt the hand of her Arab prince slide between her buttocks and onward through her legs. She groaned and shifted against his touch. His mouth kissed her neck before he spoke to her.

'Now I will show you how I punish those who do not live solely to serve my will.' His breath was as warm as the wind. 'Come.' His hand stayed where it was, one finger crooked so its tip was embedded in her vagina. His thumb pressed between her buttocks and against her anus.

By virtue of the way he was holding her, he guided her away from the borrowed Englishness of his stable yard. The building he took her into was unique to Sri Lanka.

175

Gold, blue and turquoise glinted from walls, floor and ceiling. Sweet-smelling smoke rose from head high braziers. Naked flames threw dancing shadows upon the walls.

Stone figures, bright with colour and gilt, were touched by the flickering light. It made their sloe eyes appear to blink, and their crooked arms to move as though dancing to an ancient tune.

Some of the statues were of temple dancers, their arms and legs bent at odd angles, their fingers expressive. Bright red nipples some two inches long, leapt forward from breasts as round and firm as grapefruit. Cascades of beads and pearls fell over large, round buttocks. Lips smiled promises and eyes stared enticingly forward. Slant-eyed Buddhas, their mouths leering, their bellies round and heavy, sat benignly in sheltered alcoves, their gaze forever fixed on the stone dancers who forever enticed.

'Don't you find it breathtaking,' exclaimed Ben. His eyes glittered with excitement in the flickering amber light. His voice was thick. 'Don't you get a sense of the past? Imagine the primeval urges of dancers who made those contorted movements. They went even further, you know. They used to put their legs over their shoulders, and with their feet hooked behind their head, expose their sexual parts as if it were their only part. They made themselves look as if they were made of one organ alone and with one sole purpose in life; to be impaled on a male member. Fascinating don't you think?'

'Fascinating.' Penny's voice was like a mere breath. Perhaps it was the flickering of the flame torches, but at times she could almost believe that the dancers were made of flesh and blood rather than cold stone.

She groaned as more of Ben's finger slid into her vagina and the tip of his thumb pressed more firmly into her anus. Because of the way he was doing this and the way the rest of his fingers were holding her sex, she arched her back so that her breasts thrust more firmly forward and her buttocks jutted out more prominently behind her.

'I collected these from all over Sri Lanka,' Ben said proudly and in a voice that seemed not to recognise what he was doing to her. 'All the dancers came from here, but some of the Buddhas came from India as did my most formidable acquisition. The most formidable, most bloodthirsty of goddesses.'

Something in his voice made Penny tremble. What else did she have to see before she was lying beside or beneath him, his body hard and hot against hers. A single question arose in her head. 'I wonder at you collecting such things. I thought you were a Moslem.'

'You are quite correct, but I am also a curious man,' he answered, his voice dark and low. 'I am a man who is intrigued by the supposition that religion and sex can be combined in much the same way as man and woman can be combined. I am fascinated with the many aspects of sexuality, with the history of blood sacrifice, and of religious prostitution. For my pleasure, you will now experience some of these delights. Chasek was not as loyal tonight as he should have been. You will assist me in chastising him, and when that is done, we will go to my quarters.'

Penny's mind reeled. Did Chasek's behaviour really constitute a punishable offence? And had Ben orchestrated some really terrible punishment that she could simply not take part in?

At the end of the long barn-like structure where the floor was dust and diminishing light threw long shadows, sat the stone goddess which Ben was obviously in awe of.

Braziers of fire stood either side of her, their flames throwing patches of light over her terrible features. Black-edged eyes stared from a frightening face; a blood red tongue slavered over her chin. Like the other statues, jewellery fashioned from the same rock as her fell over her round, hard breasts, and from each side of her body, three arms stuck out to form a crescent shape. Each of the six hands held a sword.

'Kali,' murmured Ben. 'Drop down! Worship her!'

So saying, he released her sex which was now wet with fluid. With a heavy hand, he pressed Penny's shoulder, and with him, she fell to her knees. For the first time, she was truly afraid.

Ben Said had a fanatical stare in his eyes. 'See,' he went on, 'how beautifully terrible she is. Is that not the blood of her victims on her tongue, dripping after she has drank of their life?'

Penny was trembling. 'Ben, what are we doing here? Please tell me.' Her voice rasped in her throat.

It had never been in Penny's nature to be afraid of anything. No matter what the adventure, she had always been game to try it. But this time, beneath the eyes of this terrible goddess and beside a man who seemed to worship the bloodthirsty Kali, she was *very* afraid!

Because he heard the fear in her voice, his hand ran down from her shoulder to her elbow. 'Come, my dear Penny. Do not be afraid. It is not you who is to be punished. Besides, I can assure you that Chasek will enjoy whatever we do to him.'

But where was Chasek?

As he helped her to her feet and guided her forward, Penny at last saw him.

Before the spread legs of the horrific goddess was a stone altar, and on that altar, face down, was Chasek, his wrists and ankles tied to the base of the altar, his bottom higher than his head.

As shadows from the burning lamps danced over Penny's naked body, Ben led her forwards. Once they were stood beside Chasek, Ben let go of her.

'See how his body glistens,' he murmured with a hint of menace. He ran his fingers over Chasek's back and down his spine. Chasek shivered. 'He shivers at my touch,' laughed Ben. 'He shivers because he knows what I am going to do to him – what you are going to do to him.'

178

Entranced by the bronzed beauty of the male flesh laid out so bare and so firm before her, Penny gazed spellbound. Even if she could have moved, she would not have. It was pleasant to look upon the man before her; so sweet to imbibe the essence of him, to smell him and feel that smell settle on the back of her tongue.

As Penny gazed at this spectacle, she was vaguely aware that Ben was undoing the zip of his trousers. As thick as her wrist, the penis of Prince Ben Said, international playboy and racehorse owner, leapt like a prime young steed from his flies. A crown of white fluid sat like a pearl on its head. Inwardly, Penny groaned. She had a powerful urge to lick it, to taste its masculinity, to roll it around on her tongue and let it slide down her throat.

She saw Ben's hand rub his erection as if trying to coax that much more stiffness from it. Thoughtfully, as she relished what it might feel like in her mouth, in her vagina or in her anus, she ran her tongue over her lips, then gasped when she saw what his intentions were.

Instead of offering such an object to her, he placed himself behind the supine Chasek. Taking the object of her interest in one hand, he placed its head against Chasek's behind then thrust forward.

Chasek cried one weak cry before his voice became a continuous moan. Ben, his trousers around his knees, rammed himself into Chasek.

'See how the goddess smiles?' cried Ben.

Penny looked up at the face of the bloodthirsty goddess. Perhaps her smile had changed, but only, decided Penny, because the flames in the iron braziers were dancing more fiercely.

'Are you going to sacrifice him to her?' Penny asked fearfully, fists clenched, legs ready to run. 'Are you going to kill him afterwards?'

Without interrupting the tempo of his thrusts, Ben threw back his head and laughed. Was it her imagination, or had she heard Chasek laugh too.

Ben looked directly at her, his shoulders still, his hips

thrusting backwards and forwards, backwards and for-wards. 'I am sacrificing my seed to Chasek. After I am finished, Chasek will be sacrificing his masculinity to you. In turn, you will be sacrificing your femininity. By such actions will the goddess be pleased. Is that not right, Chasek?'

Chasek grunted his agreement then continued to moan as if he were in ecstasy.

His mood was infectious. As his groans filled her ears, Penny ran her hands over her naked breasts, her belly and her thighs. Once fear had left her, her flesh tingled with need.

Ben, his eyes bright, mouth smiling, watched her play with her own body. Chasek too was watching. He groaned more loudly as Penny furled back the lips of her sex and stroked provocatively at her rising clitoris.

'Shut him up,' ordered Ben.

'What?' She frowned and stopped playing with her passionate little nub which even now was getting hard with desire.

'Shut him up. Use his mouth to pleasure yourself.'

This was completely unexpected. Penny's breasts rose and fell more quickly. The thought of Chasek's tongue on her sex filled her mind and sent the blood rushing hot and furious through her veins.

Now she knew that Chasek was a willing participant in this scenario, she made her way to his head. Placing a hand on either side of him, she brought his mouth to face her mound and, jerking her hips forward, she gasped as she felt the light flick of his tongue upon her sex. She closed her eyes, murmuring luscious sounds that sounded almost like a melody.

Pleasure coated her. There was a brittleness about that pleasure, a feeling that if she opened her eyes the sugar-fine coating would crack and disappear. So she kept them closed and, just as incessantly as Ben jerked against Chasek's buttocks, she jerked against Chasek's mouth.

To Penny's annoyance, Ben cried out just as the full

thickness of Chasek's tongue was dividing her labia and doing arousing things to her clitoris.

She heard Ben make those last sweet cries of satisfaction that accompany the diminishing waves of a climax. Nevertheless, she continued to thrust her pubic lips against Chasek's mouth. She had no intention of letting this chance go to waste.

'Look at this,' Ben interrupted.

Regretfully, Penny opened her eyes. 'Wow!' she exclaimed, her eyes filled with the sight of Ben's penis which he had laid on the nape of Chasek's neck so she might study it more closely.

Although he had only just reached a climax, she could see that Ben's phallus was recovering at a rate of knots. Already fresh blood was creating a new erection, and, as he cleansed it gently, wiping a length of silk soaked in a fresh-smelling infusion over its head and shaft, Penny saw its size increase further.

'Come,' said Ben as he pulled Penny away from Chasek's mouth. 'Let me make this thing more interesting. Let me help you take Chasek's masculinity.'

'How are you going to do that?' she asked, though she didn't really care. She was only regretful that Chasek's sweet mouth had left her juicy lips and left an ache behind.

'Put this on, my dear.' Ben smiled as he fastened a leather belt around her waist.

Astounded, Penny looked down as Ben passed another strap through her legs and fastened it to the belt at the back.

From the front of this device protruded a leather phallus which must have been at least six inches long.

Ben smiled. 'Now you are a man so can use Chasek as a woman.'

He saw her look of astonishment. Gently, he folded her hair back from her face, kissed her and fondled her nipples. She was putty in his hands.

'Don't worry,' he said softly. 'Chasek has been looking forward to this. Haven't you seen him watching you

181

with a glum expression? You will enjoy this, I guarantee it, for as you are invading his body, I will be invading yours. The strap that passes through your legs has a large gap in it – a gap big enough for me to ease myself through and into your body.'

Full of the sensations left by Chasek's tongue, Penny lowered her eyes, touched the false penis that thrust forward from her body, then touched the real one that thrust forward from Ben.

'I know which I prefer,' she said softly.

With Ben's help she positioned herself to enter Chasek's upturned rear. As the first inch or so entered, she gripped Chasek's haunches and felt his muscles flinch beneath her scraping fingernails.

The warmth and hardness of Ben's body came closer. She frowned as she heard something rustle like silk. Did Ben Said, prince and playboy, wear silk shorts?

The question was irrelevant. Penny was far too gone to care about what Ben wore. She only knew his penis was one of the best looking of its kind she'd ever seen and she wanted it – badly!

Sexual excitement sent shivers of desire throughout her body as the tip of Ben's penis nudged gently but firmly between her buttocks.

Chasek groaned as she thrust, and her own voice echoed the same sound as Ben entered her body. This, she told herself, is exactly as Chasek is feeling.

Ben was in her anus, and she was embedded in that of Chasek. She was between two men, receiving from one and giving to another. The thought of it, besides the actuality, was highly erotic.

Back and forth they jerked, each stroke in tune with the other, their groans mingling like an unending song, and like a song, their passion mounted, their senses reeled with the intensity of what was happening.

Like a psalm or an ancient, pagan chant, their cries of climax were rendered in unison and soared above them.

It is as Ben said, thought Penny to herself. We are sacrificing our climaxes on this altar. We are worshipping this many-armed goddess in a way she would appreciate.

When it was at last all over, Ben Said released Chasek's bonds then took hold of Penny's arm and guided her out of that place.

'What about . . .?' she began.

'My servants will take care of him,' said Ben abruptly.

'Was that Chasek's chastisement?' she asked.

He smiled a secretive little smile that told her chastisement, pleasure and goddess worship were pretty much the same thing as far as he was concerned.

She looked back. Chasek was standing up. Penny gasped. At last she knew the reason for the sadness in his eyes. Was it merely a trick of the light, or was Chasek a eunuch, having only a stem and no hanging fruit?

She did not have time to look more closely. Ben Said had hold of her elbow and was gently but firmly guiding her out of the place of dancing idols and sloe-eyed Buddhas.

'We will now go to my quarters, and we will sleep together,' he told her.

It was when Ben Said was undressing that Penny found out his secret. Beneath his smart trousers and silk shirts, Ben Said wore lace underwear – women's lace underwear, and he was quite unrepentant about it.

'It's the secret of my continuous erection,' he explained. 'The touch of silk against my scrotum is a continuous reminder of women and sex. I am always alert. Always ready for action!'

Penny, her eyes full of the size and hardness of his latest erection, pulled him to her. 'I'm not complaining,' she exclaimed. 'Whatever turns you on is fine by me!'

Chapter Seventeen

Sasha was flat on his belly in the middle of a grassy field that was hidden from the road by a row of silver-leaved poplars. His car was parked beneath them next to the long low black creation that was driven by Nadine.

'Now. Tell me when you have to pick them up, my tight-bottomed Frenchman.' Nadine had already got him to take his clothes off, kneel and kiss her hairless pubes. Now she was standing on him and her voice fell to earth like a low rumble of thunder.

Sasha closed his eyes and a sweat broke out over his body. It wasn't the result of fear or even because the heels of her boots were digging into his buttocks. The sweat was a mixture of his failure to resist the allure of Nadine's deep purring voice and the sweet pleasure of attempting to please her. He felt no actual shame at his submission. He was only annoyed with himself that he had once again failed to resist her.

Before Nadine had rung and demanded that they meet, he had composed a speech telling her that their liaison was over. Never before had he even thought about disobeying her but since meeting Penny, things had changed. Her face haunted his dreams. The feel of her body seemed to be with him constantly.

Was he in love? He wasn't sure. He only knew that since meeting Penny he had wanted her like he'd wanted no other woman before. But that didn't mean he could disregard the powerful charisma of Nadine Alicia Beaumont, a sexual vampire among women.

Even now he tried not to answer her, but it was hard – very hard.

'Tell me!' Nadine growled and dug her heels that much more deeply into his naked buttocks which in response bunched to rock hardness.

He swallowed hard before he spoke. He tasted salt as he licked his lips. 'Orly. 2.15,' he gasped. 'I am to join them and accompany Miss Bennett to Louisville, Kentucky.'

A cloud of lilac circled Nadine's head as she exhaled a mouthful of cigar smoke. Around some women such a cloud could be described as a halo, but not when it circled Nadine. She was over six feet tall, lean limbed, angular featured, her shoulders square and her white hair crisp as corn stubble over her head. She was dressed from head to toe in black lycra. Steel spurs at her heels relieved the blackness of her boots just as the dull grey of her eyes relieved the whiteness of her face. Silver bands circled her thighs and ran outwards from her neck like a spider's web over the short black cape she wore.

Her waistcoat was of an open-work design and nipped in neatly at her waist. Almost as if they were buttons or small brooches, her nipples peered sharply through two of the fretwork holes. She did not attempt to cover them, but only stood silently, thinking. Her hands rested on her waist. In one she held a silver-handled whip which was a thing she carried as frequently as some women would carry a handbag. The usual cigar was clenched firmly between her perfect white teeth. Her lips were curled back and her eyes were narrowed, her lids hooded.

'So,' she said thoughtfully, cigar still clenched between barely parted teeth as she spoke. 'What is the nature of this visit to Kentucky?'

Sasha could not resist answering. He could resist nothing Nadine asked of him. 'The races,' he blurted. 'I think she's going to the races there and to see Mr Aran's stud farm.'

He felt Nadine's feet move slightly, though her heels did not leave his buttocks. Her whip trailed menacingly through the cleft that divided his cheeks. He shivered with apprehension as he remembered the sting of that whip.

'And is the decadent Arab going too?' Nadine snarled.

Sasha paused, then jerked and cried out as the end of the whip dug into his anus. He took a deep breath and tried to stop the words coming out. It didn't work. 'No,' he answered. 'I have been told that only Miss Bennett is to fly to Kentucky.' He bit his lip hard in retribution for proclaiming what he knew. He had detected a hint of conspiracy when he had received his orders to take Penny to the airport. As always they had come by telephone. He didn't quite know what had made him suspicious. He only knew that things were not quite as straightforward as they might be. But Nadine must know that too. If he hadn't known her really well, he would have wondered why she was so interested in charting the progress of a very sexual young woman. But he did know her and knew she had a possessive nature.

He had also met Penny Bennett so could understand her feeling as she did. Hadn't Penny made him feel the same?

Sasha breathed a sigh of relief as Nadine stepped off his behind. He attempted to get up, but a booted foot landed in the small of his back.

'Stay there! Do you think I have come all this way without getting some enjoyment from your body?'

Sinking back to the earth, Sasha clenched his fists and took short, hesitant breaths. Rough grass, stones and dusty earth was the bed beneath his body. It was uncomfortable, hard in places, rough in others. Sharp stones dug into his belly, and prickly-leaved plants made his penis hotter, harder and far redder than it would otherwise have been. He knew that Nadine would know that, knew she had chosen this spot for that very reason.

'Now,' she said tantalisingly as she again trailed the whip over his naked behind. 'Now I will be cruel to you as only I know how. After that, we will discuss your trip with Miss Bennett and arrange where to meet in Kentucky.'

'You're coming?' He couldn't help sounding surprised. Why would she want to come? Did she love Penny Bennett herself or was there some other reason for her interest?

Such thoughts were quickly dispatched as Nadine, well prepared as ever, forced metal pegs into the ground and fastened him to these with leather straps around his wrists and his ankles.

Ashes sprayed his face as she dropped the cigar stub. Dust rose from the toe of her boot and flew into his face as she ground the used tobacco into the earth. This, Sasha knew, was a signal, a sign that she was about to commence enjoying herself.

When she used him like this he attempted to put himself in her position, to imagine how her body and mind were responding each time the whip reddened his flesh. By doing that, he too could enjoy the experience. It was as if he were taking his pleasure from her rather than the other way round.

There was no point in attempting to look into Nadine's face at such times. Only Nadine's eyes ever showed any emotion. The rest of her face always remained stone-like.

All the same, he knew instinctively she would be relishing the jerking of his muscles, their increased prominence each time the whip landed; how it laced over the contours of his body, his muscles bunching and quivering, his penis hardening each time it landed.

By closing his eyes tightly, he became more aware of the heat of his balls against his body, the tightening of his anus as the whip stung his flesh. Muscle bunched against muscle and penis pulsated against the rough earth and rougher plants. Pain became pleasure. There was nothing in Sasha's looks to indicate that he enjoyed submitting to a woman. He was masculine, good looking and loved to push his virile member between a woman's legs. But there was something about Nadine that was not woman. There was also something about her that had to be obeyed.

When she finally finished whipping him, he was breathing heavily, his breath hot and wet against his shoulder. He opened his eyes. Experience told him she was not finished yet.

'I need a smoke,' he heard her say. 'Now where shall I put my whip while I light up.'

Immediately he tightened his buttocks, yet it was no use. Without any consideration for the sanctity of his person, she pushed the end of the whip into his anus. He cried out, and she laughed, pleased to see his muscles harden and gather in tight bunches all over his back.

So she smoked, and as she smoked she narrowed her eyes and looked thoughtfully at the rank of upright poplars whose leaves fluttered delicately as a car swept by.

'I hate France,' she muttered. She also hated not knowing what her brother was up to. She would not believe he had tired of Penny. There was far more to this than met the eye and she was determined to find out what it was.

When she had first heard that Penny had gone with Ben Said to Sri Lanka, she had thought of following and spying on them. But Ben Said lived in a huge palace that crawled with servants and peacocks. Besides, Sasha already knew exactly how much time Penny would be spending with the dark-eyed prince. And that in itself seemed strange. It was almost as though a schedule had been worked out in advance. Of course, she thought to herself, I could ask the prince or any member of the syndicate, but that's not my style. I will not do that. No, she would bide her time, use Sasha to full advantage, and eventually she would know everything there was to know.

In the meantime, she would finish enjoying the lean, bronzed pilot, and then she would travel to Kentucky.

Chapter Eighteen

*E*ven before Penny arrived on Ben Said's private jet at Orly Airport, she was thinking of Sasha. They were to meet up in the Departure Lounge and take a transatlantic flight to the States.

Customs clearance seemed to take forever and the guy who was checking her luggage had obviously picked up on her impatience and slowed down accordingly.

His brown eyes raked her from head to toe. He spread his hands over her suitcase as if he was attempting to feel its contents through the soft brown leather.

Unwilling to appear intimidated, Penny returned his look. He eyed her body and the clothes that covered it. The trousers were tight and accentuated the length of her legs. The jacket was fitted and had only three buttons that fastened beneath her breasts. She wore earrings but no necklace. Only her cleavage and a hint of nipple took the eye between her waist and her throat. Above that, her face was radiant, her eyes shining, her hair glossy and fastened with a gold band at the nape of her neck.

She saw the man wet his lips before he unfastened the suitcase. She saw him blink and his moustache quiver as he eyed the contents.

He glanced at her from over the top of the suitcase lid.

His eyes were shining. 'You have beautiful things, *Mademoiselle*. Sexy things.'

The boldness of her returned gaze did not falter. 'I like beautiful things. I like sexy things, and I am the things that I like – beautiful and sexy.' She smiled provocatively, then realised she had made a mistake.

The man's skin became shiny. His cheeks reddened. He cleared his throat before he spoke. His voice was less strident than it had been. 'What a delight it must be to see you in these beautiful things, beautiful lady.'

Just as she had expected, he drew out a fragile item in red lace that was little more than a triangle at the front. The waistband and the piece that passed between the buttocks were mere strips of satin.

His eyes held hers as he crumpled the delicate object in the palm of his hand. Slowly, he raised his hand to his nose and sniffed. As he inhaled her sexual perfume, he closed his eyes.

'Have you had enough?' She leant forward and rested her hands on the counter as she spoke. Her breasts fell forward, her nipples peering provocatively from beneath the suede jacket.

His attitude changed. 'I think I will have to investigate this a little further, *Mademoiselle*. I need to know whether your underwear and the other articles you have in this suitcase breach any law of the Republic of France.'

'Hogwash.' She didn't stress the word, but it didn't matter. 'I'm leaving the country, not coming into it, so what bearing does my underwear have on your country?'

The customs officer was not impressed. 'No. It is not hogwash. This way, mademoiselle.'

She took a deep, impatient breath. His expression did not change. He waved her through a door that he held open for her, then she followed him along a corridor painted a boring cream and sickly green. He opened another door and they went down some steps. The next door looked like the door to a cell. Sudden fear made her stomach muscles tighten. She took a deep breath as colder air rushed out and chilled her face. Once they had entered, the customs officer locked it behind them.

Nervously, Penny rubbed at her arms.

'What is this place?'

The man did not answer.

The room was bare except for two chairs and a table. There was also a small cupboard in one corner and no window. The customs officer put the suitcase on the table and turned directly to her.

'Now, *Mademoiselle*. Please undress and I will search you just in case you are taking something other than naughty underwear out of this country.'

'Who are you kidding? Do you think I don't know what you want?'

He stood rigid, unbending. His shoulders were broad, and although she'd seen better-looking men, this customs man in his dark uniform with its shiny buttons, didn't rate too badly. Besides that, from the time she had left Sri Lanka, she had thought of Sasha and thinking of him had made her hot with desire. Now it was not just a tumble in the hay she wanted. On the flight over she had lain back and imagined many weird and wonderful scenarios with many weird and wonderful people. This man and this scenario was one she had not thought about.

She slid off her pale beige boots, her trousers and her jacket. Once she was naked before him, she saw his jaw clench and fully expected him to reach for her. But he did not do that. Instead, he went to the cupboard. He turned, and as though it were the most important task in the world, he ripped open a sterilised package and drew out a pair of lightweight rubber gloves – the sort doctors and surgeons use.

As goose bumps ran over her body and her nipples became affected by the cold air, Penny swallowed and muttered 'Oh no' in her head. He's really going to search me, she thought to herself, and shivered.

She stood stock still. Only her eyes moved as he walked around her. His face came before her and for the first time, it was hard to look into his eyes. Fear made her gaze at his shoes.

'Open your mouth.' His voice was firm.

She did what he asked and almost gagged as his fingers probed beneath her tongue, around her teeth and into her throat.

'Hold your hair back from your ear,' he ordered.

She did as he asked, felt his finger probing around and in one ear. It reminded her of the action of a lover, that in-between moment when tenderness is replaced by a bruising passion.

'Now the other, please.'

Once her ears had been searched, he lifted each breast.

Now she was surprised and had to say something. 'How can I hide something beneath my breasts?'

'Smugglers tape things beneath bosoms – especially if the bosom is very big; big bellies too. I once caught a big Algerian woman who had drugs taped beneath her bosom which reached almost to her waist – except she did not have a waist. She had a belly that hung over her thighs like a huge apron. She had more drugs taped beneath that. There were more between the lips of her sex and her buttocks. Even more inside her body.'

He was slow in removing his hands from her breasts. She tried to read his face so she could see what was coming next. In her own mind she knew what was coming but did not really want to admit it.

As she watched him take the suitcase from the table and put it on a chair, there was no escaping the inevitability of what was to come.

'Get up on the table,' he said. As he pointed at the table, he looked directly at her. His eyes blazed, but his face was still set like iron.

Shivering again from both the coldness of the room and with apprehension at what was to come, Penny got up on to the table.

'Lay flat on your back, then raise your legs.' He spoke the order as if he were merely explaining to her how best to reverse a car into a driveway. As she obeyed, he raised two iron bars from the side of the table from which hung two ankle stirrups.

'What are you going to do?' she asked, her stomach tightening and her knuckles turning white as she clung to the sides of the table.

'Just making sure you don't kick me while I carry out my investigation,' he replied.

Penny gulped. I didn't need to ask that, she thought. I already knew what he was going to do, but still I had to hear him say it. She was naked, the table hard against her back, her legs raised and parted and her ankles strapped firmly to the two iron uprights. Her sex was open to his gaze and the probing of his fingers.

She gasped as the smooth coldness of his rubber-covered fingers pulled her pubic lips further apart. One finger entered her and she groaned.

'Nothing so far,' he said, his gaze fixed on the satin flesh. His free hand grasped one haunch, his thumb pressing against the place where her bottom met her thigh. 'Now you are wet enough, I can use more fingers.'

He did just that.

'Oh no!' she cried out as two then three fingers were inserted.

He pushed them up and down, his thumb beating against her clitoris each time he rammed his fingers into her.

No matter that he was supposedly searching for contraband, his fingers were finding something else entirely. Pinpoints of sexual arousal were created by his fingers and his thumb. They multiplied and spread throughout her senses.

She closed her eyes and raised her bottom away from the coldness of the table. She groaned as he continued to wriggle his fingers inside her.

This is so perverse, she thought to herself. So deliciously perverse, and she felt no shame whatsoever.

Just when she thought she could do nothing else but come, he withdrew his fingers. Fluid trickled from her sex and seeped like warm treacle between the cheeks of her buttocks.

Penny, her eyes wide and bright, was breathless. 'Why did you stop?' Her cry echoed around the room.

He began to undo the ankle straps that held up her legs and did not look at her. 'Because I have found nothing except desire in you. No drugs, no contraband. Not there anyway. Turn over on to your belly. Slide your feet to the floor.'

He helped her turn over, then caught hold of her ankles so she slid down the table and her feet landed on the floor. He adjusted the stirrup bars so that they lay along the sides of the table, then he grabbed hold of her wrists, stretched her arms and fastened the straps that had held her ankles around her wrists.

As her sex filled with wetness, her nipples dipped against the smooth coldness of the table.

'This table is so cold,' she cried out.

'*Très bien*,' proclaimed the customers officer, and went on with what he was doing. Penny felt her legs being spread and more straps fastening her ankles to the table legs.

He pushed a wad of her own clothes – those beautiful lace items from her suitcase – beneath her hips. Tautly stretched between the straps that fastened her wrists and those that fastened her ankles, her body tingled and her breath came thick and fast. Her spine swept in an exaggerated curve, and her buttocks were thrust upwards.

Instinctively, she clenched her buttocks together. Never had she felt so naked, so vulnerable. As her hair escaped the pins and band that held it, aspects of the room around her disappeared. Touch and sound were now her only contact with the room and the man in it.

A grating sound of a jar being opened made her grit her teeth. Cold cream, her brain screamed, and her body became more taut.

With one hand he forced her buttocks apart. With the other he applied cold cream around her anus.

195

Penny sucked in her breath. The cream really was cold and his finger was rigid with intent as it burrowed its way into her. She could not help but clench her buttocks. She could not help but cry out, her back arching more as her buttock muscles clenched the intruder.

He retreated, pushed, retreated and pushed again. His finger was using her anus as a man's cock should use her vagina. Even without seeing his face, she knew his expression would be ecstatic.

Still shrouded by her hair and moaning long and low, she became more alert to touch and to sound.

His finger was still in her, hard, bony against her soft flesh. But where was his other hand?

The sound of the disentangling of metal teeth came to her. He was undoing his zip!

Suddenly, her nipples ached with passion and her vagina seeped with fresh juices. 'Yes,' she heard herself say out loud. 'Yes.'

Hot and hard his penis pushed into her vagina. She welcomed its warmth, welcomed its determined invasion and tilted her bottom towards both it and the finger that still had her.

Finger and penis moved in the same tempo and his balls slapped pleasurably against her wide-open sex. As he moved on her, she moved on the table and the pile of underwear that he had shoved beneath her. Some of that underwear had piled into tight, hard knobs, and to her great delight, those knobs were at the exact same point as her clitoris.

As her body moved up and down the table with the frequency and fierceness of his thrusts, her nipples rubbed against the smooth surface of the table.

She moaned, mewed and cried out all sorts of words that might or might not goad him to greater things or to the final spasm of a beautiful climax.

Scintillating, tingling sensations ran from her stroked clitoris, through the valley of her sex, and even around to the submissive muscles of her anus.

When he came, she felt the soft down of his thighs

tense against the back of hers. His chest would be hairy, she decided. So might his back, and just imagine how thick the curls would be around his penis which she could feel was very thick and very long.

'I don't like hairy men!' she cried out. It was a cry of defiance. And yet, in a way, it was also one of triumph because regardless of her taste in men's bodies, she was experiencing one of the best orgasms she had ever had.

At last, it was all over.

'I am now satisfied, *Mademoiselle*. You may dress and take your luggage with you.'

He did not kiss her, did not even look at her as he escorted her back to the main customs hall.

'*Merçi Mademoiselle*.' He saluted, but his eyes were already sliding sidelong to the group of long-haired musicians who had just entered and were wheeling their instruments before them on a large collection of airport trolleys.

'Thank you,' she said, once all her belongings were returned to a trolley and the care of a porter.

As the luggage rolled out of sight and onwards to a transatlantic 747, Penny's eyes searched the VIP reception area. The double doors opened and Sasha stepped through.

'Sasha, I . . .!'

'Come with me,' he said, his words rushed, his eyes burning with desire.

His fingers closed tightly around hers and she went with him.

He dragged her into the shuttle that would take them to their designated departure lounge. Once aboard, his arms were around her and her arms were around him.

Desire, inflamed by what she had already endured, burned more vibrantly. There was a hot wetness to his lips, a firm demand in the tongue that entered her mouth and lay heavy upon hers. No lips felt like Sasha's lips, no body was as hard, as urgent against hers. She wanted him badly. She wanted to feel his naked flesh against

197

hers, the crispness of his pubic hair, the tensing of his buttocks as he rammed himself into her.

'Where can we go?' she cried, her breath half strangling her words. 'I must have you, Sasha. I must have your body, must have you in me!' she cried breathlessly.

'Here and now,' he murmured. 'I will have you here and now.'

Penny had been aware from the moment they had stepped aboard that they had the shuttle carriage to themselves. But surely it would stop and pick up other passengers before reaching their drop off point? And what about the windows? Wouldn't people see them as they passed?

Sasha held her chin and looked deeply into her eyes. 'I know what you're thinking. I've bribed the driver not to open the doors until I push that button up there.' He pointed. 'See?'

She looked and saw it.

'And,' he added, after kissing her, 'the windows are a third of the way up the side of the carriage. Those outside can only see us from the chest up.'

'I'm convinced,' she said hurriedly as she clapped her hands over his behind and thrust her belly against his. 'Now do it to me – here! Now!'

They undid each other's trousers. Hers slid easily to the floor and she was thankful there was no underwear to worry about. His trousers remained where they were, but his penis leapt out eagerly and Penny gripped it tightly.

There was no time for finesse, for sweet overtures and leisurely caresses. They were in a public place. Blurred places and people flashed by as their ardour took control.

'I'm desperate for you,' gasped Penny between kisses.

'I'm having you, *ma chérie*,' murmured Sasha as his hands covered her buttocks and he eased himself into her.

She murmured sweet nonsense as he entered her body. Murmurs turned into moans and gasps for more as he rammed his full length into her.

Wrapping her arms around his neck to gain support, she raised one leg. One hand that had been on her buttock now took hold of that thigh and gripped it tightly. As naturally as night follows day, Penny raised the other leg and Sasha took hold of that too so she was suspended against him.

With his hands holding on tightly to her thighs, she wrapped her naked legs around him, enjoying the increased intimacy of his pubic area against hers, the more subtle yet sensitive pressure of his thrusting.

She was vaguely aware of the shuttle having come to a stop. People were crowding forward, their hands tapping on the glass in the hope that those inside might be able to open the carriage doors and let them in.

But those inside had no interest or intention of letting them in. They were lost in their own embrace, their own whirling, ecstatic sensations.

Penny's naked thighs were entwined firmly around the handsome young pilot. Eyes closed, lips hot for his, Penny did not care that faces were pressing against windows, hands gesticulating that they wished to come aboard.

With cat-like eyes, she smiled at them, wondered if those outside were seeing two lovers in a passionate clinch, or whether they could see more. Perhaps, she thought, they can see my naked bottom reflected in the glass opposite.

Such a thought did not embarrass her. On the contrary, it excited her more. What could be better than making love in a public place with the public looking on?

Her legs trembled when her climax came, and she threw back her head, eyes closed as the waves of pure pleasure swept over her.

Sasha stiffened, then showered her lips, her cheeks and her neck with grateful kisses. Between kisses he told her how much he had looked forward to this moment, how much he wanted to have her again and again and again.

Once her trousers were back on and his were zipped

up, they clasped each other tightly. Penny rested her chin on his shoulder, gazed over his shoulder, then smiled and hid her eyes in his hair.

'You'd better press that switch,' she whispered huskily against his ear. 'There's a whole platform full of people clamouring to get aboard.'

His hand covered her breast. He squeezed it gently, nibbled her ear then murmured breathlessly into it. 'Oh, no, no, no, *ma chérie*. Who cares about them. Let us do it all over again. Let us do it here, let us do it on the plane, and let us do it in the stables in Kentucky.'

As she shook her head, her hair fell in a dark cloud around her bare shoulders. 'No, my darling Sasha, I think we should wait. This carriage is getting too hot.'

'Hot!' Sasha exclaimed with a frown. 'Why is it hot?'

She nodded at the scene she could see in the window opposite. 'Because airport security are racing down the steps and they're carrying guns.'

Sasha moved quickly and immediately pressed the red button. The shuttle shot forward and those left on the outside stared with a mixture of stunned disbelief and outright annoyance as the motor hummed into life and the shuttle scooted away. Inside it, Penny and Sasha laughed together.

Once they were seated on the 747 to Boston, Sasha asked her how she had enjoyed her stay in Sri Lanka. She told him only the things she wanted to tell; Ben's treatment of Chasek and the fact that he wore women's underwear beneath his immaculate clothes. She also told him something else she had noticed about Chasek. He had no balls. None at all.'

'A eunuch!' he exclaimed. His thighs clenched reflexively as he spread his fingers over his crotch. 'Poor man.'

Penny's eyes glinted. 'Who worries about the fruit when the flower is still blooming?'

Sasha frowned and shook his head. He looked puzzled. 'What do you mean?'

'Nothing,' she answered, and did not tell him that although Chasek was not complete, he had been castrated at such an age that his libido was already developed. Chasek could not produce the fruit of copulation, but he could still perform. He still had the flower!

'I also visited the stables while I was there. Besides his interest in thoroughbreds, Ben Said breeds Arab horses you know.'

'No, I did not know. Did you find that interesting?' He sounded surprised.

'Of course I did. Why shouldn't I? After all, horses are my business, so to speak.'

Sasha was looking at her strangely. 'I didn't know that.'

'Well they are.' Unwilling for him to see her puzzled expression, Penny turned and looked out of the aircraft window. The lights of Paris were now far below them. The sky they were flying into was very black and heavy with cloud.

'No need to snap, my pretty Penny.' Penny's fingers curled into her palm as Sasha covered her hand. 'Is this why you are going to Kentucky?'

'Yes,' she said, her eyes looking out at the blackness of the night. 'I am going to see the horses, though of course they are racehorses – blue blooded thoroughbreds – not their desert ancestors.'

'Not to see Aran?' His fingers tightened over her knuckle. It was as if he were daring her to say otherwise.

Penny thought about her answer. Much as she adored Sasha, she did not wish to give away the true reason for her globetrotting. 'Not to see Aran,' she finally said, but did not see Sasha's look and could not wonder about what he was thinking.

Although Sasha now had something to report to Nadine, he let it ride. At this moment in time he was with Penny. There was not a moment to lose. They were alone in a double seat in first class.

Penny shifted in her seat and breathed softly as his fingers traced delicate circles on the inside of her knees. She turned her dark-lashed eyes to him and gave him a look of encouragement.

'Relax,' he said softly. 'We have a long flight.'

'There's not much oxygen up here,' she said with a smile. 'I think my clothes are too tight to cope with it.'

The dark warmth in Sasha's eyes mellowed to that of brandy. She saw his smile and, before closing her eyes, she felt his fingers moving up her arm, then roving beneath her jacket.

She felt her buttons being undone, a hand diving beneath her jacket and massaging her breasts. If this is what the trip is going to be like, then I hope it takes twice as long as usual, she thought.

They both managed to make their way along the aisle to the toilets at the same time. Both squeezed into the same toilet which wasn't much bigger than a kitchen cupboard.

As she peed, Sasha continued to play with her breasts. She for her part took his penis out from his trousers and took it in her mouth.

'Oh, no!' he murmured above her. 'Not now.'

But she did not stop sucking on him until she had finished using the lavatory.

Still standing, he took her place and stood before the bowl to relieve himself. As he started to pee, she handled his balls which caused him to groan and also caused his delivery of fluid to be intermittent.

Once he'd finished, he turned round to face her.

'Oh, Penny. I have dreamt of this moment, but not here. I dreamt of taking you to my home in the Camargue and having you in every way possible on the cold, red tiles of my house.'

'I can't wait till then,' she murmured breathlessly, and their lips met in a hungry, lustful kiss.

Her breasts were already exposed. One small, quick action, and her trousers were off.

With agile efficiency, and her arms around his neck, she walked her feet up the walls behind him, her back braced against the locked door behind her. 'This is ecstasy!' she exclaimed. Her sex was wide open before Sasha's lustful gaze.

Looking down over her breasts and her belly, she could see her fuzz of pubic hair. She could also see the tip of Sasha's penis, purple and glistening, as it neared her open portal.

It was hard not to breathe heavily in such a confined space, but what she was experiencing and what she saw were so arousing. How vulnerable she looked, her sex so widely open because her legs were braced halfway up the walls of the small cabin.

The tip of his penis kissed her sex lips and sent eddies of electricity over her body. Guided by Sasha's hand, the stiff rod moved up and down her moist, satin lips, pressed firmly against her clitoris, then rammed quickly and smoothly into her waiting vagina.

At first he steadied her by gripping her naked behind, but once his erection was inside her, his hands went to her breasts and his fingers pinched and played with her nipples. Besides her legs, she used her hands and arms to brace herself that much better within the confines of the tiny compartment.

Only once did someone knock at the tightly closed door. 'Is anyone in there?' grunted a low, gravelly voice.

'Sorry,' Penny called back. 'I've got a bug in my stomach.'

'A bug!' whispered Sasha, his face unbelievable and laughter not far from his voice. 'Is that what you call it?'

Penny flashed her eyes and laughed. 'Well I could hardly say I'm having sexual intercourse now, could I?'

They did their best to keep their chuckling down, but it wasn't easy.

There was the sound of someone grumbling outside. Then there was the sound of a flush and shuffling as the person – who sounded female – used the other toilet.

Penny made her way back to her seat first. Once she got there, she glanced back up the aisle to see if anyone had noticed they had been gone for nearly four hours. No one appeared to be looking her way. Some were asleep, some reading, and only one or two looked to admire her striking blue eyes, her breathtaking expression and luscious figure. But a smile was all she got from them. They were all normal, ordinary people. Then one above all others caught her eye.

There was a nun supposedly sleeping in about the eighth row back. She was lying sideways on, head against the headrest. Only the top half of her head showed above the seat in front. Suddenly, her eyes blinked open and Penny started.

As she slowly sat down, Sasha came back to his seat and noticed her expression. 'What is the matter, my darling Penny?'

A face of harsh lines and angular features was filling Penny's mind. It was a while before she answered.

'I thought I saw Nadine Beaumont,' she said slowly. She craned her neck and raised herself slightly from her seat. She looked back to where the nun was nestling. The top of a black cowl was all that now showed above the blue and red headrests.

Sasha fell silent. It was not until they were seated again that Penny wondered at him not asking about who Nadine actually was, but then decided he was probably too tired to care.

Chapter Nineteen

*F*rom Boston they were to fly to Louisville, the centre of Blue Grass Kentucky racing.

White, one-storey houses with sloping red-tiled roofs were the norm in the lush grasslands. Aran McKendrick's house was three-storey, more opulent than most, and reminiscent of something from *Gone With The Wind*. It had four Doric columns along its frontage and a wide verandah where a Virginia creeper curled in sensuous twists of gleaming red.

Crimson, rust and yellow leaves fluttered in piles around the driveway that led to his house. In front of the house was an old-style hitching post carved into a horse's head.

Penny, a little tired from the journey, thought she was dreaming when she first saw Aran. He was wearing buckskin that was pale gold in colour. Beaded fringes hung around his shoulders, down his arms, around his hips and down his legs. He wore tan-coloured cavalry boots, a matching belt complete with six-gun and a ten gallon hat that was the same colour as his boots. He reminded her of old fashioned Western heroes; Kit Carson, Daniel Boone. She smiled to herself. Aran lives in a fantasy, she thought to herself.

As she got out of the car, Aran beamed widely and raised the glass of whisky he was holding.

'Miss Bennett. I'm sure glad to see you.'

'Aran,' she said, as he embraced her and kissed her cheeks. As he did so, his tunic opened from neck to waist. The scent of his maleness mixed with the buckskin. It made her tingle. The tingling spread when she saw the crisp, yellow hairs that covered the solid flesh of his chest and swept in a thin line into the waistband of his trousers.

Perhaps it was the fresh air, or perhaps it was the smell of a virile man, but Penny was instantly revived. Almost of its own accord, her body snaked against his.

Aran licked his lips. 'Hell, but you sure are a ball of fire, honey. Don't you think you'd better rest before we get more acquainted?' His voice was husky and the ice in his whisky rattled as his hand shook.

Penny instantly thought of Sasha, a room of her own and a long dark night. So she agreed with him.

Her room was a cool mix of white and cream and made her think of youth and of the fresh sensuality of virgin sex.

Forgotten sweetness was fondly remembered as she lay in the blue-blackness of night. She was not alone for long. Sasha came softly creeping to enter her bed and her body.

She remembered being sixteen and a boy with wild eyes and equally wild hair sneaking into her bedroom while her parents slept. She remembered his scent, a masculine aroma that once inhaled, subdued any revulsion she might have felt. Jan, the wild young leather boy who had smelt of maleness and of motorbike oil, had ignited the fires of her burgeoning sexuality. Now she was older, nowhere near as innocent, and Sasha was doing the same thing.

In the morning they were to go to the races. Penny dressed carefully. The air was warm, so she wore a lemon silk dress that rustled as she walked. It was a simple design; boat-necked, short skirt, and short sleeved. She had teamed it with a boxy suede jacket of

Cobalt blue and she wore thigh length boots to match. Intertwined with a blue and lemon silk scarf, she piled her hair on her head.

In the mirror she looked dazzling, her eyes bright, her dark hair touched with the crimson warmth of old brandy.

Speculatively, she gazed out of her bedroom window before leaving her room. The white washed stable blocks gleamed in the sunlight. She could hear horses whinny, hear their hooves crunching gravel beneath their weight. There was a rich-blooded sweatiness in the air.

Would Superstar be here? she wondered, and felt a sudden pang of guilt.

She had almost forgotten her true reason for being here. Alistair had not entered her mind for several days now. She didn't feel guilty about enjoying the sex she had encountered, but she did feel guilty about not even thinking about him.

A knock on the door made her stop thinking.

'Come on, Penny, baby. The car's waiting.'

It was Aran. Today he did not wear the buckskin. Instead, he wore an open-necked shirt, a blue sports jacket and trousers in a softer blue. His blonde hair was slicked back away from his face and his eyes danced over her body.

And what have you got in store for me, plastic cowboy? Penny thought to herself.

'That's my horse there,' he told her once they were at the races. The horse he pointed to was a chestnut, just like Superstar. Penny held her breath.

'He's beautiful. Big and rangy; strong muscled. Just like you, Aran.' There was seduction in the sidelong look she gave him.

She saw his eyes blaze, saw him gaze at her spellbound, but she also saw a secret in his eyes. It annoyed her that she could not quite make out what it was.

They watched the race from his private box – just the two of them. Champagne, strawberries, and bowls of spiced chicken were provided – all set on a low table that had been spread with a crisp white tablecloth.

'I've bet five hundred on my horse. His name's Indian Chief,' he told her as he surveyed the runners and riders through a pair of high-powered binoculars. Then he turned to her and smiled. 'I've also put five hundred on for you.'

'That's very kind of you. I hope he wins. I don't know how I can ever repay you if he doesn't.'

He winked. 'I'll think of something. Does this sort of thing excite you?' he asked, and nodded in the direction of the waiting horses.

'Of course,' she answered truthfully. 'Who can fail to be affected by the sight of a brace of blue-bloods all straining at the bit.'

He grinned and shook his head. 'You certainly know your horseflesh, Penny Bennett.'

'And you, Aran McKendrick, appear to be a man addicted to the track. I bet your greatest wish is to own the next winner of the Kentucky Derby.'

'You're so right, honey. So right!' he said breathlessly. He sounded awe struck and looked it too.

Barely holding their mounts in check, the jockeys were steered towards the starting gate, their mounts snorting, legs prancing with pent-up energy.

The noise of the crowd fell to almost nothing. Both Penny and Aran leant forward over the rail. Aran was using the binoculars, his attention firmly focused on the starting gate.

A thought came to Penny's mind. She could not possibly let Aran concentrate too much on the horses. Alistair and his mission had returned to her mind. She needed to make Aran both want her and trust her. She had to be in control.

'Aran,' she said. 'I think you are neglecting me.'

'Sorry, honey, but I've got to . . .'

Before he could turn round fully, Penny grabbed the strap of the binoculars and tied them tightly at the back of his head. 'Stay where you are,' she ordered.

She heard his quick intake of breath and saw his fingers tense over the binoculars which were now immovable from his eyes. She congratulated herself. Aran was very similar to Leonard.

She stepped behind him, passed her arms around his waist, and undid his trousers. They were up above the crowd and there were metal railings between them and the people below. No one gathered there would see the size of his erection, the heavy hanging of his balls, and the crisp profusion of pubic hair that tangled like wild brambles on his lower belly and between his thighs.

Penny hitched up the front of her dress and pressed her naked pussy against the warmth of his behind. As she pressed against him, she reached round to his front and held his penis in one hand, his balls in the other.

'They're off!' roared the crowd as the starting gate twanged open.

That's true, thought Penny to herself, but did not voice such a basic pun. This man was to be enjoyed, not humiliated.

As she pulled on the hot, hard penis, she fingered the raised contours of his veins, followed their bending, twisting path. Matching this tempo she squeezed, let go, then again squeezed his hair-covered balls.

His body tensed, excitement increasing with the running of his horse and the riding of his body by a beautiful woman.

Penny pushed his expensive jacket and his soft, silk shirt up his back. In turn, she pulled her dress up and felt the warmth of his flesh against her nipples.

Aran, without a word of protest, kept his binoculars fixed on the horses as they rounded the far curve. His knuckles were white.

The crowds down below were yelling, screaming for their number, insulting the jockeys, threatening the racing animals with the abattoir and the cannery if they did not do their best to be first past the lollipop.

Penny rested her chin on his back, her hands tormenting his thick stem and his leaden balls. From over his shoulder she watched the racing horses, and with each pull on his member she thumped her pussy against his behind. It felt good and she purred with happiness. His bottom was warm, his muscles hard, but there was always room for improvement.

'I want to ride you like this, Aran darling. Tighten your buttocks,' she said softly against his ear. 'My clitoris needs something hard to hit against.'

Her heart leapt with triumph as Aran acceded to her demand. His buttocks tightened and his flesh pressed against her. Delicious sensations were aroused in that hard little button that sat like a priceless ruby between her sex lips. She murmured against the hardness of his back as desire embroidered her flesh.

'Oh, Aran,' she murmured rapturously, taking as much pleasure from using this man as any man might a woman. 'Your body is so hot. But it can't be as hot as a woman's can it? Surely it can't.'

'I don't know!' His words were barely audible. They were merely a rushed exclamation from a dry throat, a throat in a body that was a slave to lust. There he was, standing there naked from the chest down, his trousers sat around his ankles.

'Then I will experiment,' said Penny, and looked over her shoulder at the ice bucket.

Still holding on to his cock, she reached for the bucket. From beside the bottle of champagne, she took a large ice-cube. At first she put it in her mouth and trailed it over his back. As she did this, she continued to play with his cock and his balls. His body tensed, and she heard him gasp.

Pink lipstick transferred to the ice cube as she ran her mouth down to his behind. Still holding on to his cock and his balls, the ice-cube – guided by her mouth – went down into the crack between his buttocks. His bottom and thighs began to tremble as trickles of water ran from the melting ice-cube.

Penny guessed that his reflex was to tighten his

buttocks, yet his desire was for her to take the ice-cube down to his anus.

Leaving her right hand pulling on his cock, she used her left to help hold his buttocks apart. When she got to his anus she balanced the ice-cube on the tip of her tongue, then pushed it in.

She heard him groan. He did not resist. However, her tongue was not quite strong enough to breach his sphincter and push the ice into his behind. First with her thumb and then with her finger, she took over what her tongue had been doing and pushed in the ice-cube. As his sphincter opened and closed like the head of a daisy, a trickle of melting ice oozed out like a single tear-drop. Full of wonder, Penny took the single droplet on one finger and touched the rubbery surface with another. It dilated, then contracted like a solitary eye. It then appeared to pout. It's almost, she thought to herself with a smile, as if it is blowing me a kiss.

She repeated the exercise six more times until Aran was groaning. His anus was stuffed with ice-cubes, and his legs were trembling as icy cold water seeped from his rectum.

In the past she had received enjoyment by submitting to others. Now she was receiving just as much pleasure from someone submitting to her.

The scent of power was in her nostrils and her pussy was aching with need. She could not stop what she was doing. She had to do more to him.

Now his backside was filled with ice, she clutched a handful of crushed ice in both hands. Like before, she cruised up and down his stem with one hand. With the other hand, she held his balls in a handful of crushed ice.

His shivers intensified. His cry of surprise was drowned in the noise of the crowd down below who shouted louder as the horses made their final turn. Soon, Penny realised, it would all be over. The winner would be straining for the final stretch, and Aran would be ejaculating through the gap in the railings.

'Don't move!' she ordered.

She took a handful of strawberries and set them down before him. She took the top off the champagne, and as it fizzed up from the bottle, she let the bubbles shoot over her sex then poured some into a glass.

She pierced the strawberries, stuck them on the end of Aran's prick, then took her time nibbling and sucking them off again. In between each strawberry, she sipped at her glass of champagne.

Aran's pelvis began to move as his cock stiffened. As she sipped the last of the champagne, Aran's seed shot like whipped cream over the last of the strawberries and she sucked both into her mouth.

Well satisfied with the result, Penny got to her feet.

'A fine performance. Well worthy of a prize!' Penny exclaimed. 'What do you think?'

Trembling with relief, Aran stared down at her, his binoculars still attached firmly to his head.

I must look like a monster through those things, she thought to herself, but perhaps that's how he wants me to look.

'Anything you want, my dear. I'll give you anything you want.' His voice was as shaky as his flesh.

Penny smiled. 'A guided tour around your racing stable would be quite adequate. You can show me your very best animals.'

'Is that all?' He sounded genuinely surprised and, not for the first time, Penny wondered exactly why she was on this mission. So far no one had been concerned about her skulking around their stables. All right, she had been careful. But surely with the amount of surveillance equipment these places had, it could not have been any secret that she had been prying?

Chapter Twenty

Sasha had no trouble finding the convent where he had been instructed to meet Nadine. It had a high brick wall round it and cast-iron gates. Beside the gate a sign said CONVENT OF OUR SISTERS OF MERCIFUL DISCIPLINE. How apt, he thought, then took a deep breath before he entered the open gates which shut slowly behind him.

Legs shaking, he got out of his car and walked up a trio of white marble steps. The door creaked open and a silent nun glanced up at him, then gestured for him to enter.

Because he was shaking, he glanced at her only briefly. It came as a shock to suddenly realise that although she wore the habit, veil and cowl of a nun, her breasts hung loose and naked from beneath her stiffly starched collar.

Inside the building, what was not marble was painted white or was left as bare stone. Hideous gargoyles with women's bodies and devilish heads cavorted around a stone frieze in the entrance hall. Chains hung from the walls and a vase of blood-red flowers was set on top of some metal device that vaguely resembled a gibbet.

Sasha shivered. The nun who had let him in regarded him with glassy, but keen eyes. She had made him feel like a worm and her a thrush, keen on pulling him from the ground and eating him whole.

'I've come to see your Mother Superior,' he said, in as even a voice as he could. His gaze fell to her breasts and the nut-brown nipples. It was hard not to stare.

The nun did not smile but jerked her head in a swift nod. 'Come this way.'

He followed where she led along whitewashed corridors where lead-paned windows let in a rainbow of vivid, almost garish, light.

There were no crucifixes in this place; none hanging from the neck of the woman in black who led him along the stone-floored passageways where their footsteps echoed like the notes of a single, deep-voiced bell.

There were only stone statues of women with animal heads, bare breasts, and thigh-high boots. All carried a whip in one hand, a leash in the other. All stood on top of the bare, muscular torsos of beautiful young men: men whose faces were contorted with pain but also with ecstasy.

The nun stopped at a door that was heavy with carvings of women on horseback hunting men in flight. The men were naked, and the women wore chain-mail and armour that still allowed their breasts, bellies and bottoms to be bare.

Sasha swallowed hard when he saw Nadine. In some strange way, the nun's outfit actually suited her. Her whole body was shrouded in the blackness of it, except for her face. It was her face that held his gaze. High cheekbones, grey, cool, staring eyes, sensuous, cruel lips. A halo of ice-blue smoke circled her head in some devilish caricature of holiness. She grasped a half-smoked cigar between her clenched teeth as she came round from behind the desk. A long chain, hanging from a leather belt around her waist, tinkled as she walked.

'Do you like my habit?' she growled. Her hand slipped between his legs and squeezed his balls.

'Yes!' he gasped. An erection sprang into instant being.

'Then worship me!'

Her hand now came upon his head. She pushed him to his knees, raised one of her own legs on to a chair, then pulled up her voluminous habit so he could see her naked flesh. All she had on beneath the habit was a pair of high black boots.

He sucked in his breath as he took in the silvery sheen of her crew-cut pubic hair and the slash of pinkish red between. Her smell covered him like a fine muslin veil. He breathed in her scent and suffered a few seconds of terrible anticipation.

He knew instinctively what she wanted him to do. He sidled forward on his knees, his eyes full of the warm, juicy slit that ran from pubic bone to coccyx. There was the sound of a chain being lightly rattled as Nadine slid a collar round his neck. He guessed the chain he had heard was attached to the collar and to the belt around her waist.

Helpless to protest, he poked out his tongue and licked the wetness of her. With something akin to wonder, he kissed the satin softness of her hairless sex, sucked and nibbled at her clitoris, and tongued her slit right up to the puckered opening of her behind.

The smell of her body was intensified by the robes that fell around her limbs. He closed his eyes and felt he was drowning in her. Her buttocks were lean and firm beneath his palms.

'Enough!' she said at last, and swung her leg down from the chair, her black robes back around her limbs.

Sasha stared up at her. Even fully clothed, Nadine was impressively sexual. And yet, although she dominated the room, she was not the only one in it.

Sasha gulped when he saw the two young men. Nadine saw him look but only smiled before speaking.

'Do you like Rudi and Emile? They are my slaves. I chose them especially for their pricks, their bodies and their complete submission to my will. Come, study them more closely.'

She reached out her hand, and he took it.

This morning, I dressed myself carefully, he thought

to himself. I thought I looked good – even enticing. Now I feel overdressed.

Sasha was wearing a black turtleneck, plain blue jeans and black leather boots. He looked neat, he looked handsome, but he was definitely a touch conservative compared to the other guys. They were naked except for strips of leather and chain that held them.

'This is Rudi,' said Nadine with a grin. 'And that one's Emile.'

Sasha judged there was no point in him saying hello. After all, neither of the two young men before him were in any fit state to answer.

Their wrists were fastened to an overhead bar. They wore leather masks which covered their mouths but left their eyes to express emotion.

Their bodies shone with scented oils that filled the air with the sort of smells that calmed some people but must be assumed to arouse someone as debauched as Nadine.

Sasha was aware of his throat being dry; of being afraid of what might come next.

'Do you like my penile harnesses?' Nadine sounded really serious as she pointed to a series of straps which wound tightly around each man's balls and penis thereby trapping the whole lot and pushing it firmly forward. 'I only allow them to erect when I say so. I like to keep them imprisoned like that for days. I like to present some scenario before them that really arouses them, like me and some piece of pussy really getting it together. I usually whip her pretty little backside first before I suck her nipples. Then I have her lie down before them with her legs open so they can see my fingers go into her pussy and bring her off.'

Both young men began to moan. Their trapped members began to erect.

'Sinners!' Nadine exclaimed, and tapped each penis with a riding crop until their stiffness subsided.

'You see how quickly they obey me, my darling Sasha?' She kissed his cheek and one finger stroked his chin. 'Just like you do – or perhaps not as well as you do. So far I have encouraged you to have orgasms. I have always let you come, have I not?'

'Yes. You have always let me come,' replied Sasha, and gulped. It amazed him that despite the menace of this place, this woman, and the scene before him, he could not stop his penis from hardening. 'When was the last time you let them have an orgasm?'

Nadine smiled slowly. 'Three days ago. Each time they have shown signs of thinking lustful thoughts, I have whipped their cocks until they dare not raise their heads.' Her eyes opened wide as she laughed. 'But now you are here. They are hungry, and I am hungry. The time has come to eat.'

'Disrobe!' she ordered, and flicked at his arm with her whip.

Sasha tried to control his lust, but just the scent of Nadine, that female perfume and the hint of rich Havana, was too powerful for him.

Once he was naked, she walked around him as if he were a piece of horseflesh. Every so often she would tap his body with her crop, caress his balls with it, lift the tip of his penis, or run it firmly but provocatively between his buttocks.

'Right,' she said at last. 'You all have my permission to erect. You will all be allowed an orgasm, but only as I choose.'

With a sweeping flourish, Nadine took off the black robes but retained the wimple and veil. She also kept on her boots and refastened the leather belt around her waist so that Sasha remained attached to her.

Sasha stared. His legs felt weak, but his penis felt strong.

Nadine took hold of his chin. 'You don't often see me naked, do you Sasha?'

'No,' he said softly as his penis reached out and tapped the lean flesh of Nadine's leg.

She threw her cigar to one side before she kissed him.

Her mouth opened and her tongue slid on to his before her lips left him.

'You don't often fuck me either, do you?'

'No,' he returned, his voice barely above a whisper. A fear had come upon him, a fear that he might ejaculate at the mere thought of fucking Nadine let alone actually doing it.

'Well,' she said with a slow smile. 'Today you are going to put that beautiful prick of yours into my body. How does that grab you, my darling boy?'

Sasha stared into her eyes and gulped. Haphazard thoughts in both French and English ran through his mind. His senses were reeling, his pulse was racing. There was Nadine's body, so lean and so white before him, the breasts small, the legs long. And between those legs was a slash of pink that glistened like satin. This was what he was being offered. She was actually saying that she was about to let him enter her.

'Lay down,' she ordered, and pointed to a spot between the spread legs of one of the tortured young men.

Sasha lay down precisely where she pointed and found himself looking up at a pair hanging balls and an erecting penis.

Because of the chain that connected them, Nadine slid down with him, got astride him and like an open glove, slid her sex over his penis.

Sasha cried out and attempted to reach for her. At first Nadine resisted him. As she bounced up and down on his member, she raised her arms and laughed up into the face of the man above him.

'See, Emile? See? I am fucking this man. Imagine how his penis is feeling as my muscles squeeze his rod. Imagine how hot the blood is as it rushes fiercely up his shaft. Can you imagine it, my dear Emile? Can you really imagine it?'

Sasha could hear the man above him grunting and groaning as a result of Nadine's taunting. But he didn't care about the bound man. He didn't care that Emile's penis was stiffening against the exquisite torture of the leather straps. He closed his eyes and let the touch and smell of Nadine take him over. But even though she was dominating his senses, something inside had changed. Behind his closed eyelids, it was not the sharp-featured Nadine he was seeing, but someone with a warmer complexion, sparkling blue eyes, and a mane of tumbling, dark hair.

Nadine leant forward. 'Touch me,' she said hotly, her eyes wild with power as much as passion. 'That's it, my pretty boy,' she cried as he pinched her nipples between finger and thumb. 'Pinch me, caress me.'

Her voice faded away as her lips closed over the rigid penis above him. As she rode him, he saw Emile's balls pulsate as Nadine sucked on the penis that had not experienced an orgasm for three days. With increasing intensity, the balls seemed to convulse. Nadine withdrew her mouth and a shower of white hot semen fell on to Sasha's chest.

Sasha wanted to shout out that he had not wanted that to happen. But his voice seemed trapped in his throat.

'Now we must deal with Rudi,' ordered Nadine. By virtue of the chain around her neck, she pulled Sasha up from the floor.

The scenario was repeated. Only Sasha was left with a hard on. It had occurred to him that Nadine would continue to ride him until he had come. But Nadine pulled him to his feet, pressed a button on her desk, and Sasha turned his eyes expectantly towards the door.

It did not open. Instead, the top of the desk tipped slowly over, and there, spread-eagled on it, was a young girl. She was brown as a conker, her hair coal-black, and her eyes dark as bitter chocolate. Like the two young men, her mouth was covered by a leather gag.

'Isn't she beautiful?' cooed Nadine, as she ran her hands over the young girl's body, then gently kissed each nipple. The girl shivered. 'Feel her. Come. We will both feel her.'

Sasha was now not just mesmerised with the presence

of Nadine; he was fired with the vision of the young girl before him. Besides that, his penis was still stiff and in need of an orgasm. The weight of fluid in his balls felt fit to burst.

'She's beautiful,' he murmured and, as Nadine played with the girl's breasts, he tangled her pubic hair around his fingers before dipping into her moistness.

'Is she wet?' asked Nadine.

'Yes,' he replied. 'Very wet.'

'Then she is ready for you. Ride her.'

Sasha did not need her to order him to mount the girl. His penis was throbbing and this girl seemed so compliant.

He got on to her, his legs between hers. Without any recourse to foreplay, he pushed himself into her. Now it was him, not Nadine, being selfish.

Nadine too straddled the girl just above her face and her hands played pleasantly then cruelly with the plump, brown breasts. Her eyes were still sparkling.

'Suck me as you fuck,' Nadine ordered Sasha and, lying himself full stretch, he did exactly as she asked.

The feel of a woman was beneath him, soft against the hardness of his body, her pubic lips open to his onslaught. The scent of a woman was strong against his nostrils and her taste was upon his tongue.

With sensitive dexterity, the tip of his tongue followed each incline, each ridge of Nadine's flesh. With fierce demand, his hips thrust again and again.

When his orgasm came, echoes of his cry reverberated off the stone walls before it was swallowed by Nadine's sex as it spasmed against his mouth.

'What about her?' he asked Nadine after she had forced him to dismount. The girl was groaning, her eyes gazing longingly up into Sasha's face. Her limbs were twisting restlessly. Sasha guessed that her climax had been fairly near. But this was another part of Nadine's game.

'I'm saving her for them,' said Nadine and nodded to the two naked men. 'By the time I've finished with her, she'll do everything and anything that I want her to do. But not yet. They have to wait. They all have to wait.'

Nearby, the eyes of Emile and Rudi were sparkling with excitement and their cocks were again standing to attention.

'So how long is Penny staying with McKendrick?' Nadine asked, sprawled on a high couch. She rolled her black robe up to her waist and motioned that Sasha should massage her naked bottom.

'One week. Then I am to take her to New York. I have to take her to an address in Chinatown and there I am to meet Mister Puteri.'

'One week exactly?'

'Those are my orders.'

The wimple hid Nadine's face, yet Sasha knew she was frowning. Like him, she was wondering why this precise timetable. What and who was behind it all? And like him she did not know the answer. It suddenly occurred to him that perhaps Penny didn't realise she was following a schedule. Perhaps she was accepting each excuse as it came; Daz Dazzler going on business, Ben Said doing the same. If that was so, then she either had a reason of her own for being used by the syndicate, or she was completely ignorant that the length of these stays was pre-ordained.

Should I tell her? he asked himself. No, he decided. Not yet. Not until I know for sure that she knows nothing. After all, it was a good job working for the syndicate. Why jeopardise it for nothing?

Chapter Twenty-One

New York was heaving with people. Al Puteri and his bodyguards – who wore make-up and smelt of perfume – met them at the airport in a stretch limousine.

'You come with us,' one of them said to her in a higher voice than his size suggested.

'And you wait for the baggage,' the other one told Sasha.

Al Puteri was courteous, though he had a strangely conciliatory way of looking at her.

'I've never been to New York before,' she said, as they drove past block upon block of skyscrapers. 'Is this what you call uptown?'

Al had thin lips and an oily complexion. Penny shuddered at the thought of his body and what he might expect of her.

'Uptown, uptight and up the ass of every slick, smooth operator in this town! Uptown looks the sort of place where the money is made and power bought and paid for. But it is not strictly so. It is certainly not to my taste and the people there are not my kind of people. I am taking you to my part of town. First we will stop at my office where I will make a telephone call. Then I will take you to see someone who has real power; the coolest controller I've ever met.'

Intrigue made Penny excited. 'So who is this man? Where does he hang out?'

'In the Orient!' Al exclaimed, and burst into hollow laughter.

'Peking!' added one of the bodyguards, and all three men laughed.

'Chinatown,' Penny muttered, and sat back against the white leather of the seat.

Chinatown took on a certain magic as darkness descended and a host of multi-coloured lights pierced the darkness.

Al made his telephone call in private, then smiled coldly at her on re-entering the room.

Penny crossed one long leg over the other, but took her time so Al Puteri might catch a flash of her pubic hair.

He glanced only briefly and his glance was contemptuous. 'I see you wear no panties, my darling. I'm afraid it cuts no ice with me. My bodyguards could have told you that, beautiful men as they are. The only reason I agreed to you coming here was because I owe someone a favour and you're it.'

Penny stared. Al sat himself down behind a big, broad desk. The two bodyguards stood to either side behind him.

Penny was sat in a single chair that had been placed in the middle of the room.

'I don't understand,' she began. 'I thought we were going to your racing stables out on Long Island.'

The swarthy face that was compelling despite being pock-marked, broke into a sneer. His gritty black eyes narrowed as he ran his gaze over the soft pink suit she was wearing. It was trimmed in navy around the lapels and the hem of the skirt. Her stockings and shoes were navy too.

'You're everything he said you were,' he sneered.

She presumed he meant Aran seeing as both he and Al were American.

'You certainly got all it takes. Sam Chi will be more

than satisfied.' Suddenly, he snapped his fingers. 'Come on my beautiful boys. Let's get this show on the road.'

Penny rose to her feet as the three men came from behind the desk. The thick fingers of the two bodyguards wrapped around her arms and pinched her flesh as they manhandled her towards the door. Al sat with her in the back seat of the car, the two bodyguards at the front.

'Where are we going?' she asked, and did her best to swallow her fear. All the same her body tensed.

'Relax, honey. You're just going to do a friend a little favour. That's all. I owe him one.'

'And I'm the payment?'

The hard eyes turned to her and the sneer returned to his lips.

'That's what I said.'

She didn't protest. Al was not the sort of man to take any lip from her. He had a hard look about him and it wasn't difficult to guess how he made a living. A whole host of things came to mind: drugs, prostitution, extortion, fraud, murder . . .

The last word whirled round and round her brain. Panic made her skin turn to ice. She sat rigidly, hardly daring to breathe.

Only occasionally did she chance a sidelong look at the fifth member of the racing syndicate. What she saw was a brutal yet compelling face; a firm jaw, a dark, slightly sweaty skin.

Rather than look at him and surmise what he had in store for her, she turned her gaze to the world outside the car. Red, gold, blue and green shop, restaurant, and house facades lined a cobbled street.

Young women with slanting eyes and long dark hair wearing satin and silk cheongsams, stared from doorways but did not smile.

Perhaps, thought Penny, they know this car, know the man who sits in it and wish they did not.

'This is it, Miss Bennett,' said Al in a cold, but respectful tone.

They entered a nightclub where a dark red luminosity

was barely enough to light the way. Music was playing and two dancers were cavorting around on the stage, their breasts bare, their skirts barely covering their behinds.

A door was opened for her and she was pushed into a room that was blue with smoke, its air scented with illicit substances and cheap perfume. The door closed and shut out the redness of the nightclub.

She narrowed her eyes. The room seemed shrouded in a bluish haze. It was hard to see anything, and yet she knew someone was there.

A puff of smoke rose like a thin, curling snake before her eyes.

'Come here please.'

The richness of the voice made her stop in her tracks. There was an irresistible resonance to it that made her immediately start to walk forward again. She had a strong urge to find out who that voice belonged to.

Through the smoke she could see a figure lying on a low couch which had a dragons head at one end while the sweep of its tail extended to the other.

'Stop there.'

She did as ordered. She was feeling confused. 'I'm sorry,' she blurted out. 'I don't know what I'm here for. I don't know what you want me to do.'

She heard someone laugh. It was a low, bubbling laugh that seemed to rise and curl with the smoke.

'I will tell you what I want you to do. Al has given you to me for tonight. You are his present to me, but as with all presents, they have to be unwrapped. Please . . .'

He gestured with one hand that he wanted her to take her clothes off. She saw the glint of gold on his knuckles and also had the impression that his fingernails were extremely long, like some ancient Mandarin warlord.

Perhaps it was the heady smell of the room, or perhaps it was the unreal nature of what was occuring that made her obey so promptly. She whimpered complicity as her own hands moved over her body, unbuttoned her top, played with her breasts, then slid beneath her waistband and sent it sliding to the floor.

She was left wearing just her navy shoes, stockings and suspender belt. Her breasts were heaving and she became very aware of her pubic hair which moved as though threads of electricity were running through it.

There was a momentary shift in the room's atmosphere as a door opened and rays of reddish light mingled with the blue smoke, making it seem purple.

In that sudden moment she saw his features more clearly. Slanting almonds of blackness stared languidly at her body. His forehead was high and his hair swept in a coal-black mane over his shoulders. Thin strips of a hanging moustache fell almost a foot long from under his nose and he was smoking a long, black pipe. The silk gown he wore was of a richer blue than the smoke and embroidered with delicate patterns from gold thread.

A wrought-iron brazier burned at each end of the couch he lay on. It was from these braziers that the blue smoke rose in such scented, swirling waves.

But there were others in the room now. She could see their muscles glistening and smell the oils they had been anointed with.

They came to her, one in front, one behind, the hardness of their bodies pressing against her, their hands exploring every curve of her flesh.

She purred and her nipples rubbed deliciously against the chest before her, while her bottom rubbed against the penis that nudged her from behind.

In turn she could not help herself from touching each of them. Their muscles were like iron beneath her fingers. Their stomachs were flat without the slightest excess of fat. Strong thighs trembled beneath her touch.

Unable to resist, her body undulating as passion began to rule her, she reached for the face of the man in front, felt the firm jaw and also felt the studded collar he wore around his neck.

She reached behind and felt the same on the man behind her. As she gasped with anticipation of what might be in store, the man before her fastened the same sort of collar around her own neck. She was aware of a leash hanging from it; aware that the two men had the same hanging from theirs.

Silently, one of the men gathered the leashes, then fell down on all fours, went forward, and passed the ends of the leashes to the man who reclined on the couch.

Penny felt hands on her shoulders pressing her down until she too was on all fours; until all three of them were.

The leash was jerked and Penny crawled forward.

'You see, my pets,' said the smoky voice. 'I have brought you a bitch to play with. Play with her. Be my little pets like you always are. Amuse me.'

The smoke and the smell of the iron-muscled men beside her acted like a drug on Penny's libido.

The men whimpered like hounds as they licked at her shoulders, her neck, her face and her ears. Not once did they raise their hands to her, but then, she thought to herself, they are not supposed to. This man, this Sam Chi, wishes us to be his pets. That is why we are on all fours. That is why we are wearing dog-collars.

Shameful as her predicament was, it was impossible not to be aroused by the licking tongues, the sucking mouths.

Penny licked them in return and tasted the oil that covered their skin and the hint of male sweat that mingled so sweetly with it.

Strangely enough, erotic sensations were heightened by pretending that hands did not exist, that they were only front legs on which to support the body.

She flexed her spine and wriggled her bottom as their mouths ran down her back. One lingered, bent his elbows, and pushed his head under her body, his teeth nipping playfully at her nipples.

The other man became more vocal as he slavered over her buttocks, his tongue easing into the crease of her behind, pushing firmly into her anus, then snuffling as both his nose and his mouth were smothered by the lips and hair of her sex.

The other man left her nipple red and tingling. He followed the route of his colleague and, like two stud dogs ripe for mating, they snuffled, licked and sucked around her sex, their tongues pushing like small pricks into her vagina and into the smaller opening above it. She yelped as their teeth nibbled at the more tender flesh of her labia and her clitoris, but even so, she opened her legs that much wider.

Her yelps became more strident as her sex became juicier. She was sticking her bottom out suggestively, inviting one of them, both of them, to take her, fuck her, ride her, mate her to distraction.

The sheer fantasy of her situation overcame her completely. No word came from her throat. When she swallowed, she felt the studded collar around her neck, the pull of the leash warning her that no word was expected. There was a strange comfort in feeling it, in knowing she need say nothing. She must be what he had said she was; a bitch, a creature for these two studs to play with.

So she whimpered imploringly, opened her eyes wide, and gazed appealingly at the person who lay so still, so silent, on his dragon couch. She saw the person nod his head.

A gasp of delight escaped her lips as one of the studs mounted her, the hardness of his thighs warm and exciting against the silky softness of her flesh.

A slippery wetness ran down through the cleft of her buttocks as the head of his penis searched for the hot, moist flesh of her portal.

Push it in, screamed a voice in her head. Push it in!

She was hot, ready for it, almost dying for it. Half expecting the other stud to come and shove his member between her lips, she opened her mouth, then hissed between her teeth as the man withdrew as quickly as he had entered.

He slid himself beneath her until she straddled his

cock. Murmuring sweet words of pleasure, Penny lowered herself on to the man beneath her. She was lost on waves of her own sexuality. Her hips were moving, her pelvis slamming against his as she rode him.

Even before the other man mounted her, she knew what was to come but was beyond caring. His arms were braced either side of her and the tip of his penis nudged shyly between her buttocks before he rammed it home.

'Take her,' said a voice. 'Take her to suit yourself. No matter if she cries out. No one will hear. Enjoy her so that I too enjoy.'

Somehow it no longer mattered that a shadowy figure watched from the dragon couch. Penny had entered her own world; the world of her own sensuality, her own sexual fantasies.

It seemed as though the smoke whirled more wildly as the tempo of their thrusts increased. Three people writhed and moved like a strange creature born of legend and existing only in dreams.

Flesh slapped against flesh. Flesh invaded flesh until Penny felt as though she were no longer an individual, but a third part of some strange creature who copulated urgently and wildly in the middle of the room.

Her body was full. Her muscles and nerve ends were shivering with pleasure.

At last it came. She cried it out, trembling with the incredible sensations that ran through her. Her climax had come but still the men carried on, though not for long. Their groans, their murmurs of desire, were drowned at last by their cries of ecstasy as shudder after shudder ran over their bodies.

They lay, all three of them, collapsed on the floor, eyes closed, breathing rapid and bodies glistening with sweat.

I could easily fall asleep, thought Penny as the flight and her journey from the airport to Chinatown took their toll.

One of the studs took the leather collar from around her neck. The other caressed her back. Their touch was gentle. So were their lips, and in the gloom she could see the respect and affection in their eyes.

Both were oriental and charismatic, if not conventionally handsome. Each had a ring in his nose in addition the collars around their necks.

'Now that's certainly something to remember,' said Penny with a sigh. 'Perhaps we could do it again some time.'

Well if Sam Chi reckons on me being shamed or submissive by virtue of this little charade, she thought to herself, then he's very much mistaken.

'Perhaps you could arrange an encore, Mr Chi,' she blurted defiantly as she got to her feet and turned to face the dragon couch.

Her defiance was wasted. The two braziers still smoked on either side of the couch and a half-smoked cigar stub smouldered beside the pipe on a low table before it. The person with the slanting eyes and the long black hair was gone.

Penny frowned. The more she thought about things, the more convinced she became that not only was something severely wrong with this mission, but also that the person who had lain on the dragon couch was not really named Mr Chi and was not even Chinese.

She sniffed the air. Above the smell of incense and sandalwood she detected a whiff of pure Havana.

Chapter Twenty-Two

*S*omething was worrying Penny. It wasn't just that she'd hardly had a chance to ingratiate herself with Al Puteri and get a look at his racing stables, it was the sudden realisation that the mission no longer seemed important.

She had thought that Alistair might have tried to make contact with her by now to find out if she'd located his racehorse. But he hadn't.

On top of that, Alistair himself did not seem so important. Was it just because she was away from Beaumont Place? Or was it because she was changing, becoming more adventurous?

Besides Sasha was becoming a habit. Even now as she lay in bed before departing for Rumania and the castle of the sixth member of the syndicate, the Countess Lenushka, Sasha was here with her, his tongue lapping in a similar fashion to the two studs belonging to Sam Chi.

Because his face was against her sex, his bottom was stuck high in the air. A severe frown creased her forehead and suspicion came to her eyes as she noticed red lines criss-crossing the hard buttocks she loved so well.

Still frowning, Penny reached down and took hold of a handful of Sasha's hair and yanked his head up so his eyes met hers.

'Who's been a naughty boy?'

He blinked. 'What are you talking about?'

'Who's been beating your backside?'

He blinked again and his face became pink. 'I fell down.'

'Rubbish. Those are whip marks, my darling Sasha. Someone has been whipping your backside. Was it a punishment or a pleasure? Come on. Tell me.'

'I don't think it's any of your business!' He jerked himself from her grasp and stood up.

Looking at him made her regret upsetting him. He had a stupendous erection. She badly wanted him in her bed, and badly wanted his mouth on her sex. But now she had questioned the origin of the pink stripes, she could not contemplate backing down. Tragic, she thought to herself and, feeling suddenly angry she sprang from the bed, the sheets falling around her as her feet touched the floor.

'What are you hiding, Sasha? Why the stripes and why the hell are you reacting like this?'

He took a breath. His face was immobile yet nervous. 'I'm sorry, Penny.'

To Penny's surprise, he hung his head and his shoulders began to quake. He wasn't crying, but he was upset. That much was easy to see.

She went to him, wrapped her arms round him, then held his head to her face.

'Tell me,' she said gently. 'Tell me the truth.'

He sighed, threw back his head, then took a deep breath. The words came. 'My mistress ordered me. I have tried denying her. I have tried disobeying, but she is too strong for me. Her voice cuts through me. I swim in the sound of her voice and lose myself in the greyness of her eyes. Each and every time I leave her I tell myself that next time I will be stronger. But I never am. She contacts me, tells me what to do, torments me with pain and gives me such pleasure. I try to resist. I thought I was gaining strength from you. It occurred to me that by borrowing your strength I could resist her. It will happen, I am sure of it. I am getting stronger, but her, that woman who dresses in black, has cold grey eyes and black jewellery that swings when she whips me, she knows how to get under my skin. Nadine is so powerful, yet so compelling.'

Penny froze. 'Nadine? You know Nadine?'

He nodded and she saw the shame in his eyes. Had he betrayed her mission to Nadine? Is that why she had heard nothing from Alistair?

'You didn't tell me you knew her. When did you last see her?'

'I last saw her here. In Louisville.'

'What is she after – besides the undoubted joy of beating your behind?' asked Penny.

His long lashes fluttered over his cheeks before he looked her in the eye. 'She wanted to know what you were up to. I heard her mutter something about not believing her brother.'

'But you didn't tell her anything?'

'How could I? I do not know what reason you have for allotting so much time to each member of the syndicate, but I could not help noticing that you are working to a pre-arranged timetable.'

Penny's mouth dropped open. 'Timetable? What timetable?'

'I was given a timetable of how long you were supposed to stay in each place with each member of the syndicate. Everything was organised in advance.'

'Who gave you the timetable?'

He shook his head. 'It was faxed to me. It came from London.'

Although Sasha's body was warm and so close, Penny was feeling distracted.

She frowned as she tried to think through what was going on here. If there was a timetable, it meant everything was pre-arranged. Everything!

'Is it not time we started getting ready to depart?' asked Sasha.

'Yes.' She nodded her head slowly. Her eyes looked

thoughtful. 'It is time. I don't want to miss my flight and keep Countess Lenushka waiting.'

Sasha came with her to the airport, but she was to fly on alone to Bucharest where she would be met and taken to the medieval castle which had been in the countess's family for several generations.

'So, how long did you say I am to be with the countess?'

'Three days. That's all. Then I will meet you at Orly,' Sasha confirmed.

She nodded. She and Sasha had come to an understanding. Both of them were being used, that was definite. Nadine was using Sasha to find out what she was up to. Now it was her turn to use Nadine to find out who was behind this schedule of sex she had experienced.

A new warmth flashed between them as they kissed goodbye.

'Three days,' Penny whispered. Sasha stroked her hair and looked into her eyes. That one look spoke volumes.

Splendidly dressed and pacing impatiently, the countess was waiting for her when she landed in Bucharest.

'Darling, darling,' gushed the Countess Lenushka on first sight of Penny.

Dutifully, Penny accepted the kisses the countess showered on her – and the hands that patted her backside and clasped her breasts in welcome. The appearance of the woman was overwhelming and she reeked of wealth and privilege.

Lenushka was dressed in a swagger coat of mint-green cashmere, a matching skirt with a darker shade running through it, dark-green beret and matching shoes. Her jewellery was unashamedly ostentatious and plentiful.

'You look wonderful,' Penny said to her. 'Your outfit is splendid and your jewellery is amazing. I wish it were mine.'

A look of pure delight came over Lenushka's face.

'Well,' she exclaimed breathlessly, 'How nice of you to say so.'

Penny was not at all prepared for what happened next.

'Please. Take my earrings, my dear girl. Take my bracelet, and my necklace too!'

With a laugh in her voice, Lenushka took the earrings from her ears, the necklace from her neck, and the bracelet from around her wrist. She took Penny's hands between hers and pressed the jewellery into them. 'Here, my dear girl. Seeing as you so admire my sparklers, you must have them. I insist.'

'But I can't!'

'Yes you can, my sweetness. Of course you can. I say you can.'

'But I'm not carrying a handbag and the taxi driver has already taken my luggage,' Penny protested.

Lenushka's eyes opened wide and so did her mouth. 'Oh, my dear girl. Then you must do what my mother did when she smuggled her gems out of Rumania and went to America during the war.'

'What was that, countess?'

With a wicked grin on her lips, Lenushka leant forward. 'She put them in her knickers.' Her voice was little more than a whisper.

Penny blushed.

The countess winked. Her smile had lost none of its wickedness. 'Or you could always put them somewhere even safer.'

'You don't mean – ?'

'Of course I do, my dear Penny. Come on. You can do it in the taxi.'

Penny was wearing a short black skirt and a cropped black top. She also wore long black stockings that reached to some four inches above her knees and were held up without the use of suspenders.

'There,' said the countess once the taxi was in motion. 'The driver is looking straight ahead so it will be no problem to slip my baubles into your jewellery box.

Quickly,' she said, her fingers already pulling at the hem of Penny's skirt. 'I will help you.'

Penny gasped as Lenushka's red-painted fingernails pushed her knees apart, then pulled her legs forward so she sank lower into the seat, her hips tilted upwards. She used both hands to pull Penny's knickers down so that her bare bottom felt the chillness of the seat.

'Are you sure this will be all right?' Penny asked querulously, her eyes wide as they followed the progress of the necklace.

'Of course. It will make them shine better.'

Penny groaned slightly as the countess slid the end of the necklace into her vagina. She groaned a little more and arched her back as, one by one, the fingers pushed the rest of the necklace in.

'That was the biggest piece,' said Lenushka with a big smile. 'I've left the end hanging out for easy access. Now for the smaller pieces.'

Playfully, she tapped at Penny's clitoris – which seemed to be hardening for the occasion.

The bracelet was next. Penny became aware of the weight inside her and the delicious thrill as each piece was pushed slowly inside her. Last of all came the earrings.

Penny was breathing heavily. Her eyes followed the path of the earrings. 'Do you really think you should?' she asked a little nervously. 'They're not as big as the rest. What if you can't get them back out?'

Lenushka held both earrings up and looked at them thoughtfully.

'You are quite right, my darling Penny. I think it will be more sensible to clip these on the outside of your flesh. I think they will look much nicer if I clip them on to your pubic hairs. What do you think?'

'I think you could be right.'

Penny pulled her skirt up further so she could see the mound of hair being adorned with two of the most astonishing jewels she had ever hoped to own.

'They look beautiful,' she said softly, her eyes full of

236

the sparkling gems which glinted so brightly from among the dark hair of her sex.

Lenushka sighed, clasped her hands together and looked almost saintly. 'You look very beautiful, my darling girl. In fact I could eat you right here and now. But I won't. We have a train to catch, a schedule to meet; there will be time for all that later. Now, pull your knickers back up so my jewels do not fall out.'

The train journey to Lenushka's castle was leisurely because the rail tracks followed a tributary of the Rhine. They journeyed through deep, green valleys where red geraniums bloomed on chalet balconies and the sound of cowbells drifted on the crisp air.

Flat plateaux eventually gave way to sheer rock cliffs and dense vegetation. In the distance, the Carpathian Mountains rose blue and mauve against the sky.

'We are coming to my home,' explained the countess as she raised her head from Penny's breast and glanced briefly out of the window.

Because Lenushka was wealthy, they had a compartment all to themselves. The countess had taken full advantage of the situation – and of Penny. She had rolled Penny's top up above her breasts, lain her head on one breast and sucked at the other. Sleep had come to the countess as they travelled, but still she had intermittently sucked on Penny's nipple, her hand firmly clamped to Penny's crotch.

Chapter Twenty-Three

*D*ark trees covered the lower slopes of the Carpathian mountains. The castle was perched high on a rocky ledge, its thrusting towers capped with red tiles.

The road that led to the castle wound lazily through the valley as if in no great hurry to get to where it was going.

Evening was coming on fast and deep shadows were creeping ever nearer the castle as the sun slid behind the jagged mountain peaks, and snow was beginning to fall.

In the car which met them from the train, the countess persuaded Penny to take off everything except her knickers and surround herself with sumptuous furs that were silver, dark brown, and rich copper in colour. The furs were lined with silk and both textures tantalised her naked flesh.

'Let me see how the jewels sit in you,' crooned the countess and, dutifully, Penny opened her legs and slid the crotch of her underwear to one side. The intensity of such decadent indulgence making her moan with ecstasy and snuggle deeper into the sumptuous feel of the furs covering her.

Lenushka's index fingers probed delicately at her clitoris as if that too were another precious gem. 'Throw the furs from your body. Let me see you in your full nakedness,' said the countess, her eyes bright, her lips wet and glossy.

Penny did as she asked and lay there exposed like that for most of the journey while the countess amused herself by taking more jewels from her luggage and festooning them over Penny's body.

Once the castle had been reached, loose jewels were retrieved and repacked. The two earrings were left tangled in Penny's pubic hair, and one each of another set were fixed firmly to her nipples.

'Make sure my jewels do not fall out of your receptacle!' the countess exclaimed.

Dutifully, Penny pulled her pants back up.

'Do I keep the furs?' asked Penny, as she stepped out of the car.

'Only until we get indoors,' returned the countess with a wave of her hand and a casual lilt to her voice.

Narrow and daunting, the doorway to the castle threw its shadow over their arrival. The sun had gone completely now and Penny wondered – just for the briefest of moments – whether dark and devilish creatures really did come out at night in the Carpathians and suck the blood of virgins.

If it's only virgins, she thought to herself, there's no danger of it happening to me!

Inside the great hall of Lenushka Castle, the furs were taken from her by a cluster of servants who all had black hair, black eyes, and dresses that might very well have done a turn in a Hammer horror film.

Penny stood motionless, wearing only a pair of black lace panties. Her eyes took in the eerie light and the Gothic architecture of the place. The jewels that adorned her breasts and her pubic hair flashed brightly in the inconsistent glow of a great log fire.

The castle was old, of course, and the style was most definitely eastern rather than western European.

A high mantle was held by two evil-eyed satyrs over the roaring fire.

There were hooks set above the fire, and a man-size spit before it. Or woman-size, thought Penny and shivered despite the orange warmth from the fire dancing over her flesh.

Chains hung from the waists of the two stone satyrs, and huge phalluses stuck out from their lower limbs above balls that were more suited to bullocks than men.

There was a huge table set with food running down the middle of the room on which black and red candles shed a flickering, amber light.

Dusty tapestries lined the walls, along with instruments of hunting and torture including crossbows, axes, picks and swords. More terrifying was an object that dangled on a chain from the ceiling. It was made from metal strips to resemble a man. A man cage, Penny decided, in which a person could be imprisoned, the metal pressing against their flesh as they were hoisted above the diners who sat below.

Penny was ready to eat and rest after her journey. She was completely unprepared for what happened next.

'This girl has stolen my jewellery. Take it from her immediately!' screamed the countess.

'That's not true!' Penny protested.

It was no use. The servants sprang to obey the strident tones of the countess's voice. Cruel fingers gripped Penny's flesh; her wrists were held tightly, and so were her ankles. Yet more scratching, iron fists grasped her body around the middle.

'Oh no!' she cried out, as her black lace underwear was ripped from her body. Those who held her ankles spread her legs wide.

'It's up to you,' said the countess. 'Either we deal with this here and now, or I hand you over to the authorities.'

Penny thought for a second. She had no way of knowing how fairly – or otherwise – foreigners accused of crimes were treated in these parts, and neither did she want to risk finding out at first hand.

'Maybe we'd better just sort it out between us,' she said quietly.

Lenushka herself tore the clip-on earrings from Penny's nipples and crotch. Penny cried out again as she saw the sheer lust in the eyes of the countess. There was a sparkling darkness to them now; an uncanny dreadfulness that made her flesh quiver with fear. What else was in store for her? she wondered.

Naked, Penny was pressed to her knees, her hands manacled behind her back. Chains from those manacles were fastened to irons around her ankles. Another was placed around her neck. It was heavy and had outward facing spikes all round it.

Hands grabbed her hair and pulled her head back so that the spikes around the back of the collar touched her shoulder blades.

For a moment, Penny was sure she was going to be placed in the metal contraption that hung above the dining table and be hauled up to swing like a canary in a cage. But those who held her dragged her towards the fireplace. Her manacled hands were unhitched from each other and the chains that fell from the stone figures on either side of the fireplace were clipped to her wristbands. Once her legs were spread, other chains secured her ankles.

'That is good!' cried the countess in a very high, accented voice, and Penny shivered.

She clenched her buttocks as Lenushka's jewelled hands ran down her back and over her behind.

Eyes wide with fear, she faced the heat of the fire. Lenushka whispered of what she intended doing to her; perverted things – dreadful things. Penny drew on her inner strength. She closed her mind, and instead of seeing the gruesome things the countess intimated, she saw pictures in the flames.

In her mind, the redness of the burning logs became sunset, the intermittent blue and green flames were the coolness of the sea, and a certain shape, a certain rise of the logs lying in the fire, was the body of a man, the body she truly wanted.

'This is for stealing my beautiful stones!' cried the

countess, as a whip licked across Penny's back, her bottom and her thighs.

Penny cried out, her arms straining against the bonds that tied her, her breasts and belly reddening before the heat of the fire.

Each of the black-haired, black-clad servants took it in turn to lay six stripes across her body.

As the whip curled over her flesh, she arched her back and wished that Sasha was there to come to her rescue. But Sasha was not there, and Lenushka frightened her.

'More and more whipping for stealing my jewels,' cried the countess, and laughed.

Penny withstood the onslaught and took her strength from seeing Sasha in the flames and dreaming of the hardness of his body against hers. Soon, she thought to herself. I will see him soon.

'Now we will eat, my darling girl,' cooed the countess against her ear. The coolness of her palm caressed Penny's behind. 'How hot your bottom is, my dear Penny. It is now as red as your belly, yet no flame has warmed it. Merely my whip. My beautiful whip.'

Half fainting from her ordeal, Penny was released and each iron cuff and anklet was chained to its partner.

One of the chains that dangled from the stone statue at the side of the fireplace was fastened to the spiked collar and she was yanked to face the cold grey stone. With her legs held open by two of the servants, she was lifted before the stone monster and told to take hold of the iron ring that fell upon his forehead.

Penny gasped. She knew why they were holding her like this, knew why she had been told to hold on to the iron ring. Again she summoned all her inner strength. I must ride this stone phallus as if I am really enjoying it, she thought to herself, and closed her eyes.

In her mind she again saw Sasha and, as her body was lowered so that the stone penis invaded her vagina, she whimpered slightly, then mewed softly as she pretended it was him.

'How splendid to see you are accepting what I am

242

giving you,' said the countess with a low, and disconcerting chuckle. 'As long as you hold on to the iron ring and grip his stone feet with your toes, you will enjoy his fucking of you to the full. Feel the unbending hardness of his penis in you. Go on. Press yourself against him,' she said gleefully.

With undeniable pleasure, she pressed her hands firmly against Penny's back so that her breasts were flattened against the stone. 'I will leave you to pleasure yourself with him. I will bathe and change, and when I come back, we will eat.'

Doors creaked open and were closed before the room fell to complete silence. Only the crackling of the fire could be heard.

'Sasha,' mewed Penny, her eyes closed as she attempted to turn her predicament to her advantage. 'Sasha!'

If she flew headlong into the realms of fantasy, she could almost smell the sweet sweat of his body. She nuzzled and kissed her shoulder and murmured his name. As the image in her mind intensified, her senses began to truly believe that the cold stone against and within her body was Sasha.

She levered her breasts slightly away from the stone so that only the hard tips of her nipples brushed gently against its coldness. As she murmured sweet words of pleasure, she began to writhe on the monstrous penis that was filling her as no man of flesh had ever done.

Acting as support and almost like a saddle beneath her, she felt the rough, hugeness of the statue's balls.

Inspired by its abrasive surface, she rubbed herself on them, moving herself backward and forward so that her clitoris became exposed against it, and the juice of sexual arousal seeped on to the stone phallus.

And yet, the statue was not really doing it to her. In reality it was her doing it to the statue and thus to herself. Mentally, it was Sasha she was riding, Sasha who was so hard against her and so long lasting inside her.

As the urgency of an approaching orgasm sent spasms of delight throughout her body, she pressed her breasts against the stone. He has rough hands, a thought screamed in her mind. He has the hands of a man who uses his muscles for a living, a man who has never become pampered or soft-bodied by using purely mental power.

Sasha was in her and she was coming. 'Oh let it come,' she cried out loud, and heard her words, then her cries of orgasmic bliss, bounce off the walls and echo from the high rafters above her.

'Sasha,' she murmured in a long, drawn out sigh. 'Sasha.'

She lay her face against the coolness of the stone for no more than a few minutes before she heard doors opening and the tread of feet back and forth, then the tinkling of cutlery and the clatter of crockery.

The smell of food warmed the air, and shrill laughter heralded the return of the countess.

Penny had expected her to come closer, to fondle her body and tell her how she planned to leave her there overnight or some other dastardly trick.

But she didn't do that. Instead, there was the scraping of a chair across the stone floor then Lenushka's voice rang out imperiously.

'Let her down off there. Let her eat.'

Sighing with relief, Penny was lifted from her coupling but, instead of being taken to the table and invited to eat, she was merely set down on the floor.

She blinked as she took in the scene before her. The countess wore a dress of flowing scarlet that reached to the ground. As usual, she was bedecked with jewellery. It hung from her ears, from around her neck and her wrists – and was even entwined in her hair and around her ankles.

She was drinking red wine from a crystal glass, and food was being spooned on to her plate by a lean young man with dark skin, solid-looking thighs and wearing nothing but a black cape and a pair of black knee-length boots. His penis hung to about a third of the way down his thigh.

'Feed my slave,' she ordered him after popping a juicy fig into her mouth and wiping her fingers on his pubic hair.

The tall young man nodded and sliced meat on to a plate then added crisp vegetables and crusty bread, which he first spread with a thick layer of bright yellow butter.

Penny licked her lips. Her stomach was grumbling mildly and she had eaten little since lunchtime. Thinking she was about to be released and allowed to sit at the table, she began to get to her feet which, like her wrists, were still bound. But the young man came to her and, putting his hand on her head, forced her back down on to her knees.

To her amazement, he placed the dish on the floor then proceeded to fasten the chains from her wrist manacles to a new set which he fixed around her thighs. Chained like that, there was no way she could possibly get up. She had no alternative but to stay on all fours. That, she realised, was not his only intention: it was now also impossible for her to use her hands to eat. To her great mortification, she would have to use her mouth, stay on all fours, and eat her food like a dog. The countess really did want her to be her slave.

Pride made her pause. How dare the countess treat her like this. Penny glared at her, then saw the warning in her eyes. There would be no use in protesting her innocence. In the countess's castle, her word was law. The interlude with the stone phallus might have been very pleasant, but Lenushka's look reminded Penny of her stinging backside and the more terrible things she had threatened her with. Besides that, she was hungry – very hungry.

Dipping down delicately, bottom high in the air, she began to eat. Butter got on to her nose and was smeared around her face. Meat juice ran from the sides of her mouth and the bread left the plate and landed on the floor. But she ate most of it; the vegetables were the easiest. When she had finished, she looked up expectantly. The young man came back and took her plate. He returned again, his dark eyes meeting hers as he placed a bowl of wine before her.

She glanced at him briefly before lapping like a dog at the bowl of red burgundy, her pink backside again high in the air. She was thirsty enough not to care about how vulnerable she might look.

Lenushka got up from the table and came to her. Penny raised her head as best she could and saw silver toecaps sticking out from beneath the countess's glorious evening dress.

'My darling girl,' said the countess, her voice a low purr that was more reminiscent of a panther than a pussy cat. 'You must be ready for bed, and so, my dear girl, am I. Urish,' she said, turning to the young man who had served Penny the food and wine. 'Undo her chains, you stupid boy. This is not a dog or any low creature to be used and abused. This is a sexual animal, the sort of creature who turns any such treatment to her own advantage.'

As the chains were removed and Penny straightened up, the countess shoved one hand between her legs. 'See,' she cried as Penny cried out with surprise, 'see how wet she is already?'

Penny's cry of surprise turned to a moan as Lenushka manipulated her fingers through Penny's pubic lips.

'Come, my darling,' she said huskily as her mouth skimmed Penny's cheek. 'I will take you to my special place; a sacred place, where I commune with my ancestors and show them that although I am still very much alive and they are dead, I do not forget them. They are with me still in the form of all the beautiful, wonderful jewellery they have left behind.'

Perhaps it was caused by fear, but the mission Penny had initially set out on came suddenly to mind. 'I'm amazed you haven't lost any of it on horse-racing,' she blurted.

246

The countess stared at her. 'Horses? What makes you think I'm interested in horses?'

Penny frowned. 'Isn't that why you're a member of the syndicate?'

The countess threw back her head and exposed her bejewelled throat. 'Horses? Who gives a damn about horses, my dear girl, when sex and submission are far more interesting.'

Her face came closer.

'I take part in the things the other members of the syndicate take part in, and sometimes that involves horses, or gambling, or sailing, or even taking a safari in the Amazon jungle. But that is not the main reason for being a member; neither for me nor the other parties involved.' Her eyes sparkled suddenly and opened very wide. She pursed her glossy red lips and kissed Penny in a parody of what a kiss should surely be.

'The syndicate is devoted to sexual pleasure. Few can keep up with our sexual demands, but you, my darling girl, were recommended to us. A past member of our number wagered that you, above all others, would accommodate and keep up with our individual tastes.'

'And I have done!' exclaimed Penny with a proud toss of her head. Inside she seethed. Could it really be that Alistair had lied to her? She knew Superstar, his race-horse, did exist, but it was now obvious he had never been stolen. Realisation flooded over her. That was why Alistair had not wanted her to tell Nadine about her mission. Despite her outlandish behaviour, Nadine cared for her perhaps more so than she did for her brother. That was why there were odd looks in his eyes when he'd first told her about what he wanted her to do. Well she'd show him. And Lenushka!

'You have indeed performed well.' Lenushka's cold fingers wound around her hand. 'Come,' she said, the scarlet softness of her dress cleaving to the curves of her body. 'I will take you to my special place. But put these on first.'

Penny put on the red velvet cloak and matching thigh-high red boots that Urish, the sleek and servile young man brought to her.

Lenushka led her out into arched corridors where their footfalls echoed over cold stone walls and yet more torture instruments which stood in alcoves or around awkward corners.

Just once Penny caught a glimpse of herself in a huge mirror that was banded in ebony and cracked at one corner. The picture she presented took her breath away. There she was, her flesh unusually white and vulnerable against the red lushness of the cape and thigh-high boots. Her cheeks were slightly pink – partly because of the cold air but also because of the anger she was feeling towards Alistair. Her lips were as red as her cloak and her boots, her black hair and blue eyes made her look even more dramatic.

The corridors at last came to an end and Penny halted as she gazed down the flight of stone steps which seemed to spiral forever downwards.

'Where do these go?' she muttered fearfully.

'Not to hell, my darling girl. Only to the grave!'

The countess laughed as she wound her long fingers around Penny's wrist and pulled her down the steps. Down and down they went, round and round, their descent lit only by ancient gas lights set at infrequent intervals.

Long shadows fell at their passing, and as the cold air from far below hit Penny's naked flesh, her nipples hardened and her stomach tightened. Her red cloak and dark hair billowed out behind her.

Penny knew she could have protested. Lenushka would not have been that difficult to get away from, but whether she knew it or not, she had challenged Penny to see this thing through to the end, and Penny never could resist a challenge.

All the same, it was not a pleasant place. The lower they went, the darker it became. The smell of dust and past centuries became stronger.

Cobwebs brushed lightly against Penny's face, and

small rodents scuffled from their path until they stopped before a nail-studded door.

Lenushka, her breathing heavy and red lips parting to show her very pointed incisors, placed her hand on the black iron handle and opened the door.

The smell of decay tumbled out of the room beyond, and the coldness of the sepulchre touched Penny's bare flesh. Like a shroud, she thought, and felt sudden panic.

'Come in here, girl!'

Penny cried out as Lenushka's long nails dug into her flesh.

The countess moved at her side as if she were reaching for something. A cold, low light was ignited by a hanging chain. It was this the countess had pulled.

'These are my family!' cried Lenushka, waving her arms and laughing.

Penny stared. Row upon row of stone sarcophagi were lined on either side of the room and reached from floor to ceiling. 'Come and meet them,' Lenushka invited, and tugged her to where a grinning skull with two gold teeth stared sightless from an open coffin.

Penny's heartbeat quickened. She felt sick. This place was like something left over from a vivid nightmare. For the first time, she really did feel afraid.

'This is mine,' the countess murmured lovingly, and pointed to a monstrous sarcophagus at the end of the room.

Still gripping Penny's wrist, she walked to it and lit two tall black candles at each side. Then she turned and smiled.

'You are honoured,' she whispered excitedly. 'I am very particular as to who I allow down here. Few people have seen my last resting place. I share it only with people who please me. See how beautiful it is, how I have equipped it for double occupation?'

Curiosity got the better of Penny's growing fear. Drawing her red cloak around her, she approached the carved stone box whose lid was levered open.

What she saw surprised her. The total inside area was

lined with pink satin and, as if that were not surprising enough, small glass boxes were set into its sides.

'What are the boxes for?' she asked.

'Why! For my diamonds, my rubies, my emeralds, silly girl. Do you really think I would leave them behind? Now come. You must try it out and let me know what you think. Get in and I will get in with you.'

Penny looked at the countess with disbelief as Lenushka began taking off her flowing dinner dress. Lenushka really did mean to get in with her. Penny was not distrustful by nature, but it had occurred to her that she might be interred in there alone and the thought terrified her.

'You can keep your boots on,' the countess said. 'I will keep mine on too. Don't you think we look rather delicious with just boots on?'

'I don't believe it!' Penny exclaimed. Her eyes were fixed on Lenushka's voluptuous bosom and belly. A bright red ruby was fixed in her navel. Pearls, emeralds, rubies and sapphires were scattered among her pubic hair. 'It's truly incredible. How are they fixed?'

The countess smiled as she ran her fingers over the gemstones and also inserted one into the beginning of her sex. 'A special form of plastic surgery,' she replied in a strange voice. 'It didn't hurt my dear. Even if it had, I would have endured it because I knew exactly what the end result would look like and what affect it would have on the beholder. Don't you think it beautiful?'

Penny swallowed. 'I don't know whether beautiful is the right word. Unique might be better.' It was hard not to stop staring. The jewels caught the light and the sight of the voluptuous countess with a jewelled quim and belly button was a sight to behold.

'Come,' she said again, 'Join me in my eternal bed.' She held out her hand.

Penny hesitated then raised her hand and took that of the countess. I'm dreaming, she thought to herself. I really am. The gems are mesmerising me and leading me to where she wants me to go.

Because the satin was so cold, Penny could not help but shiver as she lay in the coffin. It was wide and the countess lay down beside her. Richly jewelled fingers took her hold of her face. Bright red lips kissed hers.

'Oh, my beautiful, darling Penny. You looked so desirable chained to my fireplace. I had thought about having Urish fuck you from behind as a dog takes a bitch, but I thought no! No, I will not do that. Has she not already enjoyed herself with the stone statue?'

'You watched? You saw what happened?' Penny felt no shame. In her mind it was Sasha's penis within her, not that of a stone statue.

The countess smiled, then kissed her again. Her lips tasted of the wine she had lately drank, and she smelt of expensive perfume.

'I watched everything you did. I was gloriously aroused by all of it. That is why I decided to save you for myself.'

Hypnotised by seeing Lenushka wearing nothing but gemstones, Penny hardly noticed that her hands were being fixed into some iron bands above her head. She was only aware of the heat of Lenushka's kiss and the resulting trickle of hot moisture that was seeping between her thighs.

'I am going to pleasure you, my darling Penny,' said Lenushka between kisses. 'I am going to enjoy you, and then you are going to pleasure me whether you like it or not. Won't that be splendid?'

Penny could hardly speak. Lenushka was not only showering her face, her neck, and her shoulders with kisses, she was also manipulating her nipples in a most expert fashion.

Penny moaned with delight as Lenushka squeezed her breasts then ran her hand over the taut flatness of her belly and through her pubic hair.

'Do you like that, my beautiful girl? Do you like my long, sharp fingernails dividing your sex lips and scratching your pink, slippery flesh?'

Penny cried out as one finger went further and

plunged into her vagina. Invaded, but welcoming, her vaginal muscles clamped around the intruder and smothered it with its honey.

The countess continued to work on Penny's sex whilst her other hand played with one nipple. Her mouth nipped and sucked at the other. Penny found herself drowning again in an odd fantasy that had suddenly became reality.

As before, on every other sexual encounter with members of the syndicate, Penny was lost in her own sexuality. Tantalising sensations crept over her skin like trickles of warm treacle.

Then suddenly, the action stopped.

'Now for this,' rasped the countess as she fumbled around Penny's waist and between her legs. 'Now you are equipped to pleasure me too.'

Penny's gasp when Lenushka squeezed her breasts was stifled by a hot, lingering kiss.

What is it?' she asked, once their mouths had parted. 'I can feel a belt around my waist. I can feel something inside my body. What am I wearing?'

'A penis!' Lenushka exclaimed as she fumbled again, then gasped with delight as whatever false appendage she had attached to Penny, was negotiated between her own legs. Once the false penis was in her, Penny was lost. She groaned with pleasure, did her utmost to elicit every sensation she could from the false penis.

'Oh, joy!' Lenushka cried out.

Penny half closed her eyes as Lenushka's mouth went back to one bosom whilst one set of red talons set to work on the other. As before, her other hand went between her legs and aroused her until she was wet with desire.

As Penny's desire turned to orgasm, Lenushka rode the false penis more fiercely until they both spasmed, cried out and the countess's head fell breathless against Penny's breast.

Her breath was warm, and so was her body. Perhaps it was that, that and the fact that Penny had not slept for some time, that caused her to doze. So weary and worn out with sex had she become, that she hardly noticed when Lenushka left her side and climbed out.

Only when stone began to grate against stone did she awake and realise that she was being entombed – alone!

'Countess! No! You can't leave me here!'

The countess laughed almost apologetically. 'Of course I am leaving you here, my dear little rosebud. I will use you again. You should feel privileged. I only bring my most favoured friends here to meet my relatives. I will be back my darling. Never fear!'

She laughed again, but the sound of her voice was soon lost. Stone scraped against stone as the lid was pulled over the coffin leaving a terrified Penny naked, wrists bound, and in complete darkness.

Chapter Twenty-Four

*A*listair Beaumont's fists were clenched very tightly. His face was red, his eyes glared. 'You can't leave me like this, Nadine. You must give me the key!'

'Like hell I will, my dear brother. At this moment in time I would enjoy the thought of you suffering the indignity of having your rubber pants cut off by someone who knows nothing of our secret games. Yes,' she growled, her eyes narrowing in the same way as a cat before it springs and tears its prey apart. 'I would seriously enjoy your discomfort and the follow on. Imagine that person running to the tabloids with the news that Alistair Beaumont wears rubber underpants. Imagine the headlines!' She shook her head disbelievingly. 'I'm ashamed of you, Alistair. In fact, I feel it is impossible for me to stay and look after your favourite fetish any longer. I can't believe you could have done this to Penny. You know damn well she'd indulge in every sexual scene thrown at her for your sake. Why did you go along with it?'

Alistair's eyes flickered guiltily and Nadine thought how handsome her brother was and wished as she had many times before, that she was not related to him.

'You know I like a wager,' he explained. 'It didn't

seem a problem at the time. I never intended that any harm should come to Penny. You must believe me.'

'You deceived her. You told her a lie. Why did you do that?'

'I thought she would perform better if she believed I had lost something I loved dearly. And anyway, you know how she feels about horses.'

Nadine shook her head. Alistair looked directly into her face to try and gauge her feelings. Nadine had always been a hard nut to crack. It was never easy to ascertain exactly how she was thinking. Up until now it had never occurred to him that she might have any scruples at all – especially about sex. Her appearance pleased him, yet it also frightened him.

Nadine was dressed in a chain-mail suit that was fashioned from the finest steel and burnished to a silvery shine. It had a high metal collar that buckled around her throat. Strips of the fine mesh-work ran down her arms and legs, but only covered the outer arms, the outer thighs and legs. Leather straps set at six-inch intervals held the chain-mail close around her flesh. Breast cups of metal gave greater emphasis to her small breasts. Silver chains hung from a matching helmet and dangled to some three inches past her chin. She looked awesome and, for once in his life, Alistair was truly humble before her.

As Nadine shook her head again, the chain-mail that covered her body sent rainbows of reflected light around the room. The chains that hung from her helmet jangled angrily as she shook her head. 'She'll never forgive you for lying to her, Alistair, and neither do I!'

With one chain-mailed finger, Nadine tapped a piece of paper on Alistair's desk. 'According to this timetable, she is now with the Countess Lenushka. Is that right?'

'If it's Tuesday,' he said sheepishly.

'It's Tuesday.'

'Then that's where she'll be.'

He shrugged his shoulders as he said it. Nadine glared. He was taking this all too casually for her liking.

255

But there was something he didn't realise, something he should have known before Penny had been consigned to the Carpathian Mountains.

'But you know what the countess is like once she gets her hands on a pretty girl. She'll keep Penny there for months and Penny will hate it.'

Alistair looked at her obliquely. 'But she won't hurt her. She's just a bit eccentric that's all.'

Nadine glared. 'Alistair, you stupid sod. That's not the point. Penny might not want to stay there. Had you thought of that? Penny will get upset, and Lenushka will get annoyed. It's not beyond probability that she'll get even more stubborn and not let Penny go at all.'

'But what can we do about it?'

'You mean what will I do about it!' Nadine's face contorted with rage. There was a tinkle of metal as Nadine threw the key to Alistair's rubber pants across the floor. This was the key that would release Alistair and allow him to relieve his sexual tension. Only Nadine, his sister, and Penny, his lover, had keys to it, and Penny had been gone a while now.

'Where is it? Where is it?' Alistair cried as he grubbed around on the floor.

'I hope you don't find it,' shouted Nadine. She stormed off, the heels of her sheepskin-lined motorcycle boots thudding on the floor as she made her way out of Beaumont Place – perhaps forever.

Swinging her leg over the silver chassis of her Harley Davidson, she donned a shiny black helmet that fitted neatly over the chain-mail one beneath it. She pulled on her leather and chain-mail gauntlets, then kick-started the engine.

In her mind she was loving her brother as usual, but also hating him. How complex, she thought, are human emotions, and how fickle. But it was Penny who was in her mind; Penny, whose flesh was so responsive to any sexual diversion whether it was implemented by a man or a woman; Penny, who gained triumph from submission.

Even as she rode her powerful machine, Nadine thought of all the joy Penny had given her and others.

After a few miles, Nadine pulled into the motorway services, parked her bike, then with long strides, raced across to where a helicopter was landing.

Amazed faces turned to watch the tall, lean woman who was pulling off her helmet as she ran. Truckers cat-called and business executives leant on their cars and merely fantasised.

Ducking beneath the whirling blades, a few strides, and Nadine was in the helicopter beside Sasha.

'Have you managed to get one, my pretty little Frenchman?

'If you mean an aircraft suitable to get us to Rumania, yes,' he shouted above the engine noise which began to scream as they climbed into the sky.

Five hours later they had landed. Chartering an aircraft to get them to Rumania had not been too much of a problem. Rumania itself was a different story. Technology had taken a back seat in the east European country, so it was a while before they managed to find a charter firm that would hire them a helicopter.

'Where are you going?' asked the swarthy man who took their money.

'The Carpathian mountains,' Nadine shouted back. 'As if it's any of your business, you horrible little man.'

The man laughed. 'Watch out for vampires! That's what all you westerners are looking for isn't it?'

His voice was drowned by the screams of an ill-serviced engine.

'Sasha, darling. Is this thing safe?' asked Nadine, as the helicopter lurched into the air.

'Nadine, my mistress. Do we have a choice?'

She didn't answer. Sasha and Nadine were now bonded by something other than their mistress-slave relationship. Both were concerned about the safety of Penny Bennet.

It was nearing sunset when they landed in the valley.

257

High above, the castle stared down, its shadow falling in a black mass over the lone road and the fields around them.

'What a diabolical place,' observed Nadine as the sun dipped behind the mountains.

'Are you armed?'

'Bet your life I am, sweetie.' She held up a knife that she'd tucked into a thick leather belt that held the chain-mail tight around her waist.

The road that meandered through the valley also wound around and up the mountain until it arrived at the gateway of the countess's castle. Once they were out of the helicopter, it was a case of walking. By the time they got to the main gateway, evening had changed into night.

'Do we ring the bell?' asked Sasha nervously.

'How else do we get in?' cried Nadine, as she tilted her head back and gazed up at the sheer walls above them. 'Who do you think we are, Batman and Robin?'

They rang and rang again.

'Batman and Robin it is then,' quipped Nadine, wishing they'd brought climbing equipment. Exasperated, she thumped her fist against the huge wooden gate. A small section gave and swung open.

'Open sesame, I see,' she said more brightly, and went in.

Sasha followed.

The hall they entered was in semi-darkness. Only half the lights were working, but they gave enough illumination for Nadine to take in the particulars.

'Wow,' she murmured intently, her eyes bright with interest. 'My opinion of this place is improving, darling Sasha.' She was looking directly at the fireplace – or rather the two naked men bound to either side of it. Their bodies were stretched to perfection and their eyes rolled – perhaps in ecstasy, perhaps in agony – at the new arrivals.

Sasha gasped as he took in the men's predicament. A weight swung from a chain hanging from each man's penis, and each weight was swaying from side to side like the pendulum of a clock.

Nadine went straight to them. 'I am impressed,' she purred, as she ran her hands over the body of each man in turn, caressing their faces and tickling their chests and stomachs. Clasping one penis, then the other, she gloated at their moaning as they erected against the metal bands that held each one. Once she was satisfied they had erected enough, she set the chains swinging again. 'A superb idea. I think I might try it out on you, my darling Sasha,' she said as she stood back to admire the cocks, the chains, and the weights that swung from them, and to listen to the two men crying out for mercy.

'Mercy?' she said in a quizzical tone as she raised her eyebrows and stood with arms akimbo, her chain-mail gleaming in the light of the flickering lamps and the dying fire. 'There is no mercy without confession. Now! Which of you delightfully tortured young men is going to tell me the whereabouts of a certain young lady who came here with the countess?'

One of the young men opened his mouth, shut it again, then cried, 'What lady?'

Instantly recognising weakness when she saw it, Nadine went to him. 'Oh, you must remember her,' she purred, in a tone that was laced with menace. 'Long, dark hair that fell like a cloak to her waist. Intense, beautiful blue eyes that showed fire but also a cool, melting submission. You must have seen her. Tell me!'

The man cried out in anguish as Nadine raked her black-painted finger nails down over his chest and his belly. With added fervour, she gripped his balls. 'You do remember! Tell me!'

'Last night. She arrived last night.'

'And where is she?'

'The crypt! She must be in the crypt!'

'Over there,' muttered the other man, his voice husky as though he were enjoying the swinging of the pendulums. 'But please, now I've told you, will you please help me off of this statue behind me. His penis is embedded in my behind, and it's a very large penis.'

Nadine exchanged looks with Sasha and raised her eyebrows. Sasha trembled. Not from fear, but purely from the excitement generated by the sure knowledge that this particular scenario was something she might try out on him.

Between them, they raised the man off the stone penis. 'And what about this?' Sasha asked, holding the tip of the man's cock in his palm which stopped the chain and the weight swinging for a moment.

'Oh no,' the man said, his eyes twinkling with wicked pleasure. 'That's no problem and I don't mind being tied up. It was just that I'd got tired of having that thing up my behind.'

'And what about you?' Nadine asked the other man.

He smiled weakly. 'Leave me as I am,' he said in a small voice. 'My mistress will be angry with me if I am not enduring what she has ordered for me.'

Nadine flicked at his penis with her fingers. The man cried out, and the pendulum began to swing again.

'Come on, my darling Sasha,' she cried, and Sasha followed.

They descended the same winding steps Penny had gone down and went through the same door. A solitary gaslight flickered and shadows danced on the walls.

'Is anyone in here?' Sasha asked, as he took in the rows of stone coffins and the odd eye socket that appeared to be looking his way.

'There are plenty of people in here,' returned Nadine, 'and all dead.'

'Not Penny!' exclaimed Sasha. 'She must be in here. The stairs came down from that door and do not go anywhere else but here.'

He narrowed his eyes against the surrounding gloom. Nadine was walking around the edge of the crypt, peering in those coffins whose lids had fallen to one side.

'Nice teeth,' she said to one grinning skull. 'Oh dear, you've got a broken nose. Should have ducked, darling.'

Sasha shook his head and chuckled. 'I love you, my mistress, even though you are a ghoul.'

'Nonsense,' Nadine replied. 'I am just interested in studying the bones of this particular dilemma. What if the countess had put our poor girl in one of these caskets?'

'You are right, as ever, my mistress. I will look too.' Sasha grimaced as he peered into each coffin. All the same, he could not help but consider that these people had once had flesh on their bones, had kissed, caressed, experienced an orgasm, and had even believed themselves to be in love.

But he was quicker about searching than Nadine, so he got to the large, free-standing sarcophagus before she did.

'Look!' he called excitedly, as he dropped to his knees. 'This casket has got the countess's name on the side. She's booked her place for eternity! And it's still got a lid.'

Nadine was at his side immediately. 'You're right, my darling slave. Quick. Help me take this lid off.'

Lenushka had moved the lid by herself, so it was easy for two to remove it.

'Who's there?' cried Penny in a plaintive voice, her eyes blinking against the sudden light, puny as it was.

'Penny! It's me. Sasha. Nadine is with me. We've come to get you out of here.'

Nadine was silent, her mouth smiling in that cruel, but characteristic way of hers as she stared down at the naked, and so very vulnerable, Penny Bennett.

'My darling,' she cooed in that old, familiar way. 'How glad we are to find you, and how pretty you look trussed up like that. I'm sure Sasha thinks so too. Ah, yes,' she said softly, her fingers running over Sasha's hardening member. 'He is getting hard already. I can feel how much he wants you. He deserves a reward. Don't you think so Penny?'

'That,' returned Penny, 'is an understatement. I love you to bits for finding me – both of you.'

'Then we will both welcome you back to us,' murmured Nadine. 'Sasha. Prepare yourself.'

'Yes, my mistress,' said Sasha, his voice husky and only just above a whisper. Eyes bright, he stared down at the supine Penny as he took off his clothes.

'Hurry,' cried Penny. 'Make me warm, Sasha. And you, Nadine. I'm freezing!'

'Oh I will make you warm, my darling,' purred Nadine.

Sasha climbed into the sarcophagus. 'This was obviously made to take two,' he observed, as he eyed the strange interior, its small glass cases and the metal rings and straps that were set into its sides.

'Enough, in fact, for three,' added Nadine, as she sprang, still dressed in her chain-mail suit, over the side. 'Now all three of us will embrace and seal the bond between us. But first, Sasha, I will bind you in the same way that Penny is bound.'

'Do you have to?' asked Penny. 'Sasha is warming me so quickly. I can feel how glad he is to be with me again, and I certainly am glad to see him – and you.'

Sasha had been caressing Penny's breasts and kissing her lips. If there had been only the two of them, he would have left her bound and thoroughly enjoyed her before releasing her to return his caresses. But Nadine had spoken and her word was law.

'Yes, my mistress,' he whispered as Nadine bound his hands and fixed his bonds to a chain ring above his head.

'This is beautiful,' cried Nadine. 'Open your legs, Penny. You too, Sasha.'

Penny and Sasha kissed and murmured words of desire. It did not matter that it was Nadine's hand and fingers playing with Penny's vagina and Sasha's cock. It was still as if they were doing it to each other.

To Nadine's instructions, they tilted their hips, and as Penny's breasts touched Sasha's chest, Nadine guided Sasha's cock into Penny's body.

'Oh, this is too beautiful,' murmured Nadine. She groaned and smiled at this copulating couple. In her mind, it was as if they were a work of art; something she, Nadine, had created.

As Penny and Sasha jerked towards each other, Nadine assisted the intensity of each thrust by pressing her hand firmly against each bottom, then pushing one finger of each hand into each willing anus.

Their jerking became fiercer as, with each thrust, Nadine wiggled her fingers in deeper. It is, she thought, as though they are my puppets, and I am the puppet master – or rather – mistress.

Faster and faster, fiercer and fiercer, her fingers went in and out of each anus. In time with her fingers, Sasha's penis went in and out of Penny.

At last, in a crescendo of climax that made each body glisten with sweat and tremble with ecstasy, the bodies thrust, fused, then fell gently apart.

Nadine untied them both, her breath racing and her pussy aching.

'Pleasure me,' she ordered, and lifted up the tunic of her chain mail.

The leggings of her suit were fastened by straps to her waist. The tunic covered only her round, white bottom, and the hairless lips of her sex.

'Oh, yes, Nadine. Oh, yes,' murmured Penny once she was freed from her bonds. She struggled to her knees and gratefully kissed Nadine between her thighs.

Sasha just groaned before kneeling behind Nadine and pressing the heat of his lips to the coolness of her behind.

As Penny pulled Nadine's labia apart and licked hungrily at her clitoris, Sasha divided Nadine's buttocks with his fingers then poked his tongue into her anus.

Like a colossus, Nadine stood above them accepting their tribute. But their tribute was a rich one, and before long she was writhing gratefully on their probing tongues and fingers until she too shuddered and shimmered with an outstanding orgasm.

'You will need proper clothes,' remarked Sasha, once they were all out of the sarcophagus.

'This will do for now.' Penny retrieved the scarlet

cloak from the floor. She was still wearing her scarlet boots. 'But I do need to get my things from upstairs.'

'Lead on,' ordered Nadine stridently, and Penny immediately thought of Henry V, though his outfit of chain-mail could never have looked as distinctly erotic as Nadine's did.

'We've been lucky so far,' whispered Nadine as they opened the door at the top of the stairs that would lead them back into the hall where the two men with the swinging cocks kept pace with the seconds, minutes and hours. 'I wonder where the countess is?'

'I think she's best avoided,' returned Penny. 'So far we've been lucky not to see her. Who knows what she'll put us through next?'

'I think,' added Sasha, passing a protective arm before both his lover and mistress, 'that our luck has just run out.'

White-faced and complete with a set of incredibly realistic false fangs, black thigh-high boots with thick straps that fastened to her belt, and a black cloak with a scarlet lining, Lenushka stood before them. Obviously she liked to think she fitted in with her background. She laughed eerily, and as though coached to do so, the two bound men laughed too.

Lenushka grinned so that her fangs were more obvious. Her eyes were bright. 'Where are you going, my darlings?' she cried.

'She thinks she's a vampire,' whispered Penny.

'She gets carried away with the part, my darling Penny. Alistair told me all about her. Besides that, I do get around you know.'

A memory of a smoky room in Chinatown came to Penny. Had that personage draped across the couch really been Nadine? Something told her not to believe it. She had been sure that the smoking person had been a man. She would bet on it. Despite the incense and dense smoke, she had smelt him, hadn't she?

But she was grateful to Nadine. Much as she might be

welcome at Lenushka's home, she was a bit over-the-top with her hospitality.

'Get out of our way,' Sasha ordered, and Penny gripped his arm.

The countess threw back her head and laughed. Sasha did not hesitate. He sprang forward and knocked her to one side. As he did so, Nadine leapt into action and caught the countess in the midriff with a well-aimed kick.

Penny for her part rushed forward to grab as much of her luggage as she could. 'Bloody hell, I've got some good designer stuff in these cases,' she muttered to herself as she headed for the door.

'Come on!' she shouted, holding it open with her hip as the night air poured in.

'Right there!' Nadine shouted back.

Sasha's eyes met Penny's. He was standing with his hands on his waist, smiling and watching Nadine. From that alone, Penny knew what he was thinking. Nadine was being incredibly imaginative, and also vengeful.

Because she was of superior strength to most women, Nadine had found it easy to divest Lenushka of her cloak, and to bind her hands. Instructed by her, Sasha had lowered the cage that was fashioned in a human shape. Nadine was now bundling Lenushka into this.

'There!' she exclaimed as she slammed the door shut.

Lenushka, her eyes wild, began to wail pitifully. 'It is my turn to have Penny, darlings,' she cried. 'Let us be fair about this. It is my turn!'

Penny, breasts still heaving from all the rushing up stairs and through the hallway, shook her head in disbelief. There were certain attractions in Lenushka's castle, but Penny's interest lay elsewhere.

'Goodbye, my darling countess,' cried Nadine.

The countess screamed curses; at least, Penny assumed them to be curses. Lenushka had lapsed into Rumanian.

Chapter Twenty-Five

*I*t was a pleasant English day and horses were swishing their tails against the flies and the breeze beneath the oak trees.

Alongside the practice track at the racing stable where Alistair Beaumont kept his best horses, he stood with his trainer, stopwatch in hand as a jockey brought Superstar up the final straight.

'Marvellous,' he exclaimed, as the horse thundered past. 'He's maintaining his time, and if his jockey sticks to the rails all the way round the course, the Derby is mine.'

Grenville, his trainer, pushed his cap to the back of his head and looked relieved. He'd put in a lot of time and energy on that horse, and any word of commendation from Mr Beaumont made him feel that it was all worthwhile. A bigger bonus would have been better, but he had to be content to accept less.

They ambled slowly back toward the stables, talking horses and racing all the way.

Alistair did glance up briefly and wondered what the cloud of dust was from the other side of the stable yard. He glanced away again as he heard the sound of a horsebox drawing away.

It wasn't until they rounded the end wall and went

through the gateway that they saw Joe Smiley, the jockey who had been riding Superstar, lying flat on the ground. He struggled up on to his elbows as they ran towards him.

'What happened?' cried Alistair.

'Someone grabbed the horse's reins, led it up into the horsebox with me on it, then pulled me off and threw me out. I landed here.'

'Who was it?' growled Alistair, his eyes wild and worried.

The jockey shook his head. 'I don't know. They only said that it was time he was retired and they had just the place for him.' He shrugged apologetically. 'I'm sorry. That's all I can tell you.'

Alistair, his face red with rage, stared into the distance where a horsebox lumbered off towards the motorway.

'Shall I call the police?' Grenville asked.

Alistair shook his head. 'No. Don't bother.' He smiled suddenly. 'I know exactly where he's likely to be. Get my chauffeur to fetch the car round. I'm off back to Beaumont Place. That's the first port of call. After that it's Angers or another of the stables belonging to some friends of mine. It's nothing to worry about. It's just their idea of a joke. I'll soon get him back.'

The setting sun turned the yellow sands of the Camargue a strawberry pink. Marbled clouds flitted over a wide sky, and the wild white horses of the region, led by a thoroughbred chestnut stallion, ran before a trio of riders.

Penny, Sasha and Nadine yelled wildly as they rounded up the neat, round mares. Superstar, nostrils flaring, penis unsheathed, would follow.

They saw him rear, his flanks turning a gleaming red in the last rays of a setting sun.

'Just look at him,' breathed Sasha, his eyes sparkling and his voice seeming to catch on the first breath of the Mistral, the wind that blows across the Rhone delta. 'See how eager he is to ride my mares?'

Penny reined in her mount and ran her hand down Sasha's back. 'See how happy he is,' she said, her eyes meeting his. 'Better in his mind to be a rider than a runner. Better in my mind too.'

They watched the dust rise as Nadine circled the outer perimeter of the herd of mares, then came galloping up to them, her horse as black as her outfit and her customary cigar hanging out of her mouth.

'That stallion is insatiable,' she shouted, before galloping off again.

'So am I,' whispered Sasha to Penny. 'And I did promise to make love to you on the cool brick floor.'

'And you will, my darling Sasha. So too will Nadine, the most experienced rider of us all,' returned Penny.

CONQUERED – Fleur Reynolds
ISBN 0 352 33025 2

DARK OBSESSION – Fredrica Alleyn
ISBN 0 352 33026 0

LED ON BY COMPULSION – Leila James
ISBN 0 352 33032 5

OPAL DARKNESS – Cleo Cordell
ISBN 0 352 33033 3

JEWEL OF XANADU – Roxanne Carr
ISBN 0 352 33037 6

RUDE AWAKENING – Pamela Kyle
ISBN 0 352 33036 8

GOLD FEVER – Louisa Francis
ISBN 0 352 33043 0

EYE OF THE STORM – Georgina Brown
ISBN 0 352 330044 9

WHITE ROSE ENSNARED – Juliet Hastings
ISBN 0 352 33052 X

A SENSE OF ENTITLEMENT – Cheryl Mildenhall
ISBN 0 352 33053 8

ARIA APPASSIONATA – Juliet Hastings
ISBN 0 352 33056 2

THE MISTRESS – Vivienne LaFay
ISBN 0 352 33057 0

ACE OF HEARTS – Lisette Allen
ISBN 0 352 33059 7

DREAMERS IN TIME – Sarah Copeland
ISBN 0 352 33064 3

GOTHIC BLUE – Portia Da Costa
ISBN 0 352 33075 9

THE HOUSE OF GABRIEL – Rafaella
ISBN 0 352 33063 5

PANDORA'S BOX – ed. Kerri Sharp
ISBN 0 352 33074 0

THE NINETY DAYS OF GENEVIEVE – Lucinda
Carrington
ISBN 0 352 33070 8

THE BIG CLASS – Angel Strand
ISBN 0 352 33076 7

THE BLACK ORCHID HOTEL – Roxanne Carr
ISBN 0 352 33060 0

LORD WRAXALL'S FANCY – Anna Lieff Saxby
ISBN 0 352 33080 5

FORBIDDEN CRUSADE – Juliet Hastings
ISBN 0 352 33079 1

THE HOUSESHARE – Pat O'Brien
ISBN 0 352 33094 5

THE KING'S GIRL – Sylvie Ouellette
ISBN 0 352 33095 3

Published in September

TO TAKE A QUEEN
Jan Smith

Winter 1314. Lady Blanche McNaghten, the young widow of a Highland chieftain, is rediscovering her taste for sexual pleasures with a variety of new and exciting lovers, when she encounters the Black MacGregor. Proud and dominant, the MacGregror is also a sworn enemy of Blanche's clan. Their lust is instantaneous and mutual, but does nothing to diminish their natural antagonism. In the ensuing struggle for power, neither hesitates to use sex as their primary strategic weapon. Can the conflict ever be resolved?

ISBN 0 352 33098 8

DANCE OF OBSESSION
Olivia Christie

Paris, 1935. Grief-stricken by the sudden death of her husband, Georgia d'Essange wants to be left alone. However, Georgia's stepson, Dominic, has inherited Fleur's – an exclusive club where women of means can indulge their sexual fantasies – and demands her help in running it. Dominic is also eager to take his father's place in Georgia's bed, and further complications arise when Georgia's first lover – now a rich and successful artist – appears on the scene. In an atmosphere of increasing sexual tensions, can everyone's desires be satisfied?

ISBN 0 352 33101 1

Published in October

THE BRACELET
Fredrica Alleyn

Kristina, a successful literary agent may appear to have it all, but her most intimate needs are not being met. She longs for a discreet sexual liaison where – for once – she can relinquish control. Then Kristina is introduced, by her friend Jacqueline, to an elite group devoted to bondage and experimental power games. Soon she is leading a double life – calling the shots at work, but privately wearing the bracelet of bondage.

ISBN 0 352 33110 0

RUNNERS AND RIDERS
Georgina Brown

When a valuable racehorse is stolen from her lover, top showjumper Penny Bennett agrees to infiltrate a syndicate suspected of the theft. As Penny jets between locations as varied and exotic as France, Sri Lanka and Kentucky in an attempt to solve the mystery, she discovers that the members of the syndicate have sophisticated sexual tastes, and are eager for her to participate in their imaginatively kinky fantasies.

ISBN 0 352 33117 8

To be published in October

PASSION FLOWERS
Celia Parker

A revolutionary sex therapy clinic, on an idyllic Caribbean island is the mystery destination to which Katherine – a brilliant lawyer – is sent, by her boss, for a well-earned holiday. For the first time in her life, Katherine feels free to indulge in all manner of sybaritic pleasures. But will she be able to retain this sense of liberation when it's time to leave?

ISBN 0 352 33118 6

ODYSSEY
Katrina Vincenzi-Thyne

Historian Julia Symonds agrees to join the sexually sophisticated Merise and Rupert in their quest for the lost treasures of Ancient Troy. Having used her powers of seduction to extract the necessary information from the leader of a ruthless criminal fraternity, Julia soon finds herself relishing the ensuing game of erotic deception – as well as the hedonistic pleasures to which her new associates introduce her.

ISBN 0 352 33111 9

If you would like a complete list of plot summaries of Black Lace titles, please fill out the questionnaire overleaf or send a stamped addressed envelope to:-

Black Lace
332 Ladbroke Grove
London W10 5AH

WE NEED YOUR HELP ...
to plan the future of women's erotic fiction –

– and no stamp required!

Yours are the only opinions that matter.

Black Lace is the first series of books devoted to erotic fiction by women for women.

We intend to keep providing the best-written, sexiest books you can buy. And we'd appreciate your help and valued opinion of the books so far. Tell us what you want to read.

THE BLACK LACE QUESTIONNAIRE

SECTION ONE: ABOUT YOU

1.1 Sex (*we presume you are female, but so as not to discriminate*)
Are you?

Male ☐

Female ☑

1.2 Age

under 21 ☑   21–30 ☐

31–40 ☐   41–50 ☐

51–60 ☐   over 60 ☐

1.3 At what age did you leave full-time education?

still in education ☐   16 or younger ☐

17–19 ☑   20 or older ☐

1.4 Occupation _____

1.5 Annual household income
    under £10,000 ☐   £10–£20,000 ☐
    £20–£30,000 ☐   £30–£40,000 ☐
    over £40,000 ☐ $0

1.6 We are perfectly happy for you to remain anonymous;
    but if you would like to receive information on other
    publications available, please insert your name and
    address *Mesha Pettus*
    104 E. Walnut St. Campsville, Ke
    _____
    _____

SECTION TWO: ABOUT BUYING BLACK LACE BOOKS

2.1 How did you acquire this copy of *Runners and Riders*?
    I bought it myself ☐   My partner bought it ☐
    I borrowed/found it ☑

2.2 How did you find out about Black Lace books?
    I saw them in a shop ☐
    I saw them advertised in a magazine ☐
    I saw the London Underground posters ☐
    I read about them in _____
    Other ___ *neither* ___

2.3 Please tick the following statements you agree with:
    I would be less embarrassed about buying Black
    Lace books if the cover pictures were less explicit ☐
    I think that in general the pictures on Black
    Lace books are about right ☐
    I think Black Lace cover pictures should be as
    explicit as possible ☑

2.4 Would you read a Black Lace book in a public place – on
    a train for instance?
    Yes ☐   No ☐

SECTION THREE: ABOUT THIS BLACK LACE BOOK

3.1 Do you think the sex content in this book is:
  Too much ☐ About right ☐
  Not enough ☑

3.2 Do you think the writing style in this book is:
  Too unreal/escapist ☐ About right ☑
  Too down to earth ☐

3.3 Do you think the story in this book is:
  Too complicated ☐ About right ☑
  Too boring/simple ☐

3.4 Do you think the cover of this book is:
  Too explicit ☐ About right ☑
  Not explicit enough ☐

Here's a space for any other comments:

SECTION FOUR: ABOUT OTHER BLACK LACE BOOKS

4.1 How many Black Lace books have you read? 1 ☐

4.2 If more than one, which one did you prefer?

_____

4.3 Why?

SECTION FIVE: ABOUT YOUR IDEAL EROTIC NOVEL

We want to publish the books you want to read – so this is your chance to tell us exactly what your ideal erotic novel would be like.

5.1 Using a scale of 1 to 5 (1 = no interest at all, 5 = your ideal), please rate the following possible settings for an erotic novel:

Medieval/barbarian/sword 'n' sorcery ☐
Renaissance/Elizabethan/Restoration ☐
Victorian/Edwardian ☐
1920s & 1930s – the Jazz Age ☐
Present day ☐
Future/Science Fiction ☐

5.2 Using the same scale of 1 to 5, please rate the following themes you may find in an erotic novel:

Submissive male/dominant female ☐
Submissive female/dominant male ☐
Lesbianism ☐
Bondage/fetishism ☐
Romantic love ☐
Experimental sex e.g. anal/watersports/sex toys ☐
Gay male sex ☐
Group sex ☐

Using the same scale of 1 to 5, please rate the following styles in which an erotic novel could be written:

Realistic, down to earth, set in real life ☐
Escapist fantasy, but just about believable ☐
Completely unreal, impressionistic, dreamlike ☐

5.3 Would you prefer your ideal erotic novel to be written from the viewpoint of the main male characters or the main female characters?

Male ☐ Female ☐
Both ☐

5.4 What would your ideal Black Lace heroine be like? Tick as many as you like:

Dominant ☐ Glamorous ☐
Extroverted ☐ Contemporary ☐
Independent ☐ Bisexual ☐
Adventurous ☐ Naive ☐
Intellectual ☐ Introverted ☐
Professional ☐ Kinky ☐
Submissive ☐ Anything else? ☐
Ordinary ☐ _____

5.5 What would your ideal male lead character be like? Again, tick as many as you like:

Rugged ☐
Athletic ☐ Caring ☐
Sophisticated ☐ Cruel ☐
Retiring ☐ Debonair ☐
Outdoor-type ☐ Naive ☐
Executive-type ☐ Intellectual ☐
Ordinary ☐ Professional ☐
Kinky ☐ Romantic ☐
Hunky ☐
Sexually dominant ☐ Anything else? ☐
Sexually submissive ☐ _____

5.6 Is there one particular setting or subject matter that your ideal erotic novel would contain?

_____

SECTION SIX: LAST WORDS

6.1 What do you like best about Black Lace books?

_____

6.2 What do you most dislike about Black Lace books?

_____

6.3 In what way, if any, would you like to change Black Lace covers?

_____

6.4   Here's a space for any other comments:

_____

_____

_____

_____

_____

Thank you for completing this questionnaire. Now tear it out of the book – carefully! – put it in an envelope and send it to:

Black Lace
FREEPOST
London
W10 5BR

No stamp is required if you are resident in the U.K.

Things I personal
Would like to
try out: